TH

CARTER

JEWEL OF HIRAM

FRANK FELTON

Description

The ghost of Snively has haunted the Milam County, Texas, countryside since the 1800's. Stories and legends fail to explain more than a century of supernatural occurrences tied to the San Xavier missions, founded to convert Apache warrior tribes on the frontier of Coahuila y Tejas. The missions were abruptly abandoned by the Spanish in 1755. Civilization would not return for more than 100 years.

One man will discover the secrets of the Legend of Snively and unmask an enigma brought to the New World with the conquistadors.

The aging narrator recounts his life, beginning as a young soldier on the beaches of Normandy in 1944. Near the end of World War II, his unit moves south to the Bavarian Alps – a fateful journey which would change his life. He discovers a glowing jewel in Hitler's bunker at Eagle's Nest, and embarks on a mission to piece together a 3,000 year old riddle. It leads him to the land where Snively roams.

From his deathbed, the narrator foretells an ominous future. He uncovers the tragic history of this jewel, crafted by the hands of Bezalel in the time of Moses, and carried by King Solomon at the founding of his temple.

Just as Moses' staff, the Jewel of Hiram is possessed of supernatural powers. It has influenced the outcome of battles throughout history, breaking the will of kings and emperors. The narrator infiltrates a reluctant cadre of men who have unwittingly kept the Jewel hidden away from the world.

But the Jewel is about to arise from almost 200 years of slumber. It will be sought by forces of good and evil, angel and demon, and its final reckoning will be unleashed.

This is a work of fiction. Names, characters, businesses, places, events and incidents are either the products of the author's imagination or used in a fictitious manner. Any resemblance to actual persons, living or dead, or actual events is purely coincidental.

~~~

Copyright 2013 by Frank Felton

All Rights Reserved

Editing by Jeanne Williams

~~~

ISBN: 978-0-9913538-1-1

To my Grandma Nell - a lifelong schoolteacher who gave one final lesson from her deathbed. Diagnosed with stage 4 cancer in 2008, she managed to live almost 4 more years. In asking me to deliver her eulogy, she unlocked a voice that had remained silent for far too long. Whether she did so knowingly, or unwittingly, I will never know.

Nervous as I should have been during the funeral, I was not. Her strength had given me the same. It was during the service that I realized this last act of Grandma Nell would change my life. It gave me the confidence to once again put pen to paper, and give voice to those who cannot speak. Death should be not proud.

A few months later, another mentor named Christine (Chris) Holcombe passed away. She is perhaps the most successful County Extension Agent in Texas history, and I came under her tutelage in the 1980s. As a high school senior, I prepared to hand in a nomination request to Representative Chet Edwards during a campaign stop in Cameron. It was part of my application to the U.S. Air Force Academy.

Before I could hand the application to Rep. Edwards' chief of staff, Brady King, I was intercepted by Chris, who snatched the paperwork from my hand, took a quick glance, folded it in half, and handed it back to me. She told me to re-write it. I was beyond upset, and frustrated, but I did as she said. She was, of course, right. I went on to graduate from the Academy a few years later.

I was asked to be a pallbearer, so I wrote a poem for Chris and read it at her funeral. On the way to the graveside, her son Andy related that he had no idea I was capable of such words.

It then struck me, like a lightning bolt – neither does the rest of the world.

Things come together in odd ways, and the Lord works even more mysteriously. I'd like to believe both of these women knew exactly what they were doing.

AUTHOR'S NOTE

Military battles in this novel are recreations of actual engagements and track with historical accuracy to the greatest extent possible. Names are changed to protect those who continue to serve on Active Duty.

I've done my utmost to remain true to the written Word. If I have erred, then so be it.

All Scripture is God-breathed and is useful for teaching, rebuking, correcting and training in righteousness.
- 2 Timothy 3:16

PREFACE: SNIVELY – FACT OR FICTION?

If you were ever to see the gods, say, see them come walking down a leaning tree, wearing shiny orange robes, this would be the place. – ***George Sessions Perry***

A legend in rural central Texas tells of a ghost that roams the countryside with a lantern, searching for, or perhaps guarding, a long lost treasure of Mexican gold. The ghost roams the rolling landscape, with its fertile blackland soil and luscious pecan groves, on the edge of the Post Oak Savannah range, nestled against the San Gabriel River. Based on sightings, the ghost has taken up residence near the same property where author George Sessions Perry once lived. Before his untimely death, this parcel of land provided a trove of literary wealth for Mr. Perry. It has a bizarre history of tragedy – murder, treasures lost, and supernatural occurrences.

Born in Rockdale, Texas, in 1910, Mr. Perry wrote an award-winning novel detailing the life of a Depression-era tenant farmer in a fictionalized version of Milam County. He described not only the hardships, but the physical beauty and state of mind, to pitch perfect harmony, with *Hold Autumn in Your Hand.* He earned the coveted National Book Award for his story. Critical acclaim for Mr. Perry's writing drew comparisons to John Steinbeck, thus, Perry went on to write for *The Saturday Evening Post*. He later abandoned novelization in order to write for periodicals, to the chagrin of his fans in Texas.

While *Hold Autumn in Your Hand* was published in 1941, the agrarian lifestyle of Milam County remains little changed to this day. To hold autumn in your hand is to preserve one's garden harvest in a Mason jar, enjoying the fruits of the field even half a turn past the September equinox and into the dead of winter. It was crucial to survival. The book's title has a sentimental feel, yet stands as a testament to the harsh tribulation of the farmer's livelihood.

Ten years after Mr. Perry published the novel, he purchased the very land that inspired it. The farm spanned 68 acres on the southern edge of the San Gabriel River, where the tributary makes a hard cut northward before its confluence with the larger Little River, itself feeding the Brazos on its way down to the Gulf of Mexico. He made a valiant effort to farm the land, with little success other than the inspiration for a new novel; *Tale of a Foolish Farmer.*

Mr. Perry ultimately met his demise under mysterious circumstances in 1957, or most likely 1956. His body was not found for several months after he went missing. He had entered a deepening depression, tortured by hallucinations of death during his time at the invasion of Sicily in World War II. His condition was complicated by alcohol. He displayed symptoms of mental illness.

Before his demise, Mr. Perry spoke the gospel as it regards the lifestyle of a bygone era. Horse and donkey soon gave way to the John Deere, lignite coal sprang forth to provide electricity and manufacturing, and the fields once filled with King Cotton are now a mix of corn, milo, and cattle. Despite these changes, the soul of rugged individualists remains deeply imbedded in this rural patch of civilized society.

In his later, unpublished writings, Mr. Perry revealed regret at having taken the easier path in life as it related to his professional writing career. He opted to pursue non-fiction journalism for major circulation on the East Coast, rather than the rustic novels of Texas which launched his career. In typical Perry allegory, he would say that he chose the less difficult sandy-land farming, rather than the harder yet more rewarding blackland soil of which his most famous novel was based. Sandy loam is far easier to till, yet lacks the fertility and ability to hold moisture so necessary to a magnificent harvest.

People around here find his self-deprecation nonsensical. They hold no grudges against him for his chosen pursuits, but will always be indebted for the mark he left behind. They will remember him for the accurate portrayal of their way of life, and the always colorful cast of characters cherry-picked from the local populace. The tombstone of Perry's beloved hound dog is all that remains today of his occupancy of this farm.

Mr. Perry's home turf boasted a heritage so colorful that he could have filled a library with novels of its history. Named for a hero of the Texas Revolution, Milam County was once the largest county in the largest state, comprising one-sixth of Texas. Both lost their titles, however, as Milam was diced into parts over time, and Texas was toppled when Alaska joined the Union in 1959.

The beautiful prose of Mr. Perry portrays the people of a relatively difficult era, but Perry's years and those beyond were far less tragic than that preceding the 20th Century. Ancestors of the Tonkawa lived here 4,500 years before Christ, settling the San Gabriel River valley. Europeans came in the 1600's, and the Spanish colonized the area with a number of missions, built to convert the Tonkawa, Comanche and Apache tribes during the 1700's. Fast forward another hundred years, and the early 1800's saw full scale settlement of Coahuila y Tejas. The United States expanded in search of Manifest Destiny. This ushered in a period of tumult for the fledgling state of Texas.

Arrival of the white man preceded the revolution of Mexico from Spain, and then of Texas from Mexico. Texas joined the Union through statehood, then seceded, fought in the Civil War and made amends throughout Reconstruction. The Lone Star State fell into economic turmoil throughout the early 20th Century. In a hallmark of such upheaval, five of the six flags of Texas were raised during a 40-year period from 1821 through 1861.

The edge of the frontier ran directly through Milam County. It was not until 1846 that Indian raids were finally put to an end with the fort at Bryant Station. Settlers were then allowed to return to their homes abandoned during the Texas Revolution, but the return of the settlers was yet a hundred years after the original Spanish missions in Milam County were constructed.

Today, the locations of the three missions, as well as a Presidio, have been discovered and documented by archaeologists from Southern Methodist University and the state of Texas. While built to establish a foothold on the frontier, in less than a decade the missions had been mysteriously abandoned. Many attribute this rapid abandonment to supernatural forces, but a closer examination of records yields a more plausible scenario. It was caused by scandal and murder within the ranks of the Spanish military.

A young Spanish Captain named Felipe de Rabago was appointed to lead the new missions at San Xavier. He was a man gifted with more dollars than sense, his family become with wealth from the silver mines of Zacatecas. As with men of his status, despite mediocre physical attributes, such position of prestige fed innate desires of the flesh. It gave way to an unhealthy pursuit of women.

This was a serious problem for the Catholic priests whom he was to protect. Captain Rabago's illicit ventures led to an affair with the wife of a well-placed Spaniard from San Antonio. By these infidelities, in 1752, the captain was excommunicated from the Church. In retribution, the husband of the woman, and a priest named Father Ganzabal, were both murdered. Evidence pointed to Captain Rabago as the primary suspect. He was sent into exile. He repented from his lascivious ways, and was eventually acquitted of the charges eight years later.

With this looming scandal and declining climate conditions across the territory, the Spanish government soon shuttered the San Xavier missions. They relocated resources further west to San Saba. As the missionaries departed, they buried valuables, including a large golden Cross. They did so seemingly to prevent the Indians from stealing these possessions as they made the trek back to San Antonio. The buildings were set afire to prevent anyone from taking up occupancy. They banished this land, Milam County, back to the fringe of the forsaken frontier.

Others claim it was the Indians who acted first, besieging the missions and forcing an abrupt burial of the valuables. In this context, the story of Captain Rabago's infidelity might have been merely political cover to mask a failed expedition. Now saddled under the weight of a terrible drought throughout the southwest, it's not beyond the realm of speculation for a government to act in such a manner.

The truth is lost to history.

The reason for the abandonment may not be known, but there is no doubt the Spanish left quickly. It is somewhat certain that in the ensuing departure, artifacts were thrown into the irrigation well near the middle of the mission and buried. There were few other options in such haste. This well was atop a hill less than a mile from where Mr. Perry's story takes place some 175 years later, at a point just east of where the San Gabriel River makes it turn to the north.

Jeanne Williams, a local reporter, writes of the exodus in the Temple Daily Telegram:

...the settlement witnessed a scary sight — a ball of fire in the sky circled the area. Some believed the fire ball represented the wrath of God, who cursed the presidio that soon was plagued by disease and a drought so severe the river dried up. The missions were abandoned in 1755 leaving behind charred ruins, intrigue and tales of hidden gold that won't stay buried.

The area would lie dormant a century nigh. Inhabitants scattered as leaves on a windy autumn day. Just as a field is plowed to make way for the season's planting, so too would the Lord clear this land for his future plans. When the Great Flood ended, the sign of the rainbow graced the skies, and Noah raised his hands to Heaven. The promise of the rainbow would be kept, but this time, the Lord's vengeance would come at the precision of a scalpel; without the brute end of a sword.

PROLOGUE

Supernatural happenings in Milam County have confounded commoners and intellectuals alike. Speculation of lost treasure is related by J. Frank Dobie, who taught at the University of Texas, as well as Cambridge. His early writings focused on the vanishing way of life in rural Texas and myths of treasure. Mr. Dobie, in his voluminous writings on Texas history, focused a few lines to the subject of Snively's gold in the early 1900's:

On the top of Sugar Loaf Mountain, in almost its exact center, there is a deep hole of considerable circumference which appears to have been covered with loose dirt. The remaining surface is comparatively level and of hard, rough rock. According to legend, this hole in the center was blasted out and used as a hiding place for a fortune in gold. This fortune was hidden by the Spaniards and is thought to have been the property of the missions.

Since that time many have searched for this hidden treasure but none has ever found it.... he once located the spot but the moment he started to dig for the treasure a great flood came down the river and obliterated all traces of it forever. Thus the elements conspire in helping Snively to protect the gold.

When the story of a wandering ghost and long lost gold was first related to me, it described a middle-aged man named Snively. He supposedly was the first treasure hunter to pursue the riches of Milam County. He was a whimsical man who spent his life in a quest for such action. Along with his recent partner, Brooker, they methodically pieced together the location of the old missions long before archaeologists from SMU began to dig. They searched for five weeks to locate the three sites using quaint historical records which described the surrounding area.

Snively was a risk-taker, a man who felt certain this trove would set him up for life. During the sixth week, Snively and Brooker found the location of what they believed to be the primary mission, the San Francisco Xavier de Horcasitas. This was the big one, the largest mission of the three, marked by a lone cottonwood tree atop a hill overlooking the San Gabriel River valley. It was Snively's belief that the treasure rested in a well at this site.

They began to dig.

~~~

Milam County, Texas, 1853

Evidence was in their favor. This was the perfect place to build a fort. It was the high ground, with close access to water. The river bottom, blanketed with pecan trees, provided a natural defense to the west, and the northern flank offered a steep drop. Open prairie to the south, and east, presented an uncompromised view for miles. The plateau of the hill was an oval, several acres in area, with a low spot where grew the lone cottonwood tree.
~~~

"This is the place. It matches all the criteria," said Snively.

"Yes, sir. The sharp bend in the Gabriel to our west. Three-hundred sixty degree view of the river valley," replied Brooker.

"Blackland soil. A clear demarcation of the sandy loam just to the east."

"Under that tree. That's got to be the well."

"I'm guessing they put a perimeter wall beginning with that steep drop off the north face, then ran it back, maybe 200 paces off the west side here."

"That tree would have been right in the center of the walls. It would have grown well with all the water coming up, spilled around the central point of the village as they carried it out."

"Reckon' that tree is a hundred, maybe 120 years old?"

"Could be."

"Well, then, shall we give her a dig?"

"I reckon'. Ain't gonna dig itself."

Certain of their find, they began to dig the well early on a hot summer day. They began to uncover pottery and other artifacts. Yet after six feet, they met the resistance of rocks and gravel.

"I don't think we're on top of it. This fill is too natural."

"Are you sure? Should we try other side?" replied the impatient Brooker.

"I think we'll have better luck."

Begrudgingly, Brooker took his shovel and moved the operation west of the tree. He'd wasted half a day in the wrong spot. This time he encountered less resistance. The softer dirt made easy digging, being a mixture of blackland soil, gravel and sand. Within two hours he dug to almost 10 feet below the surface. Yet the hot Texas sun made even the simplest tasks exhausting. The pair made conversation to pass the time.

"You know, I never asked, but what do you intend to do if we do find this treasure?" asked Snively.

"Well, truth be told, I owe quite a bit of money. Suppose I'll pay that off."

"To whom?"

"Oh, just a few folks. Here and there."

What Brooker failed to mention, is that he had a bounty on his life. Seems he had gotten in a tiff with a former partner he worked with. He'd stolen money and left town. The partner was connected to a gang of outlaw gunmen. Sooner or later, they would find him. He had no intention of paying it back, or of ever being caught. He planned to take the money and get as far from Texas as possible. It was only a matter of time before his luck ran out, or his partner discovered his true past.

"What about you?" asked Brooker.

"Me? I don't know. Well, I suppose I'll drink and gamble most of it. Maybe get married."

"Yes sir, that's what I'm talking about."

Snively wasn't telling the truth either. In fact, he was a somewhat religious man, and didn't drink. Aside from a friendly card game, he was also unlikely to gamble. He planned to tithe at least 10 percent to the church, and use the rest to fund his next hunt. While tithing was directed by the Bible, he also felt it gave him the requisite luck necessary in his line of work.

Hunting treasure was his passion in life. Brooker was merely hired muscle for this job. Snively did all the thinking, the research, and all the planning. He'd come up empty so many times before that it was proving difficult to find someone willing to go along with his odysseys.

As the sun dropped below the horizon and the digging continued, the two men became silent as they unearthed a skeleton. Soon after, a second outline of bones came into view. Snively was now certain; the legend held two bodies were thrown in with the treasure. It was unclear if this was done ceremoniously, or to make a quick burial while under attack. Regardless, Snively handled the remains delicately, intending to give them a proper burial.

Digging came to a halt as the pair struck a hard object. The skeletons gave way to a small chest, wrapped in worn leather. Within the chest were numerous items faded beyond recognition and marred by ages in the damp soil. One of the items, a cotton sackcloth, was filled with coins. When scratched away, the grime and mildew gave way to a shiny, metallic surface. The coins were made of gold. The sack weighed almost five kilograms, worth over six million in today's dollars. This was the treasure he'd long sought.

Satisfied with the day's effort, the two men hunkered down for the night, near exhaustion. They would continue digging in the morning, as the Legend also spoke of a golden Cross. Snively's partner took the first lookout shift, always cautious of who might be on his trail. Once sure that Snively was asleep, Brooker became possessed of a consuming greed.

As a coyote howled in the distance, Brooker thrust his dagger into the throat of his partner, killing Snively in cold blood. His mouth open, but unable to speak, Snively's eyes met those of his murderer. His tense body soon went limp, as the spirit loosened grip with his body. Breath still escaped his lungs when Brooker hurriedly dragged his body into the well; along with the skeletons and all other traces of their presence.

He covered the hole with lose dirt, and made his escape to the west, stealing Snively's horse and belongings as well. Brooker ventured to cross the San Gabriel River at the El Camino Real to make his way north to Oklahoma. The river crossing was just a mile from the site of the mission. The El Camino was a Spanish trail for tradesmen, somewhat similar to the Silk Road of the Orient. In modern times, the crossing has become known as Apache Pass. Recent rains made the river nearly impassable, yet Brooker did not have time to spare. He debated camping for the night, but paranoia consumed him. He pressed forward, forcing his horse into the stream. He was only 40 feet from freedom.

But the ghost of Snively was already on patrol.

As the murderer attempted to cross, his horse lost footing. It careened over the now hidden bank, spilling its rider into the breach. The sackcloth of gold, now wet, began to tear, and the gold coins were soon to be lost. Brooker's greed empowered him to risk life, and it was that price he would soon pay. With one hand on the reins, he held on desperately to the bag of gold with his other. As the raging waters pulled the horse under, Brooker loosened his grip. It began to pull him under as well.

He struggled helplessly. Water began to weigh down his clothing. His head would soon be barely above the water. He felt the sackcloth slipping free from his hand. Now faced with losing his treasure, his greed was replaced by terror, as the reality of his impending death dawned on him. He finally let go, and used both hands in a desperate attempt to remain afloat. The swirling waters of the San Gabriel would not abide. Within seconds, it swallowed him whole.

The man, nor the treasure, was ever seen again. The gold is now spread over many miles in the muddy silt of the mighty San Gabriel River. The ghost of Snively continues to haunt the land in which he was murdered. His presence noted by nothing more than a floating lantern. It traverses the pecan groves of the San Gabriel River bottom on moonless nights. Those who get too close, often meet with peril.

Or so legend would have it.

PART 1

They have a moral tendency which renders them jewels of inestimable value.

- Reverend Dr. George Oliver (1782-1867)

1. Arise

September, 2007, Milam County, Texas

He awoke to the sound of birds. They slowly chirped their way into his cerebral cortex. The sound began as a faint echo in the distance and eventually drew to a crescendo. Soon after, a more jarring noise broke him free from the subconscious. Thoughts of fantasy gave way to reality – the reality that his nightmares had not gone away.

It was a sweet sound of silence which now welcomed him to this new day, as surely as the sirens of the Odyssey. Aided by an almost motionless and serene background, it was a setting to which he was completely unaccustomed. It took a few seconds to realize he was in fact no longer dreaming. A few moments earlier, his nightmare reached a fevered pitch, as he relived the death of his close friend. The explosion of the fighter jet still reverberated in his mind, when he was pried from sleep by the sound of an airplane passing over his house.

Sometimes the mind sets a pace to reality. Other times, they are completely at odds. Today, Troy Benson's mind would re-harmonize to reality, and he would begin a path to a deeper understanding of just exactly what the hell had gone wrong in his life. His path to redemption would begin with the most basic human need—a good night's sleep.

He hadn't slept this well in quite some time, but he was now awake. He was far from the hustle of his previous career, where the prescription for success meant incessant fatigue and the daily grind. He was now in the country, more than 10 miles from the nearest town, and completely isolated from human existence.

He no longer had a career. There were no deadlines to meet, no reports to write, and no tasks to be completed. Perhaps even more, there were no mortar shells in the distance, screaming jet engines, nor warning alarms to trigger a sense of panic. Sounds of war were far removed, and in this moment of life, he felt completely at peace.

He shuttered his eyes for just a moment, to take it all in.

Out of habit, he was unable to keep his eyes shut. He was too excitable to stay motionless for very long. He harbored a quiet fear that there soon would be a knock at the door, or worse, the duty officer's screaming baritone might yell his name with orders to rise and shine. Either of those was bad enough, but what he feared most was the simple, piercing sound of the alert call. It was nothing fancy, just a simple tone telling on-call pilots to man your jet, and prepare for war.

As a pilot, he was ice cold; the latest in a line of men who could harmonize to the resonance of any machine. He was surgical in his approach to the study of flight, with an intricate knowledge of weapon systems and performance characteristics in advanced fighter aircraft. He meticulously reviewed intelligence reports. There was never a mission he undertook in which he did not prepare extensively. If there was ever a question to be asked, the other pilots came to him.

So it is said that if you know your enemies and know yourself, you can win a hundred battles without a single loss. - ***Sun Tzu***

Add to the mix his genetic predisposition for risk taking, and you have a man who Daedalus might call his own. Having grown up an orphan, he never depended on others and his leadership abilities crystallized into a reputation for true grit. Some say he lacked empathy. He could drive or fly anything, or at least he could in his own mind. Men would follow him.

He became one of the youngest pilots to ever win the Air Force Cross:

'The President of the United States of America, authorized by Title 10, Section 8742, United States Code, takes pleasure in presenting the Air Force Cross to First Lieutenant Troy Benson, United States Air Force, for extraordinary heroism in military operations against enemy forces while serving as an A-10 Pilot with the 81st Fighter Squadron, during Operation Iraqi Freedom on 15 December 2003. On that date, Lieutenant Benson was the flight lead on Shack 54, a two-ship of A-10s tasked for search and rescue alert at a forward operating location. While en route, he received tasking to provide aerial cover for a Combat Control team whose helicopter had been shot down the night before. During the next six hours he would lead his flight through three aerial refuelings, and three hours of intensive searching deep inside enemy territory.

He risked his life as he had to fly at a mere 500 feet in order to pinpoint the survivor's location. When three enemy trucks appeared to be heading toward the team, Lieutenant Benson destroyed two vehicles and directed his wingman to destroy the other, thus securing the rescue. It was his superior airmanship and his masterful techniques at orchestration that made this rescue happen. Through his extraordinary heroism, superb airmanship, and aggressiveness in the face of the enemy, Lieutenant Benson reflected the highest credit upon himself and the United States Air Force.'

No matter how many times he was called to do it, taking life had never been easy. "Old guys" in the unit, men seldom older than 40, had seen action in Desert Storm. Now lieutenant colonels, these men were line officers in the first Gulf War and all too familiar with Saddam Hussein's antics. Troy had watched the battle unfold on television as a kid in junior high. Those old guys often would regale newbies with their war stories, as the dominant American power drove Iraqis out of Kuwait, losing fewer lives to the enemy than were murdered in Chicago during the same time period.

It was the first time in history a viewer at home could watch a war unfold in almost real-time, watching a laser-guided bomb find its target through a smokestack, or an open window, leaving only a screen of static as recognition that it had fulfilled its mighty deed. He was no longer in junior high. He was by then Lieutenant Benson, A-10 flight lead, and knew firsthand that death and destruction lurked behind the static screen.

Blood and gore were redacted from the video feeds released to the media, all part of the carefully choreographed optics relayed to the public. Regardless, he never once second guessed his duty to kill. He took a vow, an oath, to defend his country against all enemies, and he held an unquestioning loyalty to the unified chain of command. Besides, at this stage in his life, the enemy was easy to spot, and Saddam Hussein was no doubt an enemy. Troy was a well-trained agent of death, sent by the country he loved and to whom he owed his allegiance.

It was a country which would soon betray him.

~~~

These thoughts of war dissipated for the moment. His body was awake, yet his mind did not want to leave behind the wonderful feeling of sleep. A moment of levity filled his soul. As his consciousness became more firm, gone too were the sounds of steel bars slamming shut for the night and echoing down the prison hallway. Even should they return, his mind was once again his own, and reassured him that those surreptitious thoughts were only flashbacks to a life behind.

At times, that nightmare was replaced by another. When it visited, a slight chill came over him, as the frigid embrace of the Reaper pulled him ever so delicately down; down to the depths of Lake Zernek. The blood left his body at an alarming rate and the feeling of panic was replaced with a
~~~

gentle euphoria as the freezing waters numbed his body. His breath ran low, and rather than fight, he simply gave in. He did not struggle; because by now he'd entered a lucid state of mind – and he knows how this nightmare ends.

Over the past six months, as the nightmares recurred, he'd manage to preempt their arrival from time to time. There is no more liberating feeling than a dream which you can control with your thoughts. Yet, he liked how this one ended, so he would let it play out – clutched from the grip of death by modern-day super heroes who wore the uniform of his country. Despite the ensuing aftermath, he owed his life to those men who pulled him from the depths. How does one repay that debt? A year in prison without any formal charges makes for a handsome down payment.

Tired of resting, he lumbered down the cabin stairs, step by step, grasping the hand rail so as to not lose his footing. Waking from a deep, rapid-eye-movement-state of slumber suddenly can give one a spinning head. His grandfather built this house many years ago. The patriarch had suddenly become a bachelor upon being served with divorce papers. It should not have been a surprise to the elder Benson, but it was. Benson men throughout history have been the type which can readily spout the genus of a particular tree, yet haven't the first clue how to identify a forest.

As such, this house was gifted with all the necessities of a 35-year-old bachelor. Situated next to a river, it stood two stories tall to prevent damage from flooding. The aforementioned hand railings on the stairs were to ensure safe passage for a drunken 35-year-old man, who might find himself more likely than not intoxicated on a Saturday night. Whether drunk or half-asleep, they came in handy.

He squinted as he neared the screen door. The early morning sun beamed directly into his face. A cool breeze found its way to his nostrils, and he soon breathed in the scent of the morning dew, tinged with the sharp fragrance of wild onion. Refreshment filled his body, and he let out a long and lung-filling yawn, raising his hands over his head, stretching his arms until he could almost touch the sky. It had to be one of the greatest feelings in the world – as sublime as the feeling of max throttle in a twin-engine fighter, or the smell of jet fuel in the morning.

Those were the things about his former life he missed. Those years were gone. He fell from grace in a world in which he had been in total control, but today, he would have reason to feel good again. It was no superficial pleasure. It was his first morning as a free man in well over a year. It was a day that would change his perception of life as he knows it.

~~~

It all went south with a court-martial held in his honor. The legal proceeding was for an act in which he exercised command authority as a commissioned officer and flight lead, in combat. He was supported by his direct chain of command, which came to his defense. He was not alone in the belief that he was completely justified, but he was
~~~

left to dry by political actors who demanded a fall guy. The act, while it saved many lives, went against the orders of that fateful day. The mission went badly, and when it did, one of his best friends lost his life. Troy nearly did as well. Thirty million dollars in military hardware was lost.

Someone had to pay. The tribunal needed a scapegoat, a decoy to detract the masses from other goings on in the 24-hour political news cycle. In other circumstances, Troy might have been lauded a hero, but on this day, he was in the wrong place at the wrong time. A genuine American citizen and patriot was thrown to the hounds by his own country.

He would eventually forgive, but he would never be able to forget the wounds left by an institution that once held his unwavering loyalty. The only iota of goodness which survived that day belonged to Troy Benson himself. For his troubles, his professional life would be completely destroyed. A moral crisis ensued which would cause him to question some very basic truths; even his own existence. Once wounded, he fell victim to a cascade of bad decisions. It would take a good deal of time to heal. The road to regain his compass would be long and difficult, yet it would set him on path to true virtue and morality.

The Lord works in mysterious ways.

That was all in the past, and he was tired of thinking about the past. What's done is done. A new phase begins today. His life is about to change. Released on probation, and no longer held prisoner by the United States government, for the first time in his life he is completely alone. He has no family remaining in this world, except for a sister that lives half-way across the country.

What he does have, besides his deflated ego, is a rather large parcel of land left him by his grandfather, Hank Benson. It was the man whose funeral he had recently been allowed to attend. A man he barely knew. That too is about to change. He will soon become more familiar with his grandfather in death, than he ever possibly could have in life.

2. Crash Carter

Be not forgetful to entertain strangers: for thereby some have entertained angels unawares. – **Hebrews 13:2**

There was a strange feeling of déjà vu as he glanced around the house. He remembered things that he shouldn't have known. There was a half-full glass of water on the table. Embers of coal burned in the wood stove. A dog stood outside, wagging its tail. She looked at him as though she had been waiting on him; waiting for food. Was this really his first day at home, in this house, on this farm? It looked as though he'd been here for weeks, perhaps months. How long was he asleep? He ushered these odd thoughts back to his subconscious. He was not so sure he could trust even his own instincts anymore.

Those odd thoughts stopped dead in their tracks. They were replaced by a much more reliable, and basic, instinct which kicked in. His brain quickly processed a well-known sensory perception. A surge of adrenaline entered his bloodstream. It wasn't exactly a fight-or-flight response, but was just as dramatic. His body froze. It took his mind a few milliseconds to digest the overload.

His heart raced with anticipation.

It was the song only a radial-engine airplane can make, and it was approaching quickly from the west. It bore down on him. The noise grew louder until he felt the feeble walls of the house began to rattle. It was close. By his judgment, it couldn't have been more than a hundred feet above ground level.

Only one thing flew that close to the ground. It had to be a crop duster, and this one sounded like the one Old Man Wernli had flown. He remembered the distinct tune very well from his days growing up out on the farm, but Mr. Wernli was long dead. No doubt some enterprising young daredevil had taken up the mantle when the old codger kicked the bucket. Before Troy could finish the thought, the yellow skin of the massive airplane appeared through the pecan trees, as the noise reached deafening levels. It was just over his head, banking hard to the right as it emerged into the clearing.

It was beautiful.

Troy ran out into the open field and watched as the aircraft returned to level flight, then pulled up and back to the left. It dove into a neighboring field in an intricate display of airmanship, darting underneath a row of power lines, and disappeared behind a hill. As the plane dipped beyond the horizon, Troy jogged up the nearby hill, from which he would have a 360-degree view of the surrounding Milam County farmland.

The plane reappeared, in a vertical climb, rolling almost inverted, and returning to the Earth with the sharpness of a razor's edge. After a few minutes, Troy had the best seat in the house. He stood in awe as the crop duster moved across the field in perfect harmony. The sharp, crisp, maneuvering meant this pilot had good hands. It was something a fighter pilot like Troy could truly respect – both of these men were masters of that craft.

It was summertime in Texas and the fields were coming into full bloom. This guy no doubt had a full day's work ahead of him, so what happened next would leave Troy thoroughly confused. As the pilot finished up a neighboring field, he turned the plane back west. He appeared to be headed directly toward Troy's location.

~~~

At the top of the hill was a rusty equipment hangar in which his grandfather kept an old airplane. It was a vintage 1954 Cessna 180 Skywagon, painted in white and green livery. By now it was so full of cobwebs and mud dauber nests that it would need some serious attention to ever get back into the sky. His grandfather, Hank, had been a pilot, and Troy had learned to fly in that plane. It was a true joy to fly growing up, and his true inspiration to become an Air Force pilot. Once he'd moved on to the fast paced life of the Air Force, slow moving puddle jumpers like the Skywagon failed to spark his interest any longer.

In fact, he'd almost forgotten about *Old Green,* as his grandpa called her. The hangar was at the end of a long gravel road that ran the length of the hill. His grandpa used that road as a landing strip. The rear elevators of the Skywagon were pockmarked with dents and dings from the main landing gear kicking up rocks. Grandpa fancied himself a barnstormer in the mold of Billy Mitchell. Just as with his approach to most things in life, Hank was an old
~~~

school pilot. He thought that real pilots flew tail draggers, and fancy new tricycle-gear airplanes were for sallies.

The crop duster made a slow, arching circle around the hill. Its airspeed slowed. It appeared to be setting up for a landing on the gravel road. Who was this guy; perhaps his grandfather's friend? No one even knew that Troy was out here. The plane continued its steady descent, lining up right on target.

Sure enough, the mysterious plane landed.

The yellow bird bounced slightly once the main landing gear touched the ground. It completed the landing roll and made a sharp U-turn while it still had considerable forward speed. It throttled up, and headed back down the road towards the hangar. Troy was now in a full sprint to get to the hangar, racking his brain for something that would explain why this marvelous beast had landed here. No one had been on this farm in weeks, ever since his grandfather died and bequeathed the property to Troy.

There was only one possibility that made sense; this guy was stealing fuel. Grandpa had a rather large fuel tank of Av-Gas up near the hangar, and this guy apparently had figured that out. The thought sent ice into his veins. He ran even faster. He wanted to see the look on this punk's face when he dragged him out of the plane and beat hell out of him. If there was one thing that disgusted him, it was a thief. What kind of lowlife bastard steals fuel from a dead man? His respect for the artisanship displayed by the pilot dissipated. He could think of no other explanation.

The plane came to a stop next to the hangar, but the propeller continued to turn. Troy was only 200 hundred yards away now. Still in pretty good shape, he figured he had about 30 seconds. He didn't know what this guy was doing, but he was about to give him a piece of his mind, and might knock out a few of his teeth. As he drew within 50 yards, he heard the engine spool down, as the pilot pulled the throttle.

The sudden audible squeal of the engine caused Troy to slow to a jog. His body tensed and he lightened his steps so as not to give the intruder any sign of his presence. The mighty radial gave a shriek as the lifeblood left its veins. A puff of smoke spewed forth from the exhaust pipes. Troy slowed to a walk, and crept up from the backside of the airplane slowly, ready for anything as he approached the side of the plane where he could see the cockpit.

The pilot caught a glimpse of Troy as he opened the hatch, giving a quick wave as he climbed out, posterior first. He had a long, thick beard, and wore a beanie cap pulled over his ears. His eyes were hidden by a pair of cheap sunglasses. He looked menacing, but at the same time, his body language communicated he was harmless.

Perhaps he knew he was caught, and was formulating his story. Troy's rage lifted slightly, but he was still on edge. He was never all that good at personal confrontation, but he was also not afraid to mete out a beating when his ire was up. He glared up at the cockpit. The man threw a bag to the ground, and the spinning propeller dwindled to a halt. It was now completely silent, and Troy readied his verbal harangue.

"Mornin'" the man yelled down.

Troy stood silent. He wanted the man to feel his disappointment. His silence communicated disapproval; this man was not welcome here.

"Mor-*ning*," the man said again, this time annunciating more clearly, in a smarter tone.

Troy still gave no reply.

"Good day for spraying, ain't it? Wind is calm; air is crisp, perfect weather!"

Troy had caught his breath. He had no idea who this guy was or why he had just landed a plane on the farm.

"But you know all about that don't you?" the man continued.

Befuddled, Troy finally replied.

"Look, buddy. I don't mean to be rude, but do I know you? Just what in the hell are you doing landing here?"

The pilot jumped down off the wing. He was a skinny fellow, dressed in camouflage pants and a long-sleeved black shirt. He ducked under the mighty wing, and walked to the back of the plane. He had a smile, revealing his teeth through the plume of facial hair; shaking his head. He put his hand up to the rear elevator, and ran his fingers along the edge. He seemed to ignore Troy for the moment.

"Heard some clinks comin' down the road. Don't look like they done any damage."

Troy reached up his own hand, as he walked around the main wing. He felt the smooth flow of the aluminum skin. There was something odd about this fellow, something familiar. He was mesmerized by the sheer size of this crop duster. She was *huge*.

"She's a beauty, ain't she? Yeah, can't believe your grandpa used this strip. It's hell on a plane."

Troy bit his tongue. He recognized this guy. He must have known him growing up. He seemed completely innocuous. What should he say next?

"Yeah."

"Yeah. What?" replied the man.

"This is a nice plane. Whose is it?"

"Well, you remember Old Man Wernli up the road?"

"Yes. Damn, I knew it. I figured this was his plane. I remember that sound."

He remembered Old Man Wernli from years back, must have been almost 20 years ago when Troy was growing up. Back then Wernli was in his 50's or 60's, but looked like he was closer to 80. The liquor done it as much as anything, as Old Man Wernli rarely saw a sober day. He did the work cheaper than anyone else, because he would usually miss about thirty percent of the field. He didn't care. All he enjoyed in life was flying, and drinking whiskey.

Wernli could have passed for a World War II vet, but he was born in 1932 and was too young for that war. A vet from the area named Van Jensen had taught Wernli to fly when he got home from Europe. At only 20 years old, Van was flying B-17's over Germany towards the end of the war. He bought a Piper Cub when he moved back home, buying land near the Bensons. Old Man Wernli caught the bug early on, and started crop dusting when he dropped out of high school in the late 1940s. A few years later, several local crop dusters had given up the dead-end gig as a multi-year drought obliterated the crops, and taken to work at the new ALCOA plant near Rockdale. From then on, Wernli had it all to himself.

"This is his?" asked Troy.

"Nah, he's dead," replied the pilot.

"I know he's dead. What I mean is, this was his plane? I mean, whose plane is it then. Yours?"

"Nah, 'fraid not. Just keepin' her warm."

"For whom?"

"For *whom*? Boy, you ain't changed a bit. All uppity and smart. That's what I always liked about you."

"Look, mister, seriously. Do I know you?"

"Yes sir. You most certainly do."

"I'm sorry. You look familiar, but I can't place it."

"Come on. Think. It ain't been *that* long."

"Alright, I suppose it will come to me. So whose plane is it then?"

"Well, best I can reckon', it's yours."

"What do you mean, mine? I don't own this airplane."

"No sir. But your grandpa owned it. I 'spect that makes it yours."

"Wait a minute. Wait a *damn* minute. Grandpa never said anything about owning a crop duster."

"I reckon not. He might a not said nothin', but he sure as hell did. He bought it from Old Man Wernli a few years back. Long time ago. He got himself too old and too broke. Hank bought it from him but let him keep flying it 'til he died."

"Well I'll be. Huh."

"*Come on.* You remember my name don't you? We grew up together."

Troy recognized the voice. It was on the tip of his tongue. There was only one person it could be. Come to think of it, he had the look of his father, Clappy, who lived across the river. He had a son about Troy's age, and they had been friends at one time, though it had been almost 20 years.

“Well I’ll be damned. You’re Crash Carter.”

3. D-Day

All warfare is based on deception. - ***Sun Tzu***

And no wonder, for even Satan disguises himself as an angel of light. - **2 Corinthians 11:14**

The battle of good and evil is ever present. It is perennial, not eternal, because you can trace this battle to the Fallen Angels, when Satan led his horde of demons against the heavenly hosts. Angels were created by God, and as such, they are not eternal. Certainly they are immortal, but they were not present at the dawn of time. Regardless, the battle has been here long before humans inhabited the planet and will continue long after.

Nitpicky, isn't it? I would agree. That is the teacher coming out in me. I suppose this is as good a time as any to introduce myself. My birth certificate says R. Cyrus McCormack, but I can't think of the last man to call me Cyrus. I've had many nicknames throughout my time on Earth. When I was younger, they called me Mac, and as I grew older and became a school teacher, it became *Mr. Mac*. Has a certain authoritarian appeal to it, I think, short and sweet. It matches my demeanor perfectly.

But my favorite nickname is that given to me, unwittingly, by Troy Benson in 1986. Some of the more interesting things in life happen that way, off the cuff. That was a rarity for Troy. He rarely wandered off the reservation, at least when he was younger. It's difficult for a methodical and emotionally closed-off person to understand that there are some things in life that must simply be left to chance. How he came up with the nickname, I couldn't say. Honestly, I think someone else came up with it, and he stole it because it sounded good. We'll get to that nickname later.

I am not much different than he is, to be honest, but I have many more years of experience. We both live in a world that is very black and white, right and wrong. It made us excellent soldiers. There is disagreement whether such uncompromising behavior is virtuous. I live by principles which have stood far longer than any modern-day relativism, revision of the Ten Commandments, or codes of law which present society aspires to follow.

I was born so long ago I can't even remember. Well before your time, for sure. Looking back, one of my fonder memories on Earth was my time spent during the 1940's. It wasn't long after Pearl Harbor that I decided to volunteer. I was several years older than most of those conscripted to service. I had previously spent time as a journeyman high school history teacher after college, ending up in Brady, Texas. I have always been fascinated by history and various languages, and teaching offered me the opportunity to engross myself in ancient history to my heart's content.

It was at Brady that I came to be mentored by a fellow educator, none other than James Earl Rudder. He was a teacher and football coach. Rudder was called back to active duty in 1941 and I decided it was time for me to leave town as well. The war underway would span the globe. It would be one for the ages, and there was important work for me ahead. However, he was an officer, and despite my education, I would be going in as a grunt. The world was at a major crossroads, with an uncertain future. It was an interesting time, to say the least.

I'd be seeing Mr. Rudder again very soon.

Perhaps it was a different day and age back then. The young men and women of America went to war because they didn't have much other choice. It helped that they didn't know any better, not completely unlike America as a whole, which herself was not much more than an adolescent coming of age. Both responded to their natural instinct to fight when times required it. In taking up the fight, this war would thrust a country to the forefront as a global superpower, shocking it from economic malaise, and establishing an era of greatness and prosperity unrivaled in human history.

First, it would require a massive investment of blood and treasure.

The world once again found itself at war. Germany abandoned the Treaty of Versailles and proceeded to invade her neighbors to re-establish national pride. That pride was lost in 1918 after the first Great War. The treaty was the genesis of this new altercation, for it hamstrung the German society so severely that it allowed the country to be engulfed by the rise of National Socialists, forever more known as the Nazis. I'm not apologizing for the German people, but a word of caution is necessary. Desperate times will always give way to irrationality. Clear thinking is the first casualty when Mr. Maslow is starved from the bottom up.

The election of a subversive government can invite world-changing shifts for an electorate who do not realize the true aims of their leadership. This has happened time and again throughout history. It will happen many times more before you ultimately annihilate the entire planet. Promised utopias never come to be, in fact, the better a promise sounds, the more likely, in military parlance, you should BOHICA. Any institution governed by mankind is subject to corruption, greed, incompetence, and quite possibly, evil itself. This is true for empires, republics, corporations, charities, and sadly, even the Church.

We were fighting for a higher cause, no doubt. But truth is, the herd was just carrying out the orders from Washington, D.C. Lost in the moral crusade were hidden dictates and political posturing which corrupted an otherwise altruistic intent. Certainly there was overwhelming good in defeating the Nazis, one cannot deny. The end justified the means.

For me, there was a much more important objective, one which had not yet been made clear to me. I had a pretty good idea, and by war's end, I knew without a doubt that I had accomplished it. My part of this tale begins on a runway in Great Britain, the summer of 1944, not really sure where I was headed, nor what I was in for.

The Nazis besieged most of Europe and embarked on the oppression and murder of millions. I knew more about the modern world, and the war, than most of the kids on that plane. Yet, none of that mattered, as we all boarded and prepared to meet our destiny for God and country. We were paratroopers with the 101st Airborne Division, 2nd Battalion, 502nd Parachute Infantry Regiment. They called us the "Five-O-Deuce", which had a nice ring to it.

It was a chilly, damp, dark morning, and I was awoken for the second time just a few hours earlier. This was after the normal duty day and we were allowed a few hours rest before the night mission. The air was dense with a cool humidity coming in from the Channel. The distinct smell of gasoline vapors filled my nostrils, one of the few pleasantries I'd experience on this night from hell.

My head throbbed as my helmet vibrated to the tune of two massive radial engines. Every rivet in the thin-skinned C-47 Skytrain vibrated as the power plants strained. They soon had summoned enough forward velocity and airflow over the wings to pull the overloaded troop carrier into the air.

We had thirty souls aboard, most about my age, except for two officers and a handful of NCOs. None of us knew much about the specifics of the overall mission. We had a small, specific task at hand. It is what we lived and breathed every day since arriving in England. Everyone on that plane knew what was unfolding, from the pilots down to the lowliest soldier. It was a massive assault, the most expansive in the annals of human history.

We'd been stationed in England for seven months. Our unit had been quickly activated after Pearl Harbor was attacked by the Japanese. That crushing surprise assault decimated the Pacific fleet. President Roosevelt gave his day of infamy speech and a formerly reticent nation seethed with bellicosity. It rallied for battle. America sprung headlong into a war she had carefully avoided, but after Pearl, there was no longer any other option. The sleeping giant mounted a pale steed to bring forth a reckoning.

The War Department hurriedly activated my unit out of Fort Benning. Our preparation was grueling. Colonel Moseley, from a long line of West Pointers, was especially demanding of his troops. After what seemed like months of division training at proving grounds across the south, we sailed for England on the SS Strathnaver in September 1943. I had been on an ocean-going vessel twice before, but mostly I'd been fishing in the San Saba River back home. That was just a rickety little fishing boat, but the Strathnaver held more bodies than the entire town of Brady. To this day, I marvel at how so many tons of steel can walk on water.

We made an emergency stop in Newfoundland after the ship ran into problems. The powers-that-be sent the SS John Ericcson to carry us the rest of the way to the United Kingdom. Once in England, our new home base was Chilton Foliat near Hungerford, as well as RAF Welford, all in Berkshire. The training continued unabated, with 20 mile hikes, training in German weaponry, chemical warfare, parachute drops, and land navigation. The rugged curriculum was to prepare us mentally and physically for the big day, our first combat drop into enemy hands.

Our goal was to pry Europe from the grip of fascism in a full frontal assault against the German war machine. One thing I had going for me is that I could read and write French. I'll agree, that was a bit of an oddity for a kid from West Texas, and I didn't normally let on such information. Far more of the boys from Texas spoke German, as the Lutherans still adhered to predominantly German liturgy. My clan, the McCormack's, may have hailed from the Scottish Highlands, but I didn't give much care for the weather on that island. It rained a lot, and was much colder than I was accustomed.

Once the Skytrain got into the air, we began a slow climb. It was a bumpy ride. The pilots had been instructed to fly low over the English Channel to avoid German radar. My foot tapped the ground, mostly because I was eager for the action. Random thoughts entered my head. I had yet to face off against an enemy armed with machine guns and hand grenades, so I imagined it. It wasn't pretty.

I was seated closest to the door. I'd be the first one out. Most of us were handling the situation as well as could be expected. The flight to our destination should have been only a few minutes, as the English Channel is not that far across. We had to wait for our assigned grouping, circling and joining up with other aircraft before the assembled force headed over the French beaches. The operation was a wonderfully detailed scheme, apparently, but we had little knowledge of its complexity. The planners must have been true geniuses to coordinate so many different forces, air, ground, and naval, to penetrate the dug-in German defensive posture.

The Germans would be taken by surprise. Men like Eisenhower, Montgomery, and Morgan plotted one heck of a strategy. The Allied Forces were about to deliver a mighty punch to the German warmongers, but for the chaps at the pointy end of the spear, it was downright terrifying. Mission Albany was under way, part of Operation Overlord, and better known as *D-Day*. I'd be one of the first to go in.

Down below were hundreds if not thousands of German soldiers embedded into the French countryside. Waiting, coiled, like a rattlesnake, they stood ready to strike at anyone who wanders too near. A rattlesnake has but one use, and that is to die. In combat there are times where you either kill, or you die. It is just that simple. Just as a rattlesnake gives warning to intruders, the German air defense artillery lit up the sky as we approached. They scattered our well-planned formations, causing the air drops to go awry. As General Patton stated; "No plan survives contact with the enemy." I could sum it up even more succinctly; *stuff happens*.

A burst of flak from the German triple-A cannons seemed to detonate right under our starboard wing. It had to be at least fifty yards out, or else the men inside would be dead already. The plane was thrust hard to the left in response to this sudden burst, the welds holding fast despite an exceptional test of *Rosie the Riveter's* fortitude. The shockwave vibrated us around like a tin can full of pebbles. The pilot veered hard back to the right in a desperate attempt to get us back on course. He was probably a twenty-two year old kid even more terrified than we were.

As more flak exploded around us, the plane felt as if we were driving over a pot-holed gravel road. "Stand! In the door!" screamed the jumpmaster, as he grabbed me by the arm and authoritatively removed me from my seat against the side of the C-47. I was just getting comfortable.

The cool blast of air was a pleasant change of pace. It replaced the stale smell of sweat, tobacco smoke, and aviation fuel. We were about to jump out of an airplane into a void of great unknown darkness, into enemy territory, at night. Jumping out of a plane didn't really scare me, but the darkness, well, that has always put me on edge.

When men are faced with such dire circumstances, they feel a connection to their own mortality. Time slows.

Senses sharpen. Some become afraid. Others see visions of heaven, or hell. Perhaps it was the stark reality of what I was about to do, but my mind soon became overwhelmingly clear. It was a Divine vision; a message from the Almighty. Unlike the other men on that plane, by war's end, my mission would be only beginning. It is a mission set in motion as the Nazis pillared and plundered the arts and treasures of Western Europe. They disturbed the resting place of a sacred artifact, and brought it to Germany. It was an object created thousands of years ago.

It was of great importance that it be found.

4. The Temple

But God said to me, 'You are not to build a house for my Name, because you are a warrior and have shed blood.' **– 1 Chronicles 28:2**

Three thousand years ago, David was a skinny youngster who would topple a much larger and more fearsome warrior named Goliath. He walked the same Earth as we do today. He was a mere human, but also a king. He fought many battles and killed many men. As such, he had blood on his hands, and was unfit to build the Lord's Temple in Jerusalem. It would be left to his son, Solomon.

King David rose to his feet and said: "Listen to me, my fellow Israelites, and my people. I had it in my heart to build a house as a place of rest for the ark of the covenant of the Lord, for the footstool of our God, and I made plans to build it." **– 1 Chronicles 28**

King David established Jerusalem as the capital of the Kingdom of Israel. In the millennia since, spiritual foes have waged war over a small piece of land in this city. It is one of the most enduring and bloody confrontations in human history. Soldiers have fought not only the physical, but an intellectual battle throughout the ages in search of Divine truth. Myths and legends endure as real truth became lost to history.

Chronologies of great leaders, passed down through the remains of their kingdoms and caliphates, are all the world has left of what once stood on the Temple Mount. Ancient stones yield precious little detail about what happened here three thousand years before. Declarations made today, by any man, are mere speculation.

Perhaps the most contentious location in Jerusalem is the peak of Mount Moriah, known as the Foundation Stone. It rests beneath the Dome of the Rock on the Temple Mount. This is where Abraham was to sacrifice his son, and where Solomon would later build the First Temple after his father David passed on the designs to him.

Judaism believes the Foundation Stone is the spiritual junction of Heaven and Earth. The concept of an omphalos stone was previously seen during the Hellenistic age of Ancient Greece. Christians claim the Stone is where Abraham bound his son Isaac for sacrifice, who would further the Church of Christ. Muslims believe it was Abraham's eldest son, Ishmael, who was bound, and would later become a forefather of Muhammad in the Islamic faith.

The clash of these Abrahamic religions amongst each other, and from outside enemies, would continue for thousands of years. Jerusalem would be besieged, conquered, and crusaded against by various warring factions. All this bloodshed for a piece of the navel of the world:

And the sanctuary in the center of Jerusalem,
and the holy place in the center of the sanctuary,

and the ark in the center of the holy place,
and the Foundation Stone before the holy place,
because from it the world was founded.
-Midrash Tanchuma

This Temple itself would become one of the most revered sites in all of human history, and to this day, the Temple Mount in the Old City of Jerusalem is claimed as one of the holiest sites of the Muslims, Christians, and Jews alike. Countless souls were sacrificed, slaughtered, or saved, both upon the site, and in the name of those revered by peoples who claim this tragic piece of earth. It would become the cornerstone of an enduring society known as Freemasonry, which passed on through spoken word the legends which escaped the inner walls of the *sanctum sanctorum*.

Only remnants of that first Temple exists today, but the Foundation Stone beneath the *sanctum sanctorum* still remains under the Dome of the Rock. It contained the Ark of the Covenant. There have been many efforts to rebuild the Temple. Some Jews and Christians await the third, and final, incarnation as related in the Bible, bringing them squarely opposed to Muslims.

Before this sad course of bloodshed succeeded, many men devoted their lives to the design and building of the first Temple. It was a thousand years before the birth of Christ, in 982 B.C. An army of stonemasons toiled faithfully to finish the masterpiece of a grand architect named Hiram.

Now I have sent a skillful man, endowed with understanding, of Hiram my father's, the son of a woman of the daughters of Dan; and his father was a man of Tyre, skillful to work in gold, and in silver, in brass, in iron, in stone, and in timber, in purple, in blue, and in fine linen, and in crimson, also to engrave any kind of engraving, and to devise any device. ***–2 Chronicles 2:3-16***

~~~

Jerusalem, 982 B.C.

As a week's work came to completion, King Solomon, the son of David, sought counsel with the leader of the Temple's construction, and admonished him accordingly:

"Brother Hiram, the work of the brethren is nigh complete. You shall direct them to retire from labor to refreshment. Pay the craft their wages if ought to be due them."

"I will carry out the orders as directed, worshipful king," replied the master craftsman, Hiram of Tyre.

"Your creation will be the most revered site in the Kingdom of Israel. It shall stand as a testament to the sweat of your brow. I shall soon honor you, and you will return to your home with great reward."

"Thank you, most worshipful."

King Solomon brought forth a jewel of consummate splendor, which had rested in the Ark from times before. He would soon confer upon his master craftsman Hiram this gift to reward loyalty, vision, and perseverance in a
~~~

colossal undertaking which would transcend the ages. It was not to be.

Hiram had yet to complete this masterpiece of masonry, and thence return to his homeland, when he was murdered by jealous ruffians. They sought to gain untold secrets of their Craft. This would be the earliest rumblings of the Lodge of Freemasons, who met with the strong grip of the Lion's paw of the Tribe of Judah.

King Solomon now churned with rage. He brought forth swiftly his vengeance and pursued the ruffians. Their day of reckoning came quickly, with an austere penance. The king exacted blood to offset that which they had taken. After the execution of all responsible for the murder of Hiram, he mourned the loss of his friend, who had laid forth the grand designs of his Temple upon the great trestle board.

But Hiram was not a man. He was a servant of God. He was an angel, a fact which escaped even the wisest king ever to rule. The murder of Hiram's earthly body merely freed the angelic form from the bondage of flesh, enabling his powers to be released. His spirit remained to complete the assigned mission, and he continued to guide the Temple to completion.

The Temple's construction was finally brought to end. Upon this grand achievement, King Solomon sent the jewel to the King of Tyre. It was a jewel that was meant for Hiram, leader of the stone masons. It was made of the finest materials, diamonds and gold, rubies and emeralds. As it was to be a gift to the master craftsman, it would now belong to his King. The King of Tyre kept the jewel in his treasury and enjoyed a long and successful reign as King, spawning a progeny that would enshrine his legacy throughout Antiquity.

But before the Jewel was sent to the King of Tyre, a strange thing happened.

*The priests brought in the ark of the covenant of Yahweh to its place, into the oracle of the house, to the most holy place, even under the wings of the cherubim. For the cherubim spread forth their wings over the place of the ark, and the cherubim covered the ark and its poles above. Then the house was filled with a cloud, even the house of Yahweh, so that the priests could not stand to minister by reason of the cloud: for the glory of Yahweh filled God's house.**—2 Chronicles 5:7-8;13-14***

King Solomon carried the jewel with him into the Temple, and the Holy of Holies. This was the *sanctum sanctorum*, the room which contained the Ark of the Covenant and where he regularly prayed to the Lord. The Ark was possessed of the power of the Divine, and instant death came to any man who laid a hand upon it, either intentionally, or accidentally.

As the King prayed for his departed friend Hiram, he clutched the jewel which he would have given to him. Unaware that Hiram was an angel, and not dead, Solomon asked the Lord to bless the soul of Hiram, the architect and master craftsmen who had laid out the grand designs of the very Temple in which he prayed.

Now when Solomon had made and end of praying, the fire came down from heaven, and consumed the burnt offering and the sacrifices; and the glory of Yahweh filled the house. The priests could not enter into the house of Yahweh, because the glory of Yahweh filled Yahweh's house. **– 2 Chronicles 7:1-2**

The Ark itself began to glow. As Solomon remained in prayer, a beam of light cascaded forth from the Ark. It found its way to the jewel clutched in Solomon's hand. *The spirit of Hiram entered the Jewel.* The angel, once again, was bound to an earthly vessel. The Jewel of Hiram began to glow.

The Temple would in due course be destroyed by Nebuchadnezzar and the Babylonians. Later, it would be rebuilt and expanded by King Herod. In 70 A.D., the Romans would finally bring down the walls of this magnificent Temple for good, but the Jewel of Hiram had begun a new journey. Over the next three millennia, the Jewel would accompany the hands of kings, emperors, marauders, men of conquest, and men of peace, philosophers, and saints. Some sought the power for *good*, others for *evil*.

Today the Jewel no longer encapsulates the angel Hiram. He would be freed from its chains in 240 B.C. to once again freely roam the earth. Yet the power of the Jewel remains. Just as the Ark of the Covenant, men continue to seek it. Its location is rarely known by man or spirit, as it wanders the Earth. Some say the Jewel can amplify God-given abilities. Others say it grants you what you most desire. Some claim that it carries within the final secret of Freemasonry, in the words of Hiram himself, which he shared with only King Solomon. Some lost it, and some cast it away, to free themselves of any connection to such sublime power.

It is here for a far greater purpose.

One man who came across the Jewel wrote in the 14th Century this translation:

Crafted by the hands of Bezalel.
A force for good, not settled by evil.
A path uncharted, free to roam,
It's keeper chosen, from the heart of man.
A power beheld, deduced by few,
Impure hearts, like cedars hewn.
Yahweh's power, deduced of the Ark
A glowing light in a world of dark.
Desire ye most, O seeker of God,
To part the waters, as Aaron's rod.
Look in your heart, it does.
A thousand times it delivers woe.
An end of man, it ushers in,
The end of time, will soon begin.

In the 1700's, Sir Isaac Newton argued that the Temple was designed with *prisca sapientia*, or sacred knowledge. He postulated that the design itself held secrets of the universe. Hidden within its arches and conic sections were the codes of a ciphered history that contained the mysteries of nature. Masonic tradition and lore date to the building of the Temple. Some say Solomon was indeed the first Master Mason.

It is somewhat fitting that the latter day protectorate of the Jewel of Hiram would be Masons, though it is likely a mere coincidence. Both had their genesis in the Temple of Solomon. The Masonic brotherhood traces its roots to that same grand building. The Jewel is free of bias to those who hold it; to race, ethnicity, religion, or fraternal belief structure, just as is Freemasonry. Both have served the hand of Jews, Gentiles, Christians, and Muslims alike. The true effect of each is determined solely by the heart of the beholder, as they amplify those gifts in due and ancient form.

This is the Jewel that I must now find, as I prepare to take a leap over the vast darkness of the French countryside.

5. Airborne

These are the men who took the cliffs. These are the champions who helped free a continent. These are the heroes who helped end a war.

- ***President Ronald Reagan** at Pointe du Hoc, June 6, 1984*

I gave one last tightening tug to my helmet strap, tapped my chest left and right with both fists, to ensure I could touch all my handles. It looked like the *Sign of the Cross*, which probably was not a bad idea at this time; a two-for-one special. Plenty of the other men were doing it, but I didn't need it. Salvation is not meant for me. This is a fact I have accepted.

With weapons in hand, a machine gun, bayonet, and a couple of grenades on my waist, I felt lightly armored compared to what may be waiting just 1,500 feet below. Locked into this human body, I was incapable of consuming the enemy with bolts of lightning from my arse. These rudimentary weapons would have to do.

A dim red light came on near the door, the only visible spectrum on this blacked out mission. It was the signal from our pilot that we were over the intended drop zone. Truth is, he knew we were not even close to our waypoint. He wanted to get us off the plane before it became a fireball. It was just a matter of time before one of those flak rounds found its target.

“Go! Go! Go!” yelled the jumpmaster.

I felt another explosion. My hatred of the darkness dissipated as I took one regular upright step with my left foot, and disappeared into the vast emptiness below. Jumping from a plane was a leap of faith, one I had taken before, but never at night. I had a one-way ticket to the ground. Now the only way out of this situation was success, or death, and I really wasn’t in the mood to die today.

I wasn’t all that scared of death, to be honest. I really hadn’t a clue where my spirit would go if it was jarred loose from the flesh. Most of the boys worried about going to heaven or hell. For me, it wasn’t so simple. As cavalier as it sounds, neither one sounded all that great. I was more concerned that I’d come back trapped in the body of a snake, or a toad, and locked in some miserable existence until I died again. I’d rather be set free to glide the air in angelic form. That is what I wished for, but alas, it was just wishful thinking.

My world became silent.

It came roaring back with a vengeance.

When you’re the first to go, you don’t hesitate. I would have been pushed out by the jumpmaster regardless, so I might as well go of my own free will and accord. The force of the wind caught me, dragging me aft of the airplane. I tumbled out of control, the sound of the engines quickly muffled by an onslaught of rushing air. This was the part I hated most; waiting for the parachute to inflate over my head. It normally took only a few seconds, but those seconds never ticked off very quickly, toying with my emotions like a cat that caught a mouse by the tail.

As I tumbled, I felt the static line weasel its way between my legs. It made my heart skip a beat, knowing that a line between the legs was not a good situation. As the line became taught, it pulled the tightly packed parachute from its fabric womb. The chute inflated, and the full weight of my flailing body was transferred to my leg straps, narrowly missing my crotch and flipping me upright.

I reached up to grab hold of the lines. I was just about to breathe a sigh of relief, when my body was suddenly pulled headlong to the right. My legs and equipment bag slung far to the left, into an ever tightening spiral as the parachute dragged me along with it. The lines of the chute had become tangled during the opening sequence, which resulted in several of them being out of place. Over the top of the canopy, they now warped its cylindrical shape and caused a wicked flagellation.

I was now spinning wildly out of control.

This was a treacherous condition. I couldn't see anything, and knew I was no more than a thousand feet above the ground. I would soon sink through 500 feet, at which point my reserve parachute would be useless. Had the pilots dove the plane too low to avoid the flak, I might well already be there. I knew one thing for certain; I didn't want to face the Germans with a broken leg. A surge of adrenaline came over me, and the training kicked in. *The Sign of the Cross*. I reached for my chest with both hands, pulling the cutaway and reserve handles at the same time.

In an instant, I was back in freefall, sliced free of my faulty main to the sound of a bullwhip. The reserve chute is designed to open quickly, but those precious few seconds ticked away like an eternity, once again. I was at one with the beats of my heart, as time slowed to a trickle. My freefall was tempered with a slight turbulence, a speckle of friction as the lines began unraveling above me. Still, I could see nothing. I did something I don't normally do; *"Dear Lord, I don't ask for much. But if you get me out of this, I promise I will...."*

Before I could finish the confessional the chute snapped open. The hurricane-force wind settled to a slight breeze. For the first time in hours, I felt a sense of serenity, caught in the eye of a passing storm. Unlike modern square parachutes, the old round parachutes are not controllable, and simply allow a paratrooper to descend slowly, straight down. This keeps a mass of bodies during large formation airborne drops from flying in to one another. With a little training, one can manipulate the parachute chords to get a nice, smooth flare out just before impact with the ground to soften the landing. I had only 18 jumps under my belt, barely the minimum for airborne duty. I lacked the experience. Even if I had it, well, I couldn't even see the ground heading up to meet me.

It wouldn't matter, because I didn't land on *land*.

~~~

D-Day was now fully underway. My unit, the Screaming Eagles, was more aptly named for a band of heathens. We jumped in just after midnight on June 6th. Our formations were scattered so severely that some units missed their mark by five miles. Some men landed in the English Channel, such as me. Some of them drowned. Those that made it safely ashore, through the web of anti-aircraft fire, met surprising little resistance on the ground. That light at the end of the tunnel, well, it wasn't the exit.

It took many hours for the unit to regroup. The Germans were as disjointed in their response as we were in the execution. Such is the nature of battle, but the fog of war gave our unit an advantage. The deception laid deep by General Eisenhower paid dividends. The 101st went about its mission assaulting the west flank of Utah Beach. Our goal was to provide covering support to the amphibious waves coming on the beaches of Normandy in just a few short hours.

Our Skytrain was one of many. While scattered, the men who drop near enough to the rally point proceeded back towards Utah. They secured the two primary supply lines, with a small group moving on to take down artillery bunkers. Most of the objectives of the 101st were cast
~~~

aside, and in the midst of battle, they took on targets of opportunity. Being inland, they were spared the carnage of the beach assaults, where thousands of our brothers in arms were killed, mowed down by dug-in artillery positions.

Yet, I would only learn of all those accomplishments many weeks later. I took no part in it. I was the first to exit the aircraft. The abrupt maneuver of the Skytrain launched me into a perigee, which combined with our altered course floated me more than five miles from our intended target. You might wonder why some people hate swimming in the ocean. For me, this is why. Try lugging a rucksack full of gear through a veritable ocean while being shot at.

Fortunately, I was a good swimmer. It took me five long hours to reach the shoreline. Most of the time, I just barely kept my head above the water. The day was breaking just as my feet felt the lovely sand soil of the French beach. I was guided by fire from the Battleship Texas. Just off shore, it sent more than 10 kilotons of high explosives screaming into the night with its 14-inch shells. They cascaded directly over my head, exploding on the shoreline. Each impact lit up the sky, and guided me towards my destiny.

This isn't where I was supposed to be, but my comrades would be landing soon. My world was getting more interesting by the minute. Sure enough, soon after I was making my boot print on the French soil, my old mentor Lieutenant Colonel James Earl Rudder showed up. He was preparing to assault the cliffs at Pointe du Hoc with his 2nd Ranger battalion. He was behind schedule, but nonetheless was leading his team down the field as both coach and quarterback. He had refused his own superiors' orders to lead his men from afar.

I'm sorry to have to disobey you, sir, but if I don't take it, it may not go. - ***Lt Col James Earl Rudder***

Or as Admiral David Farragut might have said; *Damn the torpedoes, full speed ahead.* Colonel Rudder was a proud Texan. He was not a man who led from behind. How appropriate that he fell under the protective fire of the Battleship Texas, one of the oldest and most storied dreadnoughts.

I gathered my gear and joined the fight alongside the 2nd Ranger Battalion. Two other 101st Airborne Rangers joined the fight with me, all of us having washed ashore unannounced and uninvited. We were the bastard children of the 2nd Rangers, but they welcomed us regardless. Quite a few others who landed in the Channel never made it ashore. God rest their souls.

Colonel Rudder's unit was given a treacherous assignment to assault the beach at the Pointe, scaling hundred foot cliffs to take out a German artillery battery. The Pointe tapered out into the English Channel, providing it a perfect vantage with which to spit venom at approaching Allied sea forces. Despite heavy bombing of that precise location, it remained a dug-in position of crucial strategic importance. It would certainly be the cause of many casualties once the main force arrived if Colonel Rudder were to fail.

Or so the Allies thought.

In fact, the Germans had moved the primary guns away from the Pointe just two days earlier on the orders of Rommel himself. Allied reconnaissance flights failed to pick up the anomaly due to overcast weather. Despite movement of the guns, the objective remained paramount, and the Rangers would improvise, adapt, and overcome once they took the beach.

Those guns did not simply vanish; they had to be somewhere.

The battalion lost many men just getting to the shore. Several of the amphibious "ducks" sank in the choppy seas, or had to turn back. The rangers who made it ashore pressed on. They scaled the cliffs and went about their objective to neutralize the guns. Sporadic German gunfire continued throughout, taking down numerous soldiers as they broached the beachhead. The determined Rangers pushed ahead. Launching hooks into the daunting cliffs above, they eventually gained the high ground.

Colonel Rudder would direct naval guns to destroy the recalcitrant machine gun nest that wreaked so much havoc on the beach. He sent Lieutenant Dutch Vermeer to sight it in. The lieutenant grabbed me and two others to take it down. During the fracas, a shell hit near the command post and Colonel Rudder was knocked off his feet. A captain was killed. Several men were wounded. The sight of the Colonel gave us all a charge. He was pissed off, and vehemently darted out to fire his pistol at enemy snipers in his seething rage. He was shot in the leg as a result, and we pulled him back to safety.

The biggest thing that saved our day was seeing Colonel Rudder controlling the operation. It still makes me cringe to recall the pain he must have endured trying to operate with a wound through the leg and the concussive force he must have felt from the close hit by the yellow-colored shell. He was the strength of the whole operation. ***- Lt Vermeer***

We all stepped up our game at the sight, but I'd soon share the other men's dismay that our primary objective, the main guns of Pointe du Hoc, were not here. Undeterred, Colonel Rudder split the force in two, sending one half to move out, and the other to cover the position of the command post.

He sent a message to Headquarters:

Located Pointe-du-Hoc -- mission accomplished -- need ammunition and reinforcement -- many casualties.

He received this reply:

No reinforcements available -- all rangers have landed at Omaha.

~~~

A scout group was sent to look for the large artillery pieces. We found them inland, just out of range of the
~~~

Allied bombs. Our thermite grenades would soon ensure those guns were out of commission. The war torn area had grown silent, save for the distant rumblings of a world war. The thermite grenades quickly brought us back to reality, and the objectives of the 2nd Rangers were now officially accomplished. Yet, survival was still a distant horizon.

The thermite grenades stirred up a hornet's nest, and we found ourselves locked in a two-day fight against increasing German fighters. The initial shock of D-Day had them take cover, but as their flanks were besieged by our brethren, they were squeezed back into the narrowing Pointe. They were being boxed into the sea, and we were the only thing in their path. Now bunched into a steadily decreasing position, we had less than 200 yards of real estate as the enemy closed in.

As German re-enforcements arrived, Colonel Rudder called in naval guns. The mighty dreadnoughts lobbed a much needed respite from the German assault. The accuracy of the shelling was difficult to establish. A shell landed off target, taking out several of Rudder's men, yet the constant bombardment forced the enemy away from a formidable attack.

We held off the German onslaught for two full days, besieged without food or re-supply. In a fickle turn of fate, the Rangers had landed inside the Pointe's perimeter, a near impregnable German fort which they'd strategically abandoned. We turned their assets against them. Soon, the 5th Ranger Battalion arrived and the Germans were forced to surrender.

The efforts of Colonel Rudder and the 2nd Ranger Battalion saved countless American lives. In doing so, they suffered nearly 70 percent casualties. Only 90 of his men could still fight on afterwards. I suppose you could add me as well, an adopted member of his corps. We gathered our wounded, readied the dead for burial, and prepared for the even more grudging breakout from the French coast. We would march onward, into the mouth of the cat.

Colonel Rudder would rise to the rank of Major General. He would become one of the most decorated soldiers of World War II. He earned the Distinguished Service Cross, Legion of Merit, Silver Star, French Legion of Honor with Croix de Guerre and palm, and many others. He would return home to become the mayor of his hometown, Texas Land Commissioner, and then president of the Texas A&M University system. Our rendezvous would become pivotal to world events even beyond the coming terror of Fat Man and Little Boy.

6. Eagle's Nest

My God sent his angel and shut the lions' mouths, and they have not harmed me, because I was found blameless before him; and also before you, O King, I have done no harm. - ***Daniel 6:22***

Over the next three weeks, our fighting was intermittent around the French countryside. We met German forces holed up in cities and other encampments. As the breakout from Normandy dragged on, I would return to my unit and begin preparation for our next major assault. The first trip to inland Europe would be short lived, but the Five-O-Deuce would be back very soon.

By the end of June we were sent home to England for recovery time. In mid-September we were called in for another air drop to support Operation Market Garden. This new objective was to clear a path to the German border for Allied ground forces. It would be my second combat jump. We went in on September 17th, and this jump would be my last. Luckily, this time it would be in broad daylight, without being under fire. It was much preferred to the first one.

Our objectives entailed the seizure of key roadways and bridges to secure a clear path into Germany over the Rhine. However, the operation was ill-conceived, and during the mission, the Nazis ended up destroying most of those assets before we could get close enough. It was a mission ultimately deemed a failure by historians, and achieving a logistical route over the Rhine would not be achieved fully until six months later.

Some of the toughest fighting our unit experienced was during this operation. During one particular fire fight, I witnessed a truly selfless act of bravery by Private Joe Mann. He jumped onto a grenade as we fought off German soldiers from a foxhole. I hadn't seen the grenade, but Joe did, and without hesitation, he gave his life to protect the rest of us.

That moment haunts me today. It was the first time I'd seen such an act firsthand; human being giving his own life, it doesn't happen as often as Hollywood might lead us to believe. He knew this action would be his end. I couldn't fathom why he did it. In a flash, in that brief instant, my head turned and caught a glimpse of his eyes. The mind of Private Mann became clear to me. What his mind conveyed in those eyes was stunning:

He had few regrets, but just a few. He knew his life would end. He was ready. He was confident that he was going to Heaven. He did this because of love. The love for his fellow soldiers. It was written in blood, and sweat, in the grueling heat of Fort Benning. The mutual fear he felt with them, arm-in-arm, from his fear of heights, to the assault of the beaches. Constant gunfire. An aching heart. A girl he'd never again hold. The love of his family. The longing to make them proud. The certainty of his conviction that his sacrifice along with millions of others might bring peace and justice to an unjust world.

In that instant, he made the decision to sacrifice himself. Perhaps that is the essence of what it means to be human. It has been said by those who study Ancient Greece that their gods envied the humans precisely because they could die at any moment, and that is the only thing that made living meaningful. It is a beauty those gods could never know. I was proud to see them give Joe Mann the Medal of Honor, even though it costs him everything.

After Market Garden, there was no more down time for us. The Germans were floundering. They lashed out in one more major offensive; the Battle of the Bulge. The fighting began on December 16th. By Christmas Day, during the Siege of Bastogne, I thought for certain we would be overrun by the German Panzers.

The Nazis cut off our tactical supply lines and we were ordered to conserve ammo. The last thing our group of soldiers wanted was to be overrun without having a fighting chance. We were trained to fight to the end. The goal was to make the other poor sonofabitch die for his country. The worse part was all the time we had to think about it, especially at night, as we were ordered to turn out all lights to be in total darkness. I've said it before, I *hate* the darkness.

I tried to write a letter to my dad back home, in the hopes that maybe someone would find it on my body and tell him how much I appreciated him. I never spent much time with him, and we were not close. The reality now appeared that I might never see him again. I'd had many opportunities to visit over the past few years, but never did.

Such feelings are fleeting for me, but I think my dad would appreciate this letter. I don't show emotion often, or well, for that matter. Emotion has not much of a home in my heart. I couldn't finish the letter. I just didn't have that much to say to him. He would pass away while I was overseas. The news never reached me, so I never had an opportunity to grieve.

I fell asleep that night and drifted away into a previous dream from many months before. In states of metacognition, memory recall is not always perfect. Reflecting on the oddities of such dreams can be quite telling. It seems I was lounging in a coffee house on a Mediterranean beach, when in walks none other than General Dwight D. Eisenhower. Known as "Ike", he was accompanied by his aide-de-camp.

In this dream, I am not sure if he sought me out, or if I sought him, but this was no casual encounter. The back story is hard to establish. In matters of the non-physical world, you often are subject to encounters just as you would be running into people on a busy street. His first question led me to believe it was he who had sought me for advice.

It was a loaded question, one in which he tried to ascertain whether I was on his side, or whether I would try to deceive. Espionage was in full swing, both from the Germans, and the Soviets. I've been known to be very adept at such things. Or perhaps it was just my ego. After all, why would a 4-star general seek the advice of a Private?

"Mac, I've got a conundrum here," remarked the General. "We've promised the Soviets a second front in Europe, and I've got to deliver. My question to you is, should we come in from the tip of Italy, or a full frontal assault in northern France, where the Germans are expecting us? I've got to be honest, I think we can get them on the run in Italy, and the thought of going into that hornet's nest in France frightens me. They are waiting for us in France."

Now this was a trick question if ever I'd heard one. My studies entailed a great deal of reading in European history. There are mountains of literature on great battles and warfare strategy employed in this theater. I wore the same uniform as the General. My objective, aside from being on the Allied side, was to get into German territory to recover a long lost asset. Nonetheless, the General had made an amateurish attempt to mislead me into uncovering a bias, tipping my hole card to reveal myself as a subversive agent.

Historians have debated the Western Front and a few believe the northern assault to be some great conspiracy theory. The only conspiracy is that a full-scale invasion of Italy was even considered. I measured my response, as I was talking to the great General Eisenhower, but I was nonetheless a bit offended at being patronized. I folded my hands neatly in front of me, on the table. I leaned in closer.

"General, with all due respect, I understand your question. But just how many young men do you intend to slaughter with such a half-witted strategy? Sir."

"Come again, soldier?" Ike was taken aback at this brazen act of insubordination. He was not a man accustomed to snippy retorts.

"I said, 'with all due respect', General. *Sir.*"

I patiently waited for a real answer.

"Look, Mac, I wish I could save them all, I really do. But I'm a flag officer. I send men into harm's way to protect the greater good. We're dealing with the lesser of two evils. Life is not all sunshine and rainbows; and war sure as hell not."

The General took a sip of coffee. His aide sat with a condescending gaze. He was aware of the General's feint. Ike was not going to budge, or drop his poker face, until he knew for certain just which side of the fight I was on. So I gave him my reply:

"OK, then, General, here we go. I could go through an entire list of why an Italian invasion is foolhardy, but suffice to say that northern France is your only option. You have a ready-made logistics depot in Great Britain. You can store men, machinery, and ammunition to your heart's content. I'm sure you've heard the saying 'an amateur studies tactics, a professional studies logistics?' Second, you may find it easier to get ashore in Italy, but once there you will have a distinct disadvantage--rocky, mountainous terrain, massive rivers, and a much longer hike to reach Deutschland. If you think the Rhine will be difficult to cross for a mechanized cavalry, what about the Alps? I'm sure at West Point you learned about a guy named Hannibal who tried to invade Rome two thousand years ago with Elephants. You might fancy yourself Hannibal reborn, but I assure you, sir, his victory led to losses of men and treasure that your political benefactors cannot, and will not, stomach. He was cut off by his own political class. History might smile on him, but he was...."

"OK, enough." Ike replied.

"But sir, I'm just getting started."

I am passionate about warfare and strategy. I could have rambled on for an hour, but the General got what he needed with the first salvo of my harangue. Every battle in history has a lesson, and every confrontation in the present most likely has a corresponding lesson from ages ago. The best military leaders are students of history. They study warfare and tactics, because even as weapons advance, basic principles of warfare do not. And of course, the movement of men and machinery into theater is of supreme importance in victory. Simple-minded leaders who command legions of men always get me tense. They don't deserve the rank.

This was not the case with General Eisenhower. He was a studied and intelligent man, and certainly no fool. He was, however, thorough, and took few unnecessary risks. He had simply thrown me off his trail, just as he soon would with the Germans when the Allies invaded Normandy. He was clever, and he knew the foundation of all strategy.

*All warfare is based on deception.- **Sun Tzu***

After a brief pause, I couldn't tell if the General was sizing me up as a smart-ass, or if he was genuinely contemplating my advice. I took a sip of my coffee.

I continued, "General, the only use for invading Italy is to keep them out of the major land war, and keep the Med free."

"I said. Enough. That will do," Ike replied.

"But sir, this really can't be the questions you came here to ask.

"You talk a lot, don't you Mac?"

The General sat back in his chair, looked me in the eye, and nodded. He turned to his aide. With that, the General got up from his chair, and put on his parade cap.

"OK. Brief him," he ordered the aide.

The aide jumped to his feet, and saluted sharply; "Yes, Sir, General Eisenhower."

"Have my plane ready at 1400 hours and alert my staff."

General Eisenhower turned to me.

"I'm glad we got you on our side for this one, Mac. We're gonna need all the help we can get."

I saluted sharply. The General returned the honor, and with that, he turned and began to walk out of the building.

"Thank you, sir. I have a feeling history will gaze favorably upon you long after you are gone."

With a laugh, the General replied, as he pushed open the door. He turned his head briefly to address me one last time.

"That a fact? Well that's good to know. *Good to know*. One more thing, General Patton will be there to relieve you in the morning."

The aide spent the next hour asking my advice on many dilemmas the General faced. Primarily he was concerned with how to deal with the raging egos of some of the world's most infamous leaders, from de Gaulle to Roosevelt. He even had to deal with difficult men whom were his own subordinates; other Generals he had leapfrogged to become the most powerful military man on the planet.

I didn't have all the answers, but I gave him the best advice I could muster. I was mostly right, in retrospect. As I've said before, I was always passionate about history, and politics is closely entwined with all military action. Whether it be politics of nation versus nation, or internal leadership, the same basic issues come up again and again.

The invasion would be no cakewalk, and the breakout from the beaches entering the German heartland cost many lives. You do the best you can with the tools God gave you. A General goes to battle with the army he has, not the army he wants. The same can be said for any number of elements that he must account for – politics, terrain, enemy forces, et cetera. Ike was simply trying to execute a battle plan given his available assets and a plethora of data points. It is an arduous task given this fight spanned the globe.

~~~

I awoke from my dream. It was daybreak. I had survived yet another night pinned down in the middle of Europe.

Ike was right. General Patton's 4th Armored Division broke the German line that day and saved our unit from annihilation. Aside from a few more engagements in January, my fighting days in World War II were over. We were part of some mop-up operations across Germany, but by Spring I found myself very much at ease. The sound of bombs and gunfire had abated.

Just a few more pieces needed to fall into place; I would be at the doorstep of achieving my objective. Our final duty in Europe was to head south, in May 1945, to seize one of Hitler's strongholds known as the Eagles Nest. After fighting subsided, we slowly made our way across Europe. The Five-O-Deuce was among the first to enter one of Hitler's homesteads, known by its German name as Kehlsteinhaus. It sat atop a mountain peak in the Bavarian Alps.

It is here that my story starts to get interesting. The Nazis looted large numbers of antiques, gold, art, and other
~~~

treasures from across Europe. It was one of Hitler's obsessions, although he was a failed artist in his own right. These pieces were stored in bunkers across Germany. A large cache was found in a salt mine in Austria. Many of the more famous works of art and prized pieces were taken to the homes of Hitler and the upper echelon of the Nazi party.

Hitler, and the Nazis, was not only anti-Semitic, but anti-Freemason. They disbanded the fraternity with the Enabling Act of 1933 and sent Masons into concentration camps. They raided Masonic Lodges and plundered their antiquities as well. Part of this no doubt was due to the Semitic origins of Freemasonry, tracing its lineage back to the nation of Israel, the Tribe of Judah, and the building of King Solomon's Temple.

The Monuments Men were engaged in tracking down these treasures and returning them to their rightful owners. By 1945, they had established two primary collection points to gather these treasures, at Munich and Wiesbaden. One of the secondary collection points was at Offenbach, where they processed millions of books, Torah scrolls, archives, and property seized from Masonic Lodges. In a battle that saw millions of soldiers fighting across several continents, the chances of getting all of these artifacts secured was an impossible task. It continues to this very day.

One item of Masonic significance had been stolen from Versailles, and now rested atop that Bavarian mountaintop inside the Kehlsteinhaus. It would fail to reach Offenbach, because I stashed it away and carried it home with me. While I was not inclined to pillage, it was common to take a souvenir home from the war, not for profit, but as a personal memento for the sacrifice of crossing oceans to liberate the continent from a cruel fate. I would have no trouble slipping this item back with me. It was far more than just a memento.

As the Allies moved across Europe, I volunteered to assist the Monuments Men as they endeavored to keep safe the arts and artifacts in newly liberated areas. They had less than 500 specialists across the theater. In addition to uncovering stolen items, they were tasked with collection and repatriation. They were happy to receive any volunteer assistance they could get. I first aided in searches at Berchtesgaden, and then at Neuschwanstein Castle. My zealous dedication ensured my name was passed along to other Monuments Men as my unit made its way south to the Bavarian Alps.

As we approached the Eagle's Nest, my senses honed to razor-sharp acuity. I knew we were close. I could feel the presence of that which I sought drawing at my soul. I entered the house with my commanding officer, as I was now his personal driver. Such duty had few volunteers, as entrenched sympathizers and snipers remained throughout the countryside. They'd love to take a shot at an officer. For me, to be the first inside these structures was well worth the risk.

Inside the Eagle's Nest, the energy grew stronger. The object of my obsession was near. The compound had the look of a museum, with artwork hung neatly and shelves of books adorning the lower walls. Hitler may have been a megalomaniacal dictator, and murderer of millions, but the man had a certain taste in art which was profound. It could be said that, aside from a lust for power, his desire to be an artisan drove him.

Outside the main study of the Fuhrer, I caught sight it. I knew instantly I had found that for which I was sent. Under a coffee table sat a little old chest which had a symbol which I recognized. It was the symbol of the Masons, the square and compass. This had been the symbol of the Craft since at least the 1500's. My father had a ring that he wore depicting the square and compass I had seen many times before. In time, when I got home, I too would join the Lodge. It was somewhat a family tradition for the McCormacks.

As I approached, the chest began to glow.

I hurriedly looked around to see if my commanding officer noticed. He was engrossed in casing the voluminous number of artifacts in the palace. He paid me no attention. I quickly opened the chest. It was mostly empty, except for brittle pieces of parchment, and a worn cotton sackcloth. The sackcloth glowed. I unwrapped the object inside. It was beautiful; made of the finest materials, diamonds and gold, rubies and emeralds.

As I reached for it, the glowing stopped. It was badly damaged. As I suspected, only half of the Jewel was here. It had been cut in half more than 1,700 years ago, by none other than Marcus Aurelius himself, in a failed attempt to destroy its power.

I waited for what I thought would happen. I felt numbness in my hand. My entire body felt limp, and my hand continued its journey all of its own accord. My excitement and anticipation reached an apex, as my body made contact with this Divine artifact. What happened next startled me.

Nothing.

7. The Jewel

A prudent man sees the evil and hides himself, but the simple pass on and are punished. - **Proverbs 27:12**

The great German composer Richard Wagner spent 25 years writing his masterpiece *Der Ring des Nibelungen,* commonly referred to as *The Ring.* Lauded as a synthesis of poetry and music, it follows the struggles of gods, heroes, and mythical creatures. There are similarities with J.R.R. Tolkien's *Lord of the Rings*, as both are stories of supernatural beings and common folk in a world of fantasy.

Both stories trace an eponymous magical jewel that grants powers over the entire world, but these stories were much more than just fanciful adventure. To the reader, such a story of magnificent quest is fulfilling in itself. It can cause the deeper meaning of the author to go unnoticed by the masses. One must truly absorb the work to understand the lessons.

To them it is a struggle between half a dozen fairytale personages for a ring...Only those of wider consciousness can follow it breathlessly, seeing in it the whole tragedy of human history and the whole horror of the dilemmas from which the world is shrinking today.

– ***George Bernard Shaw***

Tolkien was a devout Catholic, whose writing influenced everyone from C.S. Lewis to Led Zeppelin. He captured the imagination of the multitudes while conveying simple truths that transcend the ages. His religious beliefs are not defining characteristics of the work, but his writing is heavily vested with the themes of good and evil, fate and free will, power, temptation, and divine providence.

Once the war in Europe ended, I would have my own run-ins with fate and divine providence. Evil lurked just beyond the horizon. I couldn't see it yet, but it was always there.

~~~

Despite my theories on the location of the Jewel holding up, I was wrong about one thing. Actually, for those scoring at home, I was wrong about several things, but I'm not going to list them all out for you. I had dreamed that I would enter some type of mystical transformation, or transfer of power, when I finally beheld and made contact with the Jewel. I had traveled vast distances, across an ocean, and then marched through bullets and blood over half of Europe. As relieved as I was to reach the objective, I couldn't help but feel let down at the end.

I was perplexed. This was not what I envisioned. I pictured myself leaving this body and flying through the air. I would be empowered with abilities beyond this world and capable of conquering my enemies with supernatural powers. It was a bit of wishful thinking on my part, but I was hoping for something, anything, aside
~~~

from rucking it out as a run-of-the-mill foot soldier, confined to a human body with extremely limited abilities.

C'est la vie.

I took to heart the adage that *sometimes the treasure we seek is not the treasure we find.* Or, as my drill instructor so eloquently stated, "assumption is of the mother of all foul ups". He didn't use the word *foul.*

Perhaps this deep disenchantment in my soul is because I'd assumed I knew more than I did. The sheer fact that the Jewel was there is nothing but remarkable. The limit of mankind's knowledge is greatly constricted, but even the angels fall far short of the omnipotent understanding. I resigned myself to carry on the mission faithfully, to wait the proper time with good and wholesome intention, until the Master would make known to me the time and place.

I trudged on, one foot in front of the other. After all, I am merely a servant. My powers of knowledge and insight were gifts, but oh how I longed for that power to become physical. The quest must go on.

~~~

The war in Europe was at its end. I spent the rest of the summer of 1945 exploring the Australian Alps as I awaited my trip home. I never let the Jewel out of my sight. I managed to take the parchment from the chest as well, and I spent my downtime reading through those sacred texts. They were indeed ancient. It confirmed what I already knew. The Jewel had a marvelous history. I was
~~~

giddy as a school kid to learn more. This was all completely unpublished and unknown history, and I was likely one of the few on Earth to have ever read them - possibly the only one.

Twenty-mile ruck marches turned into pleasant hikes in the most beautiful land in the world. There was peace in the land, and the overwhelming feeling that evil had been crushed pervaded the collective psyche of the countryside. It was surreal.

Yet war in the Pacific raged on. My services would not be called upon for that theater. The Axis powers would soon crumble. In August, from a small airfield on the island of Tinian, a B-29 Super fortress called the *Enola Gay* would deploy the first atomic weapon on the town of Hiroshima. It would kill seventy thousand people in one day.

Japan surrendered on September 2nd, and the Second World War was over. It would bring a swift end to this conflict, yet usher in a new war all of its own. This would be a cold war; a war in the shadows. Mankind now had a powerful weapon which has only one use; total destruction.

As the Cold War lingered on the horizon, more than 50 million people would die during World War II. Winston Churchill described it as the most avoidable war in human history. At some level, perhaps all war is avoidable. If one is truthful with himself, he knows ultimately war can only be avoided in the near term, and will never be eradicated. It will always exist for two reasons; the fallibility of man, and the existence of good and evil. The best advice ever given to address this subject is to speak softly, and carry a big stick.

Four months later my unit would be sent home. Despite the voyage already behind me, my new mission was just beginning. I was able to smuggle the Jewel home with me, though I kept the Jewel separate from the documents just in case I came under inspection. The Jewel itself, while mangled, was easily identifiable even to the most amateur examiner as an historic artifact. There were a plethora of documents. I safeguarded them amongst my personal journals and paperwork to conceal their existence. If worse came to worse, I might be forced to lie, and use my credentials as a Monuments Men agent to cover up my crime.

Weeks later, I would realize I was wrong about something else. I believed that in finding the Jewel, I was keeping it out of Nazi hands. It dawned on me, by the time I found it, the war was essentially over. I was at a loss. Why would I be sent to recover a Jewel of such power, if there was no chance the Nazis could have used it? Certainly Hitler had no knowledge of the authority he wielded by possessing such a powerful artifact. If he did, why didn't he use it? His war was now lost. He was dead of suicide in a bunker in Berlin.

Out of the clear blue sky, bright as the shining sun, came my epiphany.

As Stalin's army moved in from the East, there was a desperate scramble to seize as much of Europe as possible by the opposing Western Allies and Soviet forces. The result of that war saw the Soviet Bloc add extensively to its list of client states, which would all eventually fall to Communism. Berlin and Germany would be split into pieces, and the stage for the next half century of struggle would be set.

At that point, America had yet to drop the atomic bomb on Japan, but espionage efforts were well underway. Soviet agents and sympathetic American communists had penetrated the Manhattan Project and the Los Alamos laboratories, stealing secrets of a nuclear weapon. The Soviets soon engaged in uranium production.

In just a few short years, in the fall of 1949, the U.S. Air Force would detect a distinct pocket of radioactive material floating innocently through the atmosphere. The die had been cast, and President Truman declared; *"We have evidence that within recent weeks an atomic explosion occurred in the U.S.S.R."*

The Cold War was upon us.

My mission was never to protect the Jewel from the Nazis. It was to safeguard it from the coming landscape of a world in which nuclear weapons could destroy all mankind. I would believe for many years that this enemy was the Soviets, but I will not be so cavalier in my assumptions this time.

Perhaps I was wrong again.

8. QUEEN ELISSA

Kingdom of Tyre, present-day Lebanon, 825 BC

Queen Elissa turned her head to steal one last glimpse of her homeland. Her eyes watered, her lips were pursed and quivering. Tears streamed down her cheeks as the ship sailed quietly into the Mediterranean night. She would never return to face the wrath of her brother, King Pygmalion; neither would she ever see her family again. In her hands, she clutched her fallen husband's most revered possession – a jewel passed on to Hiram, King of Tyre, from King Solomon himself hundreds of years ago. It was given in recognition of King Hiram's assistance in building the first Temple of Jerusalem.

The cruel and heartless Pygmalion was a man who lusted for gold and power. He desired the fortune, and authority, of Elissa's husband Acerbas, the High Priest. Days earlier, Pygmalion grew impatient in his endeavors and murdered Acerbas in the Temple of Tyre. He kept this a secret from Queen Elissa, but she came to know the truth. She was a woman of exceeding beauty, and rightfully shared the throne with Pygmalion after the death of their father, King Matten.

King Pygmalion was a compulsive liar who fabricated grand stories of Acerbas' death and sought to console his sister in mourning. The spirit of Acerbas visited Queen Elissa one night, in a dream. He told her the truth of his murder.

He warned her to leave Tyre, else she too would meet the same fate at the tyrannical Pygmalion's hand.

The spirit of Acerbas also told her where to find his gold and treasure, and the most sacred of his possessions, the Jewel of Hiram. He told her this Jewel would ensure her safe passage away from Tyre and guide her journey to a new home. The Jewel of Hiram, when crafted by Bezalel, was envisioned to become a headpiece for the Rod of Aaron. This never came to fruition, and the jewel was presented to King Solomon when he assumed the throne.

With the assistance of the ghost of Acerbas, Elissa outwitted her brother. During the night, she fled Tyre and left her homeland forever. In the vast darkness of the sea, Elissa wept, and prayed for her husband's soul, for safe passage, and for a new beginning. In the darkness, the Jewel began to glow.

She sought refuge on the shores of Africa and founded a new empire. Her dynasty would become prosperous. It pre-dated the Romans, and would soon become their greatest foe. Taking the message from the ghost of her husband, she buried his treasure within the Earth. The empire she founded was called Carthage.

Carthage prospered for many years after the establishment by Queen Elissa. The Jewel of Hiram was buried, dormant, and hidden safely beneath the earth for more than 600 years until a young Carthaginian boy found the relic in 240 B.C. The young man was hunting at night when he saw an eerie glow. As he investigated and drew near the strange light, he found that it moved away from him.

Eventually, the light descended into the ground at the base an olive tree. The earth itself became illuminated at the spot. The boy made camp for the night. While he was asleep, he felt the Earth shake. The piercing sound of crackling lumber filled the air. The tree fractured into pieces and fell to the ground. The next morning, amidst the rubble, he discovered the Jewel.

His name was Hannibal Barca. Hannibal became perhaps the greatest strategic mind of Antiquity. He desired to one day lead his country to victory over the rival Roman Republic. His vengeance toward Rome would reside with him until his death many years later.

When he came of age, Hannibal invaded Rome with his army. He famously crossed the Pyrenees, the Alps, and fought off the Gauls as he traversed their homeland. Hannibal led his forces on an arduous journey in what, at the time, was a world war. Through brilliant tactics, he fought the Romans to a stalemate, winning victories with inferior forces. His ability to outwit opponents on the battlefield struck fear into the hearts of the Romans.

At Cannae, Hannibal left one of the finest examples of his military mind. By shrinking the combat area to shape the battlefield, he then utilized his cavalry to envelope and annihilate his opponent. He capitalized on the opposing commander's hubris. The Carthaginians slaughtered more men in one day at Cannae than almost any battle in human history. Even today, the battle is revered as a masterpiece of military tactics.

Only through protracted attrition did the Romans eventually repel the invading force of Hannibal, but they did not defeat him. Rome simply refused to meet him on the battlefield ever again. His failure to fully conquer Rome was primarily from lack of national will on behalf of Carthage to continue sending money and supplies. Hannibal returned home, but the mark he left on Rome, and history, would never vanish.

The Romans eventually conquered Carthage in the Third Punic War. Following his country's defeat at the Battle of Zama, a bounty on Hannibal sent him into voluntary exile. He left his homeland for Tyre, ironically, the motherland of his country's founder Queen Elissa. From Tyre he travelled to Ephesus, where he was received by King Antiochus. The ambitious King wished Hannibal to view his assembled forces with which he planned to attack the Romans. Antiochus desired to be the greatest power in the Hellenic world. He pushed the expansion of his kingdom across the Hellespont and directly into the face of the Roman Republic.

In 190 B.C., the legionnaires of Scipio marched out to meet the encroaching threat, and defeated Antiochus at the Battles of Thermopylae and Magnesia, the latter on the plains of Anatolia in modern day Turkey. Even in exile, Hannibal fought for the Seleucid Empire of Antiochus to defeat his Roman nemesis, but to no avail. The Romans once again emerged victorious. As a result of the defeat,

Antiochus was forced to give 15,000 talents of silver to the Romans. He planned to hand over Hannibal to appease the Romans and limit his reparation, as Hannibal was the most notorious enemy of the Republic.

One step ahead, Hannibal slipped away to Crete, but not before part of this restitution was divested from his belongings. To his dismay, he was deprived of the Jewel of Hiram. Soon thereafter, Hannibal died, having never completed his life's ambition to conquer the Romans. The only thing which would bring the great society's downfall was the Romans themselves. Their gradual decline had now been set in motion and in due time it would soon no longer be a Republic. All great societies come to an end.

The Jewel found its way to the city of Rome with the rest of the seized Anatolian wealth. It was here placed into the Roman treasury, where it was among countless riches from the many people conquered by the great Republic. Here it would sit for 200 years. It would not be dredged up until a celebration for a new leader was underway, but it would not be for a consul, rather an emperor, as the Republic was no more. Rome was now an empire.

The Jewel was re-fashioned into one fit for a king and given to Emperor Nerva as he ascended to the head of the Empire. Nerva found the Jewel striking and carried it with him as a personal adornment. In a slight adjustment to the course of history, he became the first of the Five Good Emperors.

The Jewel would remain a favorite of the emperors, including Hadrian. Upon his death, Hadrian left the Jewel in a museum at his Villa outside Rome, near Tivoli. His reign was marked with relative peace, replete with constructing a defensive wall across the entire landmass of Britain to mark the northern edge of the Empire. The Jewel was unwittingly removed from Hadrian's Villa by priests following his death in 138 A.D., who were raiding his Villa to carry granite statues back to Rome for their own use. Hadrian was followed by his appointed successor, Antoninus.

The Jewel would find its end with the Roman Empire during the reign of Marcus Aurelius, the last of the Five Good Emperors. Marcus Aurelius was a philosopher king. He was a student of Stoic doctrine. He believed that knowledge was attained through reason, and truth was distinguishable from fallacy. Pulsations from objects can be received by the senses of the mind, leaving an impression on the imagination. This would lead one to knowledge. He was the only one of the emperors to hold the Jewel who understood what he had in his possession.

Make for yourself a definition or description of the thing which is presented to you, so as to see distinctly what kind of a thing it is in its substance, in its nudity, in its complete entirety, and tell yourself its proper name, and the names of the things of which it has been compounded, and into which it will be resolved. - ***Marcus Aurelius***

Marcus Aurelius died in 180 A.D. in Vienna while finishing his conquest of Germania. He recognized and came to respect, and even fear, the power of the Jewel. He saw in it the duality of man, of good and evil, and the awesome power of a supernatural force. Despite its power, the Jewel did not alter one's nature, but amplified it. His greatest concern was the possibility it could amplify the corrupted soul of an evil man should it fall to the wrong hands.

In his latter days Marcus Aurelius longed for peace. He postulated that, by destroying the Jewel, he would extinguish its power. The authority vested within could no longer be wielded, and peace might prevail. He envisioned a fate of cataclysm for Rome, not the least of which due its persecution of so many peoples. It began with Nero's oppression of the Christians, as he fiddled, while Rome burned. Rome would soon begin its descent into a 400 year decline marking the end of the Western Empire. Shortly before his death, Marcus Aurelius had the Jewel cut in two pieces, piercing it down the middle; accomplishing a seeming fatal blow.

The Emperor sent the two fragments of the Jewel to opposite ends of the known Roman world. The first he sent to modern-day Spain and the other to his friend Theophilus of Antioch in southern Turkey. Theophilus wrote *From the Foundation of the World,* which he sent to the Emperor, describing human history from Adam up to the reign of Marcus Aurelius himself.

This latter piece of the Jewel was hidden away by Theophilus inside a cave on the side of a mountain. The cave had been used by early Christians, including Peter and Paul, for worship. It was one of the earliest Churches, and today is known as St. Peter's Grotto. The Jewel would be safe here for nearly a thousand years. Its protégé in Spain would remain tucked away as well.

Yet the Jewel itself had been divested of certain powers well before it ever entered Rome, and long before it was severed by Marcus Aurelius. On the fields of the Anatolian plain, after the battle between Scipio and Antiochus, a heavenly spirit, an angel, had left the Jewel and was now free to roam the Earth. It would remain as a guardian of the Jewel, though now would be separate.

When a piece of the Jewel retired to Antioch, it would again become companioned with this angel, who had stayed behind in Cappadocia. The angel and the Jewel would be present during the infamous Crusades for the Holy City of Jerusalem. In 634 A.D., two years after the death of the Muslim prophet Muhammad, a legacy of caliphates would gain hold of the Middle East. This would eventually spark the greatest Holy War of the ages; the Crusades in the Middle East, and the Reconquista in Iberia.

In 1098, Muslim forces besieged the city of Antioch. A mystic named Bartholomew claimed he knew the location of the Holy Lance, which had pierced Christ's side, within the city. An excavation was undertaken to find it, and the Crusaders believed they had found the lance. Alas, they did not find the lance, but rather the severed piece of the Jewel of Hiram buried by Theophilus.

Nevertheless, the relic was carried at the head of the armies. It bolstered the morale of the Crusaders. They marched out to miraculously defeat the Muslim forces. Some Crusaders claim an army of angels and saints appeared on the battlefield to win the day. The piece of the Jewel stayed at the head of the army, and would go with the Crusaders into the Kingdom of Jerusalem. This is the location where it was bestowed its supernatural powers at the hands of King Solomon two thousand years before.

Forty years later, one of the greatest military leaders in Muslim history was born. Saladin would conquer Jerusalem in 1187, and his legacy as one of the most important figures in Islam would be established when he conquered the Holy city. Saladin died a poor man, having given away his wealth. Before his death, he returned the piece of the Jewel to his home, to the Grand Mosque of Damascus, and died there in 1193.

Here again, in Damascus, the piece of the Jewel was safe for hundreds of years. In 1799, an aspiring young Italian, turned Frenchmen, named Napoleon Bonaparte moved his Army to the province of Damascus. He led 13,000 French soldiers in conquest of the region. In a brutal attack on Jaffa, 1,400 prisoners were summarily executed by bayonet in order to save bullets.

The spoils of war returned with Napoleon to France a year later. The Jewel was with him when he led a coup to seize power in the country. Napoleon would not carry the piece of the Jewel into battle, but had it locked up at the Palace of Versailles where he resided while Emperor.

It was at Versailles, the estate of the French Monarchy, that Hitler's forces, while raiding Europe of its historic treasures, came into possession of the sacred object in late 1942. Once seized, it eventually found its way to Hitler's home in Bavaria, one of millions of treasures seized during the war. The date of the Nazi pillage of Versailles was coincidentally the exact date that I was drafted into the U.S. Army.

9. Return to Texas

The Lord said to Raphael: "Bind Azazel hand and foot, and cast him into the darkness. And on the day of the great judgment he shall be cast into the fire". - ***Book of Enoch***

My time in Europe came to an end. I made my way back to the small town of Brady. It was only then that I learned of my father's death. As I said previously, we were not close. I had no siblings. My mother had passed away in childbirth. There were aunts and uncles, and cousins; none of whom I had more than a distant relationship with. Dad left me a few things, and as it turned out, it would be enough to go back to school. I made a pilgrimage from Brady back to my hometown, but only to pay my respects. I had always been a loner, out of place in that small, dusty cow town on the plains of west Texas.

I re-adjusted to life outside the military. It was a welcome respite to have a roof over my head, clean clothes, and the comforts of civilized life. The nation had a renewed sense of pride. People had a feeling of hope, a stark contrast to the decade of Great Depression, and another half decade of world war.

It was a good time in the nation's history, but it was also a time when the country mourned the fallen. It settled into an era of relative peace. Nevertheless, I was restless, and I prepared for only a short stay in Brady.

When I left Brady four years earlier, part of me felt I would never return except as a visitor. In many respects, that is all I would ever be to this small town. I was beginning to think I'd never actually have a home of my own. My mission in life was elsewhere, and Brady just a temporary stop on the path. I said goodbye to my mentor, Colonel Rudder. He would soon become mayor of the town. He tried to convince me to stay around. I think he just wanted a kindred spirit; someone to reminisce with about the war. He was a great man who went on to great things far beyond Brady.

Teaching the fundamentals to school kids was no longer in my heart. I wanted to learn. I wanted to immerse myself in study and piece together this puzzle I'd found. I planned to enroll at the University of Texas in that pursuit. I packed up my belongings and headed east, towards the more economically prosperous city of Austin. Here, I would narrow my search for the remaining piece of the Jewel of Hiram. I was prepared for an arduous task, but I attacked it with aplomb.

Austin was the state Capitol. It was beginning to emerge as one of the major metropolitan centers of Texas. Despite being in the intellectual center of the state, I struggled to find a suitable course of study which would prove useful. College is rigid in many respects. If you don't have a defined purpose, you are quite likely wasting your time. Surely enough, there did not exist a graduate program in *finding lost treasure*. After one semester, I discontinued my studies.

Back in Germany, I had managed to find the first piece of the Jewel rather quickly. In retrospect it was not as tall an order as you might suspect. The Nazis had compiled all the artifacts of Europe into central locations, which made the quest much less difficult. Rather than the needle in a haystack, it was more of a needle in a five-gallon bucket. This next piece could be anywhere on the planet. That's a needle in a hay *field*.

I had to narrow the search area, and I was fairly certain the item I sought was no longer on the European continent. Call it a hunch. Marcus Aurelius sent the missing piece to southern Spain, the far western edge of the Roman Empire. From there, hallmarks of the Jewel can be inferred through a close examination of history. The Jewel could be tracked by certain unnatural occurrences which it throws up in its wake.

The missing fragment of the Jewel of Hiram had been used by forces of the Reconquista to overtake the Iberian Peninsula. The guardian of the Jewel tracked it down, and the mighty archangel appeared in Spain in the early 16th century to search for it. The apparition was seen by many in Cordova, and to this day is celebrated by the Catholic Church. It was the appearance of the archangel Raphael.

Raphael arrived too late. The Jewel had already departed Spain in the era of the conquistadors. It arrived on the shores of a land thousands of miles away. It sailed the ocean on a Spanish galleon in 1504 at the hands of a young mariner bent on conquering the New World. Its power led to the overthrow of a great civilization, and would continue to assert influence as the European conquest of the Americas took hold.

Great victories were taken at the hands of tactical and strategic geniuses, by men who were just ordinary, but suddenly gifted with supernatural wisdom and insight. The Jewel has spawned greater warriors than any institution of man has, or ever will. Such rationale leads me to believe the Jewel now exists in the southern United States.

The hallmarks I would discover point to this region plagued by centuries of warfare from the time of conquistadors to the final battles of the American Civil War. At that point, around 1836, the Jewel vanishes from the historical record. I would refine my search to this period, and what better place to start than in the land which saw the confluence of the two great conquering powers of America; the Lone Star State.

As luck would have it, I was already here.

~~~

After I dropped out of the university, I took my research to the Texas State Library. I rummaged through archives from the most tumultuous time in the state's history, looking for any telltale sign or oddity. The archives were remarkably complete. I found the history of the early 1830's intriguing, yet I found few promising leads. There were not even vague mentions of anything remotely resembling what I was looking for.
~~~

I turned my inward reflection to my original postulation that I could find the Jewel based on its inferences in the physical world. Most notably, I examined major battles. I searched for displays of tactical ingenuity on the battlefield. There were many. The surprising victory of the Texan rebels against a vastly superior Mexican Army was very telling; something was out of place and unnatural.

In fact, some historians believe that Texas' existence as its own Republic is an historic anomaly of epic proportions. This did not bode well for my theory. The Jewel is more adept at shaping the outcome of battle through military genius, not random acts or *force majeure*. But the Lord, well, he does work in mysterious ways.

I was so deep in reading ancient records that I'd become lost in a forest. I had to balance my bouts with the minutiae by instead noting such macro data as the various dates and locations of the Archive-stamped documents. There were many documents whose location varied from Austin, which seemed to imply the Archive repository was somewhat mobile. I dug deeper. I soon realized that the Archives had been moved from town to town by the wagonload ahead of major battles during the Texas Revolution.

Alas, I had my epiphany. This was the act of a tactical genius I'd searched for. While it might not have been material to the war effort, it was crucial to preserve these documents to a leader who believed in forming a republic.

That leader understood centers of gravity, and the power of information 150 years before the Internet.

Who was this man?

His name was Sam Houston. In 1842, Sam Houston fought to have the Archives moved east, from Austin. He was known as a politician, at least by me, because he was president of the republic and governor of the state. He was also a U.S. senator. Less known to me at that time is that he had been a military general. He led the Texans in a miraculous victory over the vastly superior Mexican Army. This came on the heels of the Revolution, after the Mexican Army was bogged down in a sea of mud while the Texans retreated from defeat at the Alamo. Days later, Sam Houston would lead a surprise attack, culminating in victory.

Houston not only was a statesman and warrior, he was one of Texas' earliest Freemasons. The first Lodge in Texas, Holland #1, was chartered months before outbreak of the Texas Revolution. Soon after the Revolution ended, he presided over the convention which gave birth to the Grand Lodge of Texas. The fraternal order of the Masons had grown quite large in the past 500 years, and the network of Masons within early Texas was extensive.

I hearkened back to the square and compass on the chest I found at Eagle's Nest. Markings of the symbol of the Masons adorned the outside of the rustic chest I had found, but perhaps it was just coincidence. It could be the Jewel was placed there for safekeeping and had no real meaning. Regardless, those coincidences were becoming too great to ignore.

Now, I also learned that Santa Anna, the great Mexican President and war general, lost the battle to Sam Houston at San Jacinto. He too, was a Mason. In fact, it is said that Santa Anna's life was spared on the battlefield, at least a first, because he displayed the Masonic sign of distress which the Texans honored. The sign only saved him from being killed outright. Once he was captured, he became far more valuable to Sam Houston alive, primarily for political reasons as a bargaining chip with Mexico.

What intrigued me even more is that when the Jewel disappeared from the record in 1836, its last known location was in Mexico.

As they say, even a blind hog can find an acorn, yet this information was nothing but speculation at this point. There was nothing irrefutable that told me I was heading in the right direction of finding my Jewel. If Sam Houston did, in fact, know the whereabouts of the Jewel, then his death in 1863 would be a good place to start looking. This was the only lead I had of any promise.

I took my search for information to the Lodge of Free and Accepted Masons. This just and legally constituted body was a society full of mysteries and secrets of its own accord. It is a brotherhood that models its formal Lodges in the manner of King Solomon's Temple, even to this day.

The Lodge reaches back to the same period of time and place as the creation of this Jewel, the sanctum sanctorum. Even the physical structure of each Lodge building is aligned in an East-West direction, so as *the sun is in the south at meridian height at the beauty and glory of the day, to better observe the time, to call the Craft from labor to refreshment at the will and pleasure of the Worshipful Master.*

I could not put my finger on it, but there was something about the Lodge that began to draw me in. I could not truly understand the history from the outside. I submitted my petition to join the Masonic Lodge and became an Entered Apprentice. After my initiation, the real work to become a Mason began. I spent most of my days going over the memory assignments required to be elevated in status to a Master Mason.

Masonic tradition is passed on in spoken word. It is forbidden to be written down, except in coded symbols. As such, the exercise in learning Masonic lore is much more time consuming. Conversing with fellow brethren is the only way this wisdom is passed on.

I became quite knowledgeable in the esoteric history and word of the Craft. I grew to become quite enamored of the idea that the Lodge paid homage to Hiram. He was respected as the eponymous master craftsman because he brought forth the grand designs of the First Temple from knowledge passed on to him from King David, and to King David from the Lord.

David had blood on his hands, as such, he was not worthy to build the Temple for the Lord. Solomon was wise, as was Hiram. According to the word, he was an architect and master craftsman.

Nevertheless, my pursuit was not to become an expert in Masonic tradition. It was specifically to find the lost piece of the Jewel. After nine months, my foray into Masonry produced no answers as to the Jewel's location. I could not find even the slightest hint of anything remotely resembling an ancient Jewel. Sam Houston left no evidence of any type of magnificent object. Even the archives from the Grand Lodge of Texas were a complete dead end.

As far as Masonry was concerned, this object did not exist. My hopes began to dim that I was chasing fool's gold. I often pondered starting over from scratch, and going back to church to ask for Divine inspiration. Just as a man who refuses to ask directions, I stubbornly continued my search.

I did go back to start from scratch, at least a bit. I re-read all of the papers in the chest. Their brittle and yellowed condition testified to their age. A museum would kill for such treasures, but I wasn't interested in preserving such items for posterity. I needed them to decipher the mystery. These priceless pages held the secret to the riddle I had to solve.

I sent myself in circles, tracing and re-tracing the path I knew the Jewel had taken, looking for something, anything, that might yield a clue. I could readily ascertain the history of the Jewel in my hands up the early 19th Century, as it departed Syria en route to France at the hands of Napoleon. This did me absolutely no good, of course, because I had already found this Jewel.

The other piece was split apart in 180 A.D., and the next known location was Iberia in the 16th Century. From there, it is known that it was buried with Cortez in 1836. Aside from leaving an indelible mark on the course of warfare, there is a distinct yet fleeting trademark of a physical glow, an effervescence of energy that spills out into the natural world. This was first noted by Hannibal.

The faint remembrance of that last clue is what led me to a moment of *eureka* while being told a story over lunch one day.

It is a story that exists only in folklore. It sounds downright preposterous. It is a ghost story, one of countless to spring from the fancied thoughts of the human mind. Yet, even far-fetched tales often have some element of truth. The occurrence of this story fits, strikingly, with my timeline. It is the legend of a floating lantern in Milam County. It occurs on land that Sam Houston had ready access to, and even perhaps ownership of, during the early days of the Republic.

It was the Legend of Snively; a legend with many unknowns.

There is only one way to find out for certain.

I must go to Milam County and find out for myself.

10. The Conquest

I will make mine arrows drunk with blood, and my sword shall devour flesh; and that with the blood of the slain and of the captives, from the beginning of revenges upon the enemy. –***Deuteronomy 32:42***

Recall that Marcus Aurelius split the Jewel of Hiram into two pieces and cast them asunder, to the opposite ends of the known world. The piece which I now sought had been sent to the Western half of the Roman Empire. At that time, it meant the artifact would end up in Hispaniola, or modern-day southern Spain. This part of the Iberian Peninsula reminded me of Texas, with its pastoral landscape and arid climate. It's no wonder the descendants of the Spaniards have prospered in the Lone Star State.

The Jewel's location at this juncture was unknown, until it reappeared in the New World 1,400 years later. Whoever was charged with its safekeeping in the 2nd Century A.D. took their secret to the grave, or perhaps they were never even aware of it. Hiram's Jewel would disappear into the countryside on the hills east of Granada. Eventually it would become restless, as conflict surrounded and nigh consumed it.

Across the Strait of Gibraltar, the Moors gradually moved northward into Spain from Morocco in the early 8th

Century. They inhabited the Iberian Peninsula, and over time the Muslims built the magnificent and expansive Alhambra citadel in the city of Granada. Only 10 years after the Muslims arrived began the Reconquista, an 800-year struggle culminating with the fall of Granada in 1492. It was a year which also marked the discovery of a New World, and the beginning of colonial empires.

Subtle indications within this hall of man lead me to believe the Jewel came forth from hibernation to inspire the Alhambra. Aware of the coming conflict, the Jewel would compel the building of a fortress upon itself, inspiring the Craft to build a massive complex of protective walls to keep it hidden. Master craftsmen of the Islamic faith descended on Granada to build the epic structure beginning in 889.

Over time, it grew to be more expansive even than King Solomon's Temple. Poets describe this beautiful masterpiece of masonry as a "pearl set in emeralds". Major expansions in the 11th and 14th century evolved the Alhambra into a luxurious seat of royalty. Washington Irving described it as "a most picturesque and beautiful city, situated in one of the loveliest landscapes that I have ever seen."

Just over a century after this architectural treasure was completed, the Alhambra would be the last Muslim stronghold in Hispaniola during Reconquista. It would fall, and be subjugated during Ferdinand and Isabella's conquest. This victory marked the end of a tragic period that saw ethnic and religious genocide, and hundreds of thousands displaced or killed for their religious beliefs.

The Jewel was never found by either side.

In that same year, a young adventurer met with Ferdinand and Isabella. He sought funding for a voyage to the Far East and dreamed of bringing the Crown treasures from afar. His name was Christopher Columbus. While he was given many promises by the Crown, the country was financially destitute, and could ill afford to finance his ambitious venture across the seas. Columbus would ultimately be credited with discovering the New World, but it was another young man who would find the Jewel.

One day, a young man named Fernando made a fateful visit to the Alhambra. He was born in Medellin, and spent two years in Salamanca at the university. Thereafter he worked in Seville. He was a mischievous teenager, who'd sought more in life than his parents of lesser nobility could offer. Frustrated in his schooling, he'd taken to traveling across southern Spain, hearing the tales of brave voyagers sailing off for the New World.

During his visit, as he slept, a strange vision appeared before him in a dream. He awoke, and was met with a strange light. It led him to the interior of the *Puerta de la Justicia*. This was the original entrance tower to the Alhambra. The glowing light disappeared into the base of the tower. He fell asleep. The next morning he again awoke, and saw a shiny object perturbed from the wall. He peeled away the masonry, and beheld a Jewel of consummate splendor.

He had been searching for a place in life, unsure of what profession he would pursue. This find instantly re-invigorated him and granted him a clear vision. He knew this was his destiny. Combined with the word of Christopher Columbus reaching the New World, it inspired the lanky Spaniard and gave him a mission.

The boy today is better known as *Hernando* Cortez. With the Jewel at his side, he first traveled to the Americas in 1504. Later, in 1518, he would arrive in Mexico, and realize his destiny as he overtook the Aztecs and established himself as one of the greatest Conquistadors in history.

Cortez was buried with the Jewel in 1547 in a mausoleum in Sevilla. In a bizarre twist, his body was moved numerous times; three years after his death, and then again seven years later. It would be moved five more times in total, finally ending up in an unknown location. The Jewel, once again, seemed to have been lost.

His final resting place was eventually discovered in 1947. Suspiciously, the Jewel was not with his remains. A secret document would be found which contained an inquisition into the sordid tale of Cortez' body. It was written by Lucas Alcaman, and indicated the bones were actually buried in their final resting place in 1836; more than a hundred years prior.

Alcaman was one of the most educated men in Mexico in the 1830's. His insight into Latin American history led him to determine the existence of a paranormal anomaly surrounding Cortez. There were simply too many bizarre occurrences for his success to be natural. It was this power Cortez used to conquer great peoples of the New World. The telltale signs of the Jewel are there for those looking closely.

After years of research, Alcaman consulted a rising star in the new nation of Mexico with this information. This man was none other than General Antonio Lopez de Santa Anna. He became convinced of Alcaman's theory, and he hungered for power. Together, they tracked down and located the bones of Cortez. Upon discovering the final resting place, Santa Anna would also discover the Jewel. Cortez valued the Jewel highly; it wrapped around his neck even in death. Despite the flesh giving way to rot, the Jewel remained bound about his upper cavity even 300 years after his death.

General Santa Anna would take possession of this artifact and soon become known as the "Napoleon of the West." He was elected President of Mexico on April 1, 1833. A known opportunist, he switched loyalties to those he felt could best support his chances. He would use the power of the Jewel to rule, but his ill-conceived victory would be short-lived.

Santa Anna's hubris consumed him. During his pinnacle of power, he marched his Army boldly into Texas to quell an uprising. With superior numbers, and an opposition lacking rudimentary organization, he sought to overwhelm the Texans with a brute display of force. In San Antonio, he slaughtered the Texans at the Alamo in March 1836, killing every last defender including the legendary Davey

Crockett and Jim Bowie. The rallying cry "Remember the Alamo" would remain ingrained in the Texan rebels' minds for the rest of the war, and is still regaled in folklore today.

Great misfortunes visited the Mexican Army after the initial onslaught, beginning with the sea of mud as the Mexicans pursued the rebels east from San Antonio. A vast numerical advantage and battlefield supremacy dissipated, yet Santa Anna still held the initiative. The tide of the war was changing.

General Sam Houston led the remainder of the Texan insurrection. He retreated to Harrisburg, rounding up fighters in hopes of one last desperate stand. Santa Anna and his army gave pursuit with the fervor of Varro at Cannae. It would prove to be his downfall, as a modern-day Hannibal awaited. After being chased into a corner, General Houston ordered his men to burn the bridges, preventing Mexican re-enforcements. It also prevented any opportunity for escape for either army.

The die was cast, and while the Mexicans guard was down during an afternoon siesta, preparing their battle plans; the Texans attacked. Santa Anna was caught completely by surprise. The Texans fought with relentless fury. They held fire until the Mexicans shot their first volley in a panic, which amazingly went over the head of the entire column of approaching fighters.

While the Mexicans reloaded muskets, the Texans were within bayonet range and began a hand-to-hand, bloody fight. They used rifles as clubs to deliver blunt force trauma. *Remembering the Alamo*, they continued the fight at close range, smashing skulls, firing pistols, and carving up the enemy with Bowie knives.

When the dust settled, after a mere 29 minutes, more than 600 Mexicans lay dead or wounded. Another 700 soldiers were taken prisoner. Only three Texans died. Santa Anna's army was soundly defeated. It was an overwhelming victory; a display of tactical genius by Sam Houston.

Despite his army's route, Santa Anna himself had not yet surrendered. He was found hiding in tall grass near the battlefield. He was first sighted by Jim Sylvester who was riding by on horseback. The General had donned a corporal's uniform in hopes of escape. He would have been summarily executed, had it not been for one important thing. Sylvester was a Mason, as was Santa Anna, who presented himself with the Masonic sign of distress. Knowing this sign, Sylvester spared the General's life for the moment and took him prisoner.

He was marched back to General Houston himself, still clad in the uniform of a soldier. No one knew for certain his true identity, except the Mexican soldiers. Santa Anna's disguise was betrayed by his own men. Upon his approach to the encampment, the other Mexican prisoners began to salute and say:

"El Presidente! Es nuestro General!"

Sam Houston was severely wounded; however he treated the captive President with utmost respect. Santa Anna remained defiant and proud. He was searched, and his property seized. In his pocket, he carried numerous items. He had discarded the lavish uniform of the commander in chief, save for one thing; around his neck he wore the Jewel of Hiram.

He would never hold it again.

Santa Anna was forced to sign the Treaty of Velasco, recognizing the complete independence of Texas. In exchange, his life was spared and he was granted travel back to Mexico. He would try in vain to get the Jewel back throughout the rest of his life. His legacy was in tatters. He lost half the landmass of Mexico during his foray into Texas, and was looked upon by his countrymen as a failure.

I cannot explain how or why the Jewel turned into a weakness for Santa Anna. Perhaps his arrogance and selfishness were too much for him to overcome, even with the power of the Jewel at his disposal. It by no means grants omnipotence. It can, and will, be lost. I've said it before, strengths or weaknesses are both merely assets. The difference lies in how they are deployed.

At San Jacinto, the Texans would win the day against long odds. Sam Houston would hold onto the Jewel until the day before he died, going on to become President of the Republic of Texas, and senator of the United States. As a fervent Mason, he eagerly scouted the Craft over his later years to find a suitable heir to the Jewel.

He found his heir in the person of Aiden Benson, and I'd soon learn more about him as I packed my belongings and headed to Milam County.

~~~

An interesting side note: Though the last male heir of Cortez died in 1629, he left many children and many descendants who did not bear the Cortez name. One of those descendants heard rumors of what Lucas Alcaman found, and in 1851, threatened Alcaman's life if he did not tell him the location of Cortez' body. Alcaman refused, knowing that Santa Anna long since reburied the body and took the Jewel for himself. The man would not relent, and stole volumes of work from Alacaman's shelves pertaining to Cortez.

Four hundred fifty years later, that man's descendants would continue to search for that Jewel.
~~~

PART 2

Then the angel of the Lord went out, and killed in the camp of the Assyrians one hundred and eighty-five thousand; and when people arose early in the morning, there were the corpses—all dead. ***– Isaiah 37:36***

11. The Masons

After I quit the University, I took to working for a local construction outfit. America was prospering coming out of World War II, giving way to the baby boom generation. Texas began to grow as a hub for energy and manufacturing, and few towns were more vivacious than Austin. My ability to learn quickly and handle confrontation not only ensured my gainful employment, but allowed me to work my way up the ranks of a highway crew. Despite my past as a soldier, I was, at heart, a peacemaker.

Blessed are the peacemakers, for they shall be called sons of God. – ***Matthew 5:9***

Being a peacemaker comes in handy when working construction. We worked long days in the brutal Texas sun. Nerves become frayed, and tempers can flare at the slightest semblance of offense. My abilities to defuse bad situations and my ability to think on my feet soon reverberated up the chain of command of my roadway crew. My foreman took note of my ambitious nature and promoted me to supervisor. Before long, I was running my own crew, beating deadlines and helping the company's bottom line.

A few more months in, I learned the art of the bottom line. My crews were consistently coming in under budget, and before long I was called in by management to begin outlining ways to reduce costs. I got the sense that I was being groomed for upward movement, which, while reassuring, left me feeling that I was getting too far attached to what was supposed to be temporary employment.

It was the winter of 1948 when I accompanied the boss to a meeting to bid on a new highway job. We only had a few hours to assess the project, and cut our cost projections to the bare minimum while still accounting for a profit. If the bid was too high, we'd be beaten by a competitor. Too low, and we'd win the bid but lose money as we wouldn't be able to cover our costs.

We lost the bid. In retrospect, maybe I was a bit too naïve and padded our numbers. Regardless, it was at that meeting my fate would take a turn in the right direction. It was here I met Hank Benson. He was technically bidding for the job, but in reality, he was scouting for new hires as he expanded his own construction empire. Sniping talent from his competitors was a shrewd business maneuver he liked to employ.

This was about the time I'd entertained myself with the thought that the Legend of Snively might be my next big break in the search for the Jewel. Hank left me with his contact information and asked to sit down and discuss a potential new opportunity. I figured him to be a hiring manager for a competing company, and I was not interested. I knew all of the major players in construction around Austin, and I was not keen on taking a gamble with some mom-and-pop operation. I politely turned him down.

He operated out of the town of Thorndale, which I'd also never heard of. I took a quick glance at the map, out of curiosity. I couldn't find it anywhere near Austin. I looked a bit further out. It wasn't even in a neighboring county. Finally, I located it. There it was; a tiny little town, barely a dot on the map. Hard to believe a legitimate company would operate so far from the city. Then something else caught my eye, and I had to look more closely to make sure I wasn't imagining things. Oddly enough, it was just over the border into Milam County. Needless to say, I was now very much interested. I nearly stumbled over myself to catch him before he left the site.

He invited me to come out to the local watering hole in Thorndale, called Steve's Place. Back in the early 1930's, Thorndale had been quite the destination. The sulfuric salt baths on the east side of this remote town were a place for upper class social types to come and relax. It was not altogether unlike the salt baths of Pamukkale in Turkey, where the Romans created a vast pleasure palace near Hierapolis for their elite citizens and aristocracy.

The Great Depression ended the prosperous run, and Thorndale simply became another dusty rural farming and ranching community. It had little else to offer, and the area stagnated. It was too far from Austin to see any economic activity.

That was all about to change.

I arrived on a Friday afternoon at Steve's Place in Thorndale. I walked in the front door, where Hank sat alone in the dusty, smoke-filled bar that smelled of cigarettes and burnt grease. The proprietor, Elmo Burke, cooked hamburgers as a group of locals played dominoes in the corner. The voice of Hank Williams and a lone guitar echoed from the jukebox.

The occupants at the domino table were more like inhabitants, and all gave a united, condescending glare in my direction as I walked in. The front door let so much light into the dark cavern they had to squint to see whom I was. It was as though I was a stranger in foreign lands.

Their curiosity waned as I took a seat with Hank, who extended his hand. From that point on, I was accepted by the patrons, and more importantly Mr. Burke. I'd later learn that it also meant I would be accepted in the community. In this town, it's all about who you know. Or, perhaps who you're with. In Thorndale, Hank was a man you needed to know.

Hank was seated at the table where he reviewed writings in a notebook. I recognized other papers on the table as equipment invoices. Apparently Steve's place doubled as an office for him. After a minute, he pushed the papers aside and got down to the first order of business.

"You hungry?" Hank asked.

"Starving. We had a maintainer get stuck off 35 this morning. Didn't get lunch." I replied.

"Perfect. Elmo makes burgers here that are damn near edible."

He turned his head toward Elmo, and raised his voice:

"Elmo! Couple cheeseburgers. All the way."

Elmo heard the command and glanced up through his thick glasses. He couldn't see very well. He had to nod his head downward to peer through the top of his bifocals to find who was talking. Then he'd lean his head back to look through the lower portion of his glasses, which were refractive enough to identify the person. It took him a few seconds to gain his bearing. To newcomers, he came off as rude, but to the locals, that was just Elmo. Blind or not, he was the only one allowed near the hamburger grill.

"Comin' up brother Hiram," he exclaimed, tilting his head forward and back, just slightly, as if to acknowledge a superior.

There was a heavy southern accent in his speech. Elmo hailed from South Carolina but came to Texas at an early age with his parents. He was a retired lawman, having been a sheriff's deputy for many years. *Brother* was pronounced as two separate and distinct words, with the last two letters dropped in favor of an "ah"; a southeastern twang which readily identified him as a non-native Texan. *Hiram* was condensed to sound more like *harm*.

"Cheese?" Elmo asked.

For a man who was legally blind and moved slowly, Elmo had a piercing voice that could raise Elijah from the dead. Yet, he rarely spoke, which added to his mystery. He didn't need to move quickly or talk much. He sure as hell wasn't going anywhere.

"Cheese okay with you?" Hank asked.

"Sure."

"Yep!" Hank hollered across the room at Elmo. Elmo nodded his head. Hank then turned back to me.

"See there, you gotta tell him you want cheese on your cheeseburger. Ain't that some shit?"

"Yes, I was going to ask why...."

"That's just Elmo. He don't listen too good."

"I see."

"But even now, you got about a 75-percent chance that he'll remember the cheese. It's a crapshoot around here what kind of burger you get. Know what I mean?"

"Well, sir, I'm easy to please in the food department."

"You ain't lactose intolerant, are you? Cause he also might forget and put both slices on yours."

"No sir."

"Good. You drink beer?"

"You bet."

"What kind?"

That was an odd question. This interview was starting off a bit different than I expected. I'd soon learn that Hank was not your ordinary business owner. In this bar, you might take a lot of grief over what type of beer you drank or hamburger you ordered.

Yet something else struck me as even more odd during this conversation. Why did Elmo refer to Hank as brother *Hiram*? When I heard it, I glanced around to see if someone else had walked in. There was no one.

I looked the other direction, only to see the sunlight-deprived domino players' heads buried deep in contemplation of their next bid. He hadn't address him as *Hank*. Yet Hank knew who Elmo was talking too. It didn't add up for me at that moment. Apparently I was the only one in this bar who found it strange. Elmo was definitely talking to Hank, but now as I observed more of Elmo, the more it seemed maybe he was just a little, you know, crazy.

"Who's your friend?" Elmo yelled from across the room.

"This is brother McCormack. From over in Austin. He's going to work for me."

"City boy," replied Elmo, under his breath, now disinterested to learn any more about me. He turned back to his vocation, and tossed two red meat patties onto the grill. It filled the room with the hiss of scalding meat. It would soon be followed by the aroma of caramelized

onions and the crisp scent of cracked pepper and garlic. The smoke wafted lazily to our table.

Elmo studied the grill intently, his thick bifocals covered in fog as he flipped and poked the patties with his spatula, to perfection. Once judged righteous, a slice of cheddar was place perfectly on top for a few seconds of melting which signaled the patty was ready to move off to the side. He slid it up onto the spatula with a quick flip, and placed the burger onto a waiting bun.

I am the type of person that notices everything, every little mundane detail. From the color of a shoe someone is wearing or a receding hairline that reveals one's age. I ascertain subtleties in demeanor, the type of clothes, and the general manner in which someone speaks. I could size a man up in 30 seconds, and tell you if he was friend or foe, rich or poor, arrogant, unbecoming, or downright haughty. Normally, on such a civil occasion, my antennae would not be up, and I'd be much more relaxed.

I glanced down at the ring on Hank's finger. It was the ring of a Mason. Now *that* was interesting. A man addressed as Hiram, with the ring of a Mason.

Hank now had my full and undivided attention.

12. LONE STAR BEER

I will strike you down; and I will give the dead bodies to the birds of the air and to the wild beasts of the earth. – ***David, as he approached Goliath***

Hank and I discussed our backgrounds over a few bottles of Lone Star beer. When I informed him that I had no true preference for any certain brand of beer, he was aghast. To him, that was fairly close to sacrilege. Hank was a true believer that Lone Star is the National Beer of Texas. The motto is thus explained, that *drinking any other beer is treason.* While it may seem conceited, it is anything but. Here in the land of Texas, it defines the attitude and way of life to a fault. Texas was a republic, after all, well before it became a state.

Don't Mess with Texas is another pithy saying I enjoy. I never cared for the overtly braggadocios *Everything's Bigger in Texas.* To me, bigger has always meant clumsy, and slow. Most of us tend to favor the underdog, the guy who is smaller yet faces an adversary without a hint of fear. Light and stealthy is a much better way of conducting business. If your opponent cannot see you, then you already have the advantage. I'll say this, in retrospect, Hank had the advantage right now, not just over me, but over just about everything in his life.

He had a secret.

~~~

So it is said that if you know your enemies and know yourself, you can win a hundred battles without a single loss. If you only know yourself, but not your opponent, you may win or may lose. If you know neither yourself nor your enemy, you will always endanger yourself. - **Sun Tzu**

Being unseen is useful in just about any trade, not exclusive to warfare. Jack Welch might posit that business *is* warfare, but I assure you it is not. I've been there. Nonetheless, such attributes can be effectively employed by the up-and-comer; the man on the rise who wants to leave his mark in business. There are men who bet on the come line, who have the luxury of betting with shorter stacks against a more entrenched competitor. The man who operates with minimal overhead can many times out flank a larger and more risk-averse opponent.

Those who are risk-averse only bet on sure things, exposing little, if any, in order to preserve what they have. The risk-*taker* brings a fight to his enemy, pushing him out of that comfort zone. In my first half hour with Hank, this is the general impression I got of his approach to business. *Damn the torpedoes, full speed ahead.*

In the Bible, King David was a lowly errand boy before he ever became King. The Israelites faced down the Philistines in the Valley of Elah. For 40 days Goliath dared and mocked the Army of Israel to mano-y-mano combat, flaunting his sheer size to intimidate his opponents. Unable to find someone to accept the fight, King Saul
~~~

offered a reward to any soldier who stepped forward; he offered the chance to become royalty.

The young David answered this challenge. He was lightly armored and almost completely unseen prior to accepting the task of his king to face the mighty Goliath. He carried only his sling and five stones into combat. He was ridiculed incessantly as he came forth to confront the colossal warlord. While Goliath was not fully the giant as described by legend, he was indeed a fearsome foe, such as Achilles. Just as the Greek hero, Goliath had a distinct and unprotected weakness.

David had only as much to lose as Goliath, but the potential upside for the boy was exponentially higher. He was unflinching in the face of certain death, which would prove lethal to his opponent on the battlefield. The centrifugal force applied by the sling gave rapid acceleration to the tiny object. With pinpoint accuracy, it penetrated Goliath's unprotected flank to destroy a vital center.

He directed one tiny stone into the exposed flesh of Goliath, felling him with a single payload. In an instant, a boy was transformed into a hero. Nearly the entire spectrum of military principles was demonstrated to perfection, as an entire army fell at the hands of one solitary stone. The scrawny boy went on to become one of the most legendary kings of all time.

America, as a band of outcasts, pulled off the same stunt thousands of years later. American colonists squared off against the forces of a British dictator in the late 1700's, facing a better trained and well-equipped military. Beginning with the Battle of Cowpens, the tide turned in favor of George Washington's army leading to a domino-effect of defeats for the Brits. General Cornwallis was ultimately vanquished at Yorktown, and America was born, birthed from the tip of muskets of an entire nation of King Davids.

Fifty years later, a subset of those colonists ventured to Texas and would unexpectedly outmaneuver a superior Mexican Army. It was an act of subversion against a government that sought to restrict liberty by centralizing control over the previously federated government construct. The Texans would have none of it, and Sam Houston ultimately annihilated the Mexican Army.

The Texans' new republic soon joined the United States. Despite an internal struggle for the nation's soul during the Civil War, the mentality of the Americans did not change. Eighty years later, victory in World War II had yet to transform America from underdog to superpower. As an underdog, it should have come as no surprise that America would fiercely defend itself and bring every last full measure of devotion to the fight.

After Pearl Harbor, such ferocity was moved to action. The sentiment of Admiral Yamamoto portrayed in a quote from a movie, which, while fabricated, was emblematic of the dire straits in which Japan would soon find itself: *I fear all we have done is to awaken a sleeping giant.*

What he actually said was: "it is certain that, angered and outraged, he will soon launch a determined counterattack." Nonetheless, the substance is the same. The Americans would soon plunge headlong into World War II, resulting in a great and tragic end to the Japanese Empire. The underdog Americans would press onward, marching forth to conquer the mighty warlords with unrelenting resolve.

After World War II, America would no longer be an underdog. It would face down the Soviets in the Cold War, but engaged in a perennial string of defeats in numerous wars where being the frontrunner became a major liability. While tactically superior in every category, the strategic goals were rarely met.

Korea and Vietnam became quagmires resulting in truce or outright defeat. Iraq and Afghanistan languished for a decade, even to this day, as protracted guerilla warfare inflicted a thousand small cuts in the armor of the most powerful military ever known. The common denominator in most cases was a lack of resolve by the political leadership and a disinterest by the citizenry. Such resolve will *never* exist unless there is a bona fide interest at stake which is embraced by the people.

Hank Benson's ancestors navigated the course of these battles, but none of them, save one, would be saddled with the weight of the duty placed onto his shoulders. The man sitting next to me is part of a fraternity, and I'm not talking about the Masons, or the Templar Knights, or any other group of men that have existed throughout history. You've never heard of this fraternity. Neither has Hank. Its membership is supremely elite. It is nobler than any in existence. At any time, two, and possibly three individuals even know of its existence.

For the chosen few, it is an unwanted fate. It is a destiny of solitude, fraught with peril. The pressures of such duty are akin to the force which creates a diamond from a lump of coal. At 22 years old, Hank doesn't have the slightest clue of what is in store for him, but I see it.

It is what I've been looking for.

~~~

Hank started right in on the questions. He was a bit overzealous and left no doubt this was a sales pitch to retain my services. I would find out later the cause of his aggressive pursuit. His business was set to expand exponentially. He could hardly contain his excitement, and was hiring men as quickly as possible.

I would guess his age to be mid-20s, but I would find out later, of course, he was only 22. This was extremely young for a company owner, and had I not my own ulterior motive, I doubt I'd even consider this job. Still, he had the demeanor of a man in his 30s, and was doing his best to portray an intimidating and authoritarian figure.

Honestly, I don't think Hank gave a care in the world if he succeeded or failed. He was honing his chops as a businessman. There would be plenty of opportunity ahead even if this hire didn't come to fruition. He wasn't one to swing for a base hit. He aimed for the fences with every step to the plate, and a guy like that is bound to
~~~

strike out many times in between home runs. This was his approach with me, with women, with his new venture, and with life itself.

“So. Mr. McCormack. Can I just call you Mac?”

“Sure. In fact, that’s what...”

“How do you like working in that, no offense, in that crap-hole of Austin?” Hank interrupted.

“Well, sir, it’s not too...”

“Hold on a damn minute. You don’t have to call me *Sir*. Alright? Just don’t do it. Call me *Hank* for Christ’s sake.”

“Okay, yes.....” I caught myself as I was about to say *Sir* once again.

“I mean, will do, Hank.”

“Good.”

Hank took a sip of beer; “Now, you were saying?”

“Well, I was saying, that, it’s not too bad, I guess, working in Austin. I’ve been promoted a couple times, have a good crew, and I enjoy the environment,” I replied.

Hank took a sip of his beer.

“Not too bad, huh? You enjoy the environment? Sounds like the voice of a man looking for something better. How much they paying you anyway?”

"Nothing worth bragging about. I got a decent pay raise when..."

"You ever worked down in *Chili Switch*?"

"Pardon, *Chili Switch*?"

"Yeah, you know, San Antonio. Ever worked with the Guthries?"

"No, afraid I haven't."

"They call it Chili Switch, you know, because of all the wetbacks."

I'd come to expect direct verbiage from my construction crews, but was never that fond of it. Foul language was just something you accepted. But Hank didn't have much of a filter. He just dove right in and let loose with both barrels. He continued:

"Wouldn't you rather be out here in God's country than slaving away in a concrete jungle?"

"I think, yes, I think I might."

"You know what they say about Austin don't you? Nothing but steers and..."

"You know, Hank, let me stop you right there. If you're going to talk like a kid, then at least take that ring off."

Hank was aghast. So was I. I just blurted it out. I needed to draw a line. If there is one thing that gets my ire up, it's a man that runs his mouth recklessly. I continued:

"You are a Mason, I presume. Well you ought to know that many years ago a man named Euclid admonished the Egyptians that they should live in harmony with their fellow man, and not call them *knave or servant or anything foul.*"

Hank sat back in his chair, his demeanor changed as he glared at me through suddenly suspicious eyes, yet a coy smile formed at the corner of his lips. He was intrigued. In that moment, Hank knew he'd move heaven itself to hire me, yet that subtle clue was all he'd let slip. It was enough indication for me. *Check mate.*

"What are you, a damn scientist?"

"No."

"Who the hell is Euclid?"

"He was an early figure in the foundation of Masonry."

"Never heard of him."

"Look, I'm just not much into the blasphemy, swearing, and name-calling. It's a personal thing. We're men. We're leaders. We should walk and act uprightly."

"Alright. Touche'."

"Maybe I'm barking up the wrong tree."

"No, no, now, don't get all uppity. I'm just, you know, making conversation."

I pushed my chair back from the table. Hank cut me off.

"Hold on a damn minute. Just hold on."

He pulled his chair up, closer to the table, and sat upright.

"I got it. Look, I know I come off a bit crude. I don't mean too. Let's cut through the bullshit."

"Okay. Why don't we start over then," I replied.

"I've asked around about you. I like what I see. I need a man like you in my outfit."

"What are you pitching?"

"I want you to come on down to Thorndale. I'll pay you half again what your making now."

"That's awfully rich. Sure you can afford it?"

"That's a fact. Don't you worry about the pay. I'm up to my ears in business, I just need the manpower."

"Well, alright. But first, there are a few questions I have of my own."

"Alright. Shoot."

Hank was accustomed to doing everything himself. He carried a massive chip on his shoulder. I soon realized his rugged demeanor was no more than a poorly disguised defense mechanism. It was his way to cope in a world where he felt abandoned by everyone around him, except for his tight knit group of friends. No one got into his inner circle unless they thought and acted like him, but once disarmed, he was a fairly likable creature.

We cut to the heart of the matter. It was apparent to me that Hank liked to be in control. He liked to assert himself. On the other hand, so did I. I was not one to be pushed around. Hank was not accustomed to being challenged; but he relished it. He needed men with strong backbones for his company. More importantly, he needed men he could trust, and who would tell him the truth.

"How does a guy as young as you come to own his own company?" I asked.

Hank pondered the question for a moment, as he readied his reply. He crossed his hands on the table, and delivered his answer.

"Simple. My parents died young and my grandpa raised me. Put me to work in the cotton fields. I got sick of that, dropped out of school, and started work as a truck driver when I'm 15. I learned the construction business from the bottom up. Then grandpa died when I'm 17. I inherited a big chunk of land. That's when the fun started."

He paused for a moment, with a chuckle. It was one of those laughs intended to mask something painful. I sensed a change in his mood; it was beginning to darken.

"You grow up quick when every relative you know tries to sue your ass to steal it away, all in the name of their own greed. Most kids 17 are out doing, I don't know, whatever they do, but me, I had to learn the legal system before I'm old enough to vote. Every guy I looked up to got shipped off to the war. Most of 'em never came home."

Hank took a drink of his Lone Star, and lit a cigarette. He breathed in, and let loose a plume of smoke. His eyes gazed down at the table. There was a passion in his eyes. Discussing this story opened a fresh wound. His early life was marked with tragedy; his parents died, then his grandfather, and many of his friends and mentors never returned from Europe or the Pacific in World War II. It's not hard to fathom just how much of a mental stigma death places on someone at that age.

"I'm not an arrogant prick like everyone says, you know. I've been meaning to change, but hey, just never got around to it."

"Understood," I replied.

"I guess, what I'm trying to say is, I just am who I am. And I did what I had to do."

He looked up, and stared directly into my eyes. His mouth quivered. Hank was visibly agitated. I feared I unwittingly opened up a Pandora's Box. *What he had to do* had all the hallmarks of something darker. I ventured he was not going to speak of those things to me; at least not yet.

"They threw the first punch. They got what they deserved. That's all I'm going to say."

I was somewhat startled, but in an instant, he switched gears, as if nothing odd had transpired. He went right back to being an obnoxious windbag without missing a beat.

"Anyway, construction just came easy to me. These sons 'a bitches I was working for didn't have sense to pour piss out of a boot. I was young, and a bit reckless; one night after about six shots of whiskey, I mouthed off to my boss about how I could run the operation better than him. He didn't like it. He fired my ass on the spot."

I was still trying to figure out his previous comments, but he was well past it.

"I told him to take that job and stick it up his ass. The whiskey had me fired up, much as anything, but it'd been a long time a comin'. I vowed right then and there I would start my own company and run him out of business."

Hank took another long puff on his cancer stick, and drained his bottle of beer, setting it down with a loud thud, which perked up the ears of Elmo. Hank held the bottle up over his head, and yelled at Elmo.

"Yo! Believe I'll have another. And one for my friend."

"That's okay Hank. I'm fine. Gotta drive home tonight," I replied.

"Bullshit! You'll have another. I'm not drinking alone."

"Alright, one more."

"That's how you become an alcoholic, you know. Drinking alone."

"I'll keep that in mind."

Elmo had two cold beers over to the table right soon. It was the quickest I'd seen him move, which isn't saying much.

"So, Hank, you started your own company then?"

"Yes. Went down to the bank and got Mr. Clement to loan me 20,000 dollars against my land. Bought me a truck and went into business. I undercut every sumbitch out there. Lived off peanuts and Nehi Red for awhile, but I eventually ran them out of town. Once I broke 'em, I bought another truck, then another, so on and so forth. Before you know it, I had seven drivers and a fleet of rigs. Then bought a backhoe and started bidding on road work. That's all I wanted to do. Worked 16 hours a day. I just had, I don't know, this insatiable appetite to go out and conquer."

"I must say, that's impressive, especially for, no offense, but someone so young," I replied.

"Well, people never gave me much of a chance. That made it even easier. They never gave me a second thought, and I never looked back. After a while, everything I touched turned to money. I honestly think maybe I'm just protected by the hand of God, or something."

Hank turned his attention back his beer, his eyes peering deeply into the dark bottle. His smile widened, as he took a drink. He couldn't hide his emotions very well, and even less after a few beers. I could tell there was something else he was thinking, something he just could not wait to get off his chest.

"I'll tell you something else, Mac. *Come here.*"

Hank leaned in close, and motioned with his finger for me to move in.

"There's a whole shitload of money about to come to this town."

"You don't say."

"I'm serious. Piles of it. You come aboard, and you and me, we're gonna grab as much of it as we can."

"And how do you know this?"

"It's a secret. But God as my witness, it's coming."

Hank had yet another secret; one that I'd soon know.

I had only known the man for an hour, but I already knew I wanted into his circle. I had a gut feeling that this was the right thing to do. Getting through his defenses would not be easy. This was a man who'd fought off the devil himself, it would seem, and was constantly on guard against the approach of cowans and eavesdroppers.

Hank had no family. He was an orphan in the world, but hell-bent on making his presence known. The only real family he had was a short list of friends of which I'd soon be. It was an inner circle that few would enter, and none would ever leave.

I had my foot in the door, at least for the moment.

13. HANK'S SECRET

It should come as no surprise that the history of the Masons began in King Solomon's Temple, the son of King David. Generals Washington and Houston, both, in their respective victories, were Master Masons. It was this band of brothers which held the secret to the Jewel of Hiram. It is why I found myself pursuing the Craft, way out here in Milam County, to return the Jewel to its true and rightful owner.

Nonetheless, at this stage of his life, Hank Benson knew little of his own storied past. He knew even less of Masonic history, and I questioned whether he even knew how to behave in public. He was country, a man who rarely ventured into the city. He didn't need to. Everything he needed or wanted was right here in Milam County, but just as the crushing weight of the Earth compresses pure carbon to form a diamond, so too was the life of Hank Benson being fashioned into something much more potent.

His base of operations, his livelihood, his passion, and his only real ambition in life, all resided right here in this fertile blackland soil, nestled against the San Gabriel River and under the canopy of pecan groves. He was born H. K. Benson in 1927, but from day one they called him Hank. He wouldn't learn what the H.K. stood for until many years later.

He hit the ground right outside of Rockdale, Texas, and came of age in the midst of the Great Depression. As a boy, he worked the fields for his grandfather, tending the cattle, and farmland back before machinery made the task less labor-intensive. His father worked in Galveston, visiting home only on the weekends. His mother died young, likely from pneumonia, although no one knew for certain. Shortly thereafter his father died in Galveston under strange circumstances, but it's likely he was murdered.

Young Hank then fell under his own grandfather Aiden Benson's demanding tutelage. Aiden was known around the area as *Old Man* Benson, 80 years old when Hank was born, but just as spry as he was in his 60s. Aiden Benson had many children, the last of which was conceived when he was in his mid 40s.

During the Depression, Aiden employed his numerous full-grown children and his daughters' husbands as well. He provided the modern equivalent of a welfare system several years ahead of FDR's New Deal. As Hank would say, most of those aunts and uncles didn't have the good sense to pour piss out of a boot. It was an expression of which he was quite fond.

As a teenager, Hank notoriously outworked his lazy uncles and most of the farmhands, earning nothing extra aside from their spitefulness while laboring through the hot Texas summers. The lazy kinfolk seemed to be primarily interested in passing the time, living off Old Man Benson's goodwill and stockpile of land and cattle. They had no ambition of their own. Hank never relented, nor believed in wasting a minute of time taking handouts. If he was out there, he was earning his keep.

Once, Hank had been assigned a day's labor with two of his uncles to split firewood out of a pecan tree. It fell during a spring thunderstorm. The two uncles spent half the day goofing off, skipping rocks, and just being slothful in general. Hank endured the majority of the toiling. About noon, the trio broke for lunch. Soon enough, Aiden came driving up the road in his Model-A Roadster. The two uncles, while lethargic, were keen enough to sense trouble brewing. Not wanting to be caught slacking off, they immediately jumped up and furiously went back to work, leaving their sandwiches behind.

Aiden walked up to Hank, who continued to sit on an old pecan stump, eating his sandwich. He was exhausted, having picked up half a day's worth of slack. Today, he was in no mood to be trifled with. It would be the first time in Hank's life in which he would stand up to his grandfather, and tell him to stick it where the sun does not shine.

As the old man approached, he stopped for a second, observing the situation. He observed as the two uncles worked feverishly, feigning approval. Hank quietly ate his sandwich, staring at the ground. The old man chewed on a stalk of Johnson grass, one hand in the front breast pocket of his overalls. He then turned back to Hank, whose shirt was entirely soaked through with sweat. Two half-eaten sandwiches lie where the two uncles had been loafing minutes before.

"What say, *boy*. Why ain't you workin'?"

"It's lunch time."

"How 'bout them other two? Look like *they* workin'."

"I don't know. I guess they're done eating."

"Must not been too hungry. I see them sammiches layin' there."

"I guess not."

The old man grabbed three fingers of chewing tobacco from a pouch, and put it in his mouth. Once it had nestled to his lips, he stood for a moment, chewing the syrupy leaves. He turned, and with a flicker of his head, unleashed a spittle of brownish juice, taking out a grasshopper.

"Well then, how much longer you gonna sit there?"

Hank sighed. His emotions bristled. His grandpa had a coy smile as he chewed on his tobacco. The old man knew what was going on, but the subtlety flew right over Hank's head; he was already in a defensive posture. The old man knew long before today his sons-in-law were a couple of worthless hands, but he thoroughly enjoyed pestering Hank. Toughened him up a bit. Such was the manner in which young Hank came up.

"Yeah, well, I've been at this all morning. It's lunch time. I'm not going back to work just 'cause you fuckin' drive up."

The old man let out a mighty *"Hmmph"*, a bit perturbed at hearing young Hank use the F-word for the first time. This was a seminal moment in a young man's life. While the F-word was not out of bounds for mature adults, most children in this era knew that using it was grounds for a whipping. Kids might use it around each other, but never in front of an adult.

The old man, in his wisdom, realized the boy was not the one at fault here, but he was the only one of the three who was worth the time to discipline. Instead of a whipping, Hank got a verbal admonishment. Besides, Aiden was far too old by now to administer a whipping, and Hank was, as they say in the business, built like a brick shit-house.

"You watch that goddamn cussin' *boy*."

The old man was proud that he had been stood up to; he just needed something to complain about sometimes. At his age, and with his fortune, it didn't happen too often. He turned his attention towards the two sons-in-law. The duo feverishly swung their axes; glancing back to make sure someone was watching them work.

They weren't even worth Aiden's bother to complain. It made him wish he could go back and slap sense into his daughters. It wouldn't have mattered. They simply didn't inherit the good sense of their momma, though sometimes he wondered if they could have raised them better. It was all water under the bridge now, regardless. He nodded his head, spit, and wiped the sweat from his brow. He gave a long sigh, as if to ask advice from his grandson on how to deal with his two indolent son-in-laws.

"Well, you grandmamma and Miss Maria are makin' tamales tonight. Break off 'bout six and come on to the house."

"Yes, sir."

And that was as much of an appreciation as Hank ever got from his grandfather; at least until the day the old man passed away.

14. THE NEW JOB

Hank offered me the job. I became so enthralled with his personal story I can't recall if we even talked about what the job was. I assumed I'd be a crew supervisor, which is what I had been doing, but he had something else in mind.

He recruited me into his budding business with a 20 percent pay raise and my own truck. When I inquired about the 50 percent he promised, he stated that if I lasted three months, I'd get the full 50 percent. In Hank's mind, that wasn't a renege, it was a shrewd maneuver. I'd just have to get used to it.

Even with Hank taking me under his wing, I'd still have to deal with the obligatory gossip and condescension of being the new guy. Small town folk just can't comprehend why a *city boy* from Austin would move out here. Normally the migration is the other direction. It took Elmo three weeks before he actually acknowledged my existence.

Thorndale was at least 45 miles from the bright lights of Austin. In those days it was at least a two hour drive. Hank found me a house even further out in the country, seven miles north of town on the old Schramm place and a few miles from his property. It was peaceful. The twinkling of the stars seemed 10 times brighter. I could sleep at night and hear nothing but the occasional howl of coyotes, or the hooting of owls. Hot summer days gave way to a crisp nighttime breeze, as winds through the pecan groves were cooled by moisture evaporating off the San Gabriel River.

Milam County was my new home.

Over the next two months, he hired dozens of new hands, putting me in charge of four crews. The work seemed menial, and I suspected it was just busy work in preparation for something greater. He secured several pieces of real estate and bought parking lots full of equipment. Every day revealed a new surprise, a new clue to what he was up to.

I hadn't a clue as to what he was brewing. He kept it strictly confidential, and far as I knew, he didn't tell a single soul at the Thorndale detachment. He spent quite a bit of time in meetings with people I didn't know, and traveled quite frequently down to San Antonio. He gave me orders, mostly putting together bid proposals and screening candidates to hire as supervisors and shift leads. On occasion, I was sent on a fool's errand to pick up a load of gravel. He kept us all in the dark.

His clandestine work would soon slip the bonds of secrecy. I found the answers to Hank's mystery, and so did the rest of the world, as it were, because it was all over the news one morning. It headlined the Milam County newspapers: the Rockdale Reporter, Thorndale Champion and Cameron Herald. The towns were abuzz with fervor. The vibrancy lost in the 1930s would soon come roaring back with a vengeance.

Hank's work over the past six months left him ready to cash in.

First, a little background; half a century before, in the early 1900s, Milam County had a mini economic boom when massive underground deposits of lignite coal were discovered. Unfortunately, the boom soon fizzled, as oil was discovered further east at Spindletop. Oil was much more utilitarian than the brownish, watery lignite. It could be pumped from the Earth rather than mined. Petroleum became en vogue as the fuel of choice for Henry Ford's contraptions, and would launch Texas as an energy giant.

George Sessions Perry wrote of the fateful economic landscape in the county Milam:

But these happy times had to end. The great oil fields near Beaumont had been discovered along about the turn of the century. By 1920 many of the old lignite customers had got around to installing petroleum-burning equipment. By 1925 the change-over was relatively complete. The businessmen of the town, who had invested in lignite and once prospered so lavishly, were now broke and badly in debt. The mines closed and the mining camps lay desolate and abandoned.

Saturday Evening Post, December 27, 1952, The Town Where it Rains Money

After the economic bust, Milam would join the rest of the country in Depression and return to agriculture as its primary stock in trade. Such were the tales of Mr. Perry's greatest novel. Milam's lignite coal would lose its value as economic factors beyond its control converged. Up until

1950, lignite was considered the most substandard among the many varieties of coal. Even beyond the newly found oil, lignite had a strident competitor in natural gas. Natural gas became readily available in Texas in the deep caverns which produced the oil.

Lignite is too watery to be shipped long distances, so it remained buried, unused and unappreciated, deep within the bowels of Milam County. As a result, the Sandow mine near Rockdale, named for the father of bodybuilding Eugene Sandow, closed in 1950 due to low demand. Milam would be unable to follow the United States into prosperity, even long after Fat Man and Little Boy accomplished their deeds in World War II.

~~~

I hearkened back to my second meeting with Hank. He'd invited me out to his cabin on the river. It was just three of us, Hank, Claude Guthrie, and I. We'd run trot lines up the San Gabriel that morning, and pulled in a nice haul of catfish. By noon, Hank had gotten so drunk on Jim Beam whiskey that he could barely stand, let alone form a coherent sentence. In that state of mind, he'd tell you just about anything.

I'd all but written off that discussion to drunken ramblings, until I read those newspaper headlines.

"Mac. I have, I have a secret to tell you," Hank said.

He looked me directly in the eye. His body swayed to and fro, and his arms tried to steady himself as he sat at the
~~~

table. In one hand, he held a paring knife with which he attempted to filet a fish. In the other, he had a grip on his cup of whiskey. He had a wry smile on his face. Claude giggled, and then let out a loud, obnoxious belch. They were both entirely inebriated. I stood alone as the only sober soul.

"Go on, tell him, Hank. *Tell him,*" Claude yelled.

"Alright, okay. I will. Just gimme a minute, Guthrie."

"Spill it, Hank. I'm listening," I replied.

"I don't know, Guthrie. *He might tell,*" Hank retorted.

"He ain't gonna tell. If he does, I'll cut him right open with this goddamned knife," Claude replied, tapping his knife on the table and glaring at me.

Claude turned his attention to me. He was a beast of a man; not large, but muscled and lightning fast. He'd been to hell and back during his time in the military. He was as tough as he was cocky. And I was certain he knew how to use that knife. Claude was a recent business associate of Hank from down in San Antonio.

He was a rugged former Marine who served in the Korean War. He made his way back to Texas in 1951 after being seriously wounded in combat. He fought at Chosin Reservoir, a 17-day battle which became a decisive turning point in the war. U.S. forces were outnumbered more than two-to-one, and found themselves surrounded by the Chinese army which had secretly crossed the border into North Korea. Claude's outfit was trapped in treacherous terrain and freezing conditions, but managed to fight their way through the lines and inflict crippling losses on the Chinese.

Claude's father owned a construction firm in San Antonio. He would join the family business upon his return and work closely with Hank on numerous projects. The two companies eventually merged many years later. Claude became the third leg of our tripod when he was in town, but he and I didn't always get along. Perhaps it was in no small part due to the rivalry between the Army and Marines.

I would make the mistake, just once, of referring to him as an ex-Marine in conversation, during a formal business meeting no less. I was quickly corrected. "There ain't no ex-Marines, just *former* Marines, but I wouldn't expect a little peckerhead Army Ranger like you to know the difference." Claude had impeccable delivery, amidst his spitting of tobacco juice; he got right to the point. He was confrontational to a tee, and could be a man's best friend or his worst enemy. This made him both an asset, and at times a liability for the company.

Claude was born to end lives, both as a rifleman in the Marines, and later on when such energies were manifested in the proving grounds of west Texas. He loved to hunt. Once on a trip to Uvalde with Hank and I, Claude took down an 18-point buck on a 400-yard shot with his .300 Weatherby Magnum. It was Christmas Eve, and the wind chill had to be in the teens. Vapors wafted gently over the animal as we approached. While the carcass was still warm, Claude cut out its heart with a Marine-issue KA-BAR combat knife. He then took a bite *to make sure his spirit lives on*.

Hank nearly lost his stomach as the blood dripped from Claude's lips. Claude looked to enjoy it as much as a bite of warm apple pie. I don't know if he just enjoyed getting a rise out of us, or if the man truly had a few screws loose. He claimed to be three-sixteenths Comanche. No one really knows for sure, but around these parts of the former frontier, chances are good somewhere along the line a Native American entered the blood line. What I do know is the man was at least three-quarters insane.

~~~

Back at the cabin, Hank stood ready to make his revelation.

"You ain't gonna say nothin', are you, Mac?" Guthrie demanded.

Claude had the look in his eye. It was his predatory inclination manifested. It told me I should leave well enough alone. He was not a man to be trifled with. He was big, and no doubt good with the blade. I ascertained that even inebriated, he would be a force to behold. I was not one to encourage such manner of fisticuffs, so I obliged:

"You got my word, Claude. I won't say anything. To anybody."

"Alright then, dammit. Tell him Hank. Or I will."
~~~

I'd disarmed the brutish Claude, albeit by allowing him the upper hand. He was now on my side. Claude and I were matched up against Hank. Hank nodded his head. He was giddy; ready to spill the beans.

"You see. You see, there is a fortune buried out here."

"Where?" I replied.

"Here. Right here. Right beneath, beneath the very ground of Milam County. Is going to, it's gonna to make us all rich."

"Hank," I questioned.

"What?"

"Does this have something to do with a buried treasure?"

"What the...what the hell? No, I ain't, I'm not talkin' 'bout no damn gold," he replied.

"Oh. Sorry. Must be my mistake."

"What the hell are you thinkin'? You're as crazy as that sumbitch Snively everybody lookin' for. I'm talkin', talkin' about lignite coal, brother."

And there it was.

He knew about *Snively.* It was a triumphal moment for me. It verified my longings, despite the fact that he and I were in pursuits of completely different treasures. He was talking about lignite, but I was far more interested in

Snively. I couldn't let him know it. I knew for certain I was onto something, so I let Hank ramble on.

He regaled me with stories of a light-weight metal called Aluminum. It was the most sought-after material used in the manufacturing boom of post-World War II America. It was used to build airplanes. As America grew, so did her need for more aircraft. The Korean War exacerbated this need. Hank told me that an aluminum manufacturer would soon expand production, and they would be coming to Milam County to produce that very thing, courtesy of the lignite coal beneath the ground. The coal was needed to derive massive amounts of electricity to melt elementals into liquid, thus forming this precious metal.

Milam County's economic savior was on the march.

Where he got this information, I couldn't say. He would later tell me that it came to him in a dream. Possibly, but I doubt it. Hank was not beyond spinning a yarn. I would wager a bet that Guthrie's well-placed father had connections, and they picked Hank as their point man to lay the groundwork locally.

A new process had recently been developed whereby lignite coal could be carbonized and used as a cheap fuel source. The Aluminum Company of America (ALCOA), a Pittsburgh-based steel company, utilized the same aluminum smelting formula developed by Charles Martin Hall in 1886. ALCOA would begin to build a large ingot smelter near Rockdale in the early 1950's. It would be ALCOA's largest smelter in the nation.

This company rode into town to take advantage of the abundant lignite, which they'd turn into electricity. Electricity is created, basically, by nothing more than boiling water to create steam. The steam turns a large turbine. Boiling water requires heat, which requires fuel. Most generators use a fossil fuel, others harness the water, wind or sun, and today, some even use nuclear fission. The entire process is far more technical than I can describe, and is best left to a power engineer.

Hank was set to take full advantage of this massive opportunity. He knew that the ALCOA plant would bring hundreds of millions, if not billions, in infrastructure changes to Milam County. Power plants and smelters are massive undertakings. It would require new roads, a cooling pond, railroad spurs, conveyor systems, and thousands of tons of steel to erect the smelter and power plant. He positioned himself to be a prime subcontractor, and went to work securing bids on any job, large or small.

All he needed was manpower. He needed people he could trust. Fortunately, he was a fairly solid judge of character. To him, that was the only thing that mattered. If a man lacked a certain flavor of character, Hank simply wasn't interested.

15. On the Farm

And he said unto them, Cast the net on the right side of the ship, and ye shall find. They cast therefore, and now they were not able to draw it for the multitude of fishes. ***– John 21:6***

This new challenge sounded like it might become even thornier that the one I faced with the Nazis. The goose-stepping Gestapo was easy to spot, and I had the weight of an entire nation behind me. When in doubt, I simply fired my weapon and followed the sound of gunfire. Life in the civilian world has consequences for such actions. Civilian life can be much more treacherous and difficult to decipher.

At times, I hated it.

Excited as I was at the ALCOA prospect, reality soon set in. This was going to be a ton of work. I thought Hank might have bitten off more than he could chew with this deal, but he was a master of dicing the largest tasks into manageable chunks. He fed them to me bit by bit. I consumed my share, and then some, so my portions grew steadily in size. Hank was a wunderkind, if not a genius, when it came to operational management. He was simply flawless in his approach to business.

I rarely worked less than 60 hours a week. Quite often it would grow to 80 hours. Sometimes, work never ended, and we would retire to Hank's farm to drink beer, go over schematics and work up bid proposals late into the night. He had half a dozen foremen, but I was his chief deputy and trusted counsel. I was the ear he would bend, and since he did most of his thinking out loud, my work never stopped.

Hank made sure each job was completed on time and under budget. As profits from smaller bids rolled in, he left his money on the table. He doubled down to secure even bigger jobs. Hank never took money out of the company, rather he re-invested it to grow and secure more business. By the time the breaker tripped on the main power feed when the ALCOA plant went live in 1952, Benson Construction Company did almost $12 million in gross revenue for the year.

As the sole owner, Hank began to amass a small fortune. He put nearly every penny of it into purchasing land to adjoin his farm. I once asked why he chose land, to which he replied; *because they ain't makin' any more of it.* Yet, with his fortunes on the rise, he never even bought himself a new truck. Rarely would you see the man in anything but blue jeans and a pair of dusty cowboy boots. Money never mattered much to Hank, and his tastes for the finer things in life were limited to Lone Star beer, whiskey, and mountain oysters.

It's not okay to love money, but it is okay to love to make money. ***– Hank circa 1954***

~~~

Hank was a third generation Texan. His great-great grandfather fought in the American Revolution and his grandfather in the Civil War. As odds would have it, he owned the very land upon which the Snively legend existed. The site where the San Francisco Xavier de Horcasitas stood was on a hill overlooking a little cabin Hank built next to the San Gabriel River. Hank blossomed into an avid reader of history as he neared his 30's, and he verbally relayed to me nearly everything he read of any interest.

Since Hank never stopped talking, I would become familiar with the San Xavier missions in the many fishing trips down at the cabin, and excursions on his land to shoot at deer as we discussed business. We rarely actually shot at deer unless Claude was in town, but the act of deer hunting was a primal pastime to remind us that we descend from the hunter-gathers. Or so we told ourselves. To me it felt like the old adage; *because that's the way we've always done it.* We much preferred to grill steaks from the Forbes Meat Market in Thorndale.

Now, with Claude, it was a different story. We'd be up at 0-dark-30, full camo face paint, and end up skinning a freezer full of venison steaks. Claude was a high strung individual. He and I eventually found a mutual respect for each other. I remember his funeral like it was yesterday. A fitter man I'd rarely known, yet he died at only 42 years of age from a massive coronary.

Some things just don't make a great deal of sense.
~~~

~~~

Hank's grandpa had farmed and ranched nearly 1,000 acres in Milam County. He came to own the land under bizarre circumstances. He owned all the land on the east and south side of the Gabriel, an area of several thousand acres. The Carters owned the land to the west. The Carters and Bensons had been neighbors since the late 1800's.

Hank loved the land. His second love would be the airplane. This is why he also came to love ALCOA, not because it made him wealthy, but because it made aluminum. Aluminum is the principle element of an airplane. The uneducated yet engineering-minded Hank had a lifelong obsession with silver-winged beasts. The ALCOA plant could produce enough aluminum to make almost 10,000 airplanes each year. It also made an atomized aluminum powder, used as a solid rocket propellant; another engineering marvel which Hank came to study in his spare time.

While Hank would forego the day-to-day luxuries of his money, he did indulge his sweet tooth at times. When he did, his tastes could be quite expensive. He purchased himself an airplane in 1954 and started taking flying lessons. It was his 26th birthday present to himself; a brand new Cessna 180 Skywagon that had entered production that very year.

Now, before most folks buy a bicycle, they learn how to ride. Hank had never flown a plane the day he bought his first one. He just decided one day; *why the hell not?* This
~~~

particular Skywagon rolled off the line about the same time as the *Spirit of Columbus,* the plane that Geraldine Mock would pilot to become the first woman to fly solo around the world in 1964.

According to Hank, the Cessna was a business asset, not a toy; a somewhat true proclamation. The new "company" plane was used to ferry he and I down to San Antonio at first, where Benson Construction had now formally partnered with Claude's larger outfit. More routinely, it ferried us down to the Gulf of Mexico, where we'd take his boat out into Baffin Bay and other ports of call for a weekend of sea fishing. Boats were Hank's only other vice, which isn't too bad, I presume.

Once the ALCOA plant came fully online, the work slowed considerably for me. Business was still booming, but we'd essentially built an empire from the ground up in less than five years, and the really difficult challenges were behind us. Hank's business was now a major profit center, a day-to-day business that ran like a well-oiled machine.

Life working for Hank became a true pleasure. In fact, some days I forgot what I was doing here in the first place. I had to consciously remind myself from time to time just exactly what my mission in Milam County was all about, but in the meantime, I had settled into an actual life. It was one I came to enjoy.

I admired his magnanimity with the workers, his vision, loyalty, and ability to get people to do just about anything he needed done, and like it. Though I can't remember which, Patton or Truman had a quote along those lines, defining leadership. To me it wasn't a job, it was my destiny. I was just along for the ride.

Around the time of my 30th year in this body, he made me Vice President of the Benson Contracting Company, now *incorporated*. Nothing changed but the job title. We still spent many hours down at the farm, drinking whiskey, fishing, and working out business matters. The San Gabriel River was full of catfish, in between the gar, turtles, and water moccasins. He made me the VP because I think he had the idea to step away from the company, but ultimately he couldn't relinquish total control; even to me.

Catfish were wonderful creatures. I could sit for hours just watching them eat grasshoppers that landed on the surface of the river, unaware that their doom lied just beneath. Catfish is a dish best served fried. The name derived from the long whiskers on either side of its mouth, giving the appearance of a cat. A catfish would eat anything it could get its mouth around, which was quite large in proportion to its body.

Our days fishing grew fewer and fewer over time. The climate of Milam County was undergoing a cyclical change. It stopped raining in Texas sometime in 1947. Over the next 10 years, the worst drought in six centuries would take hold of the state. For many men in Milam County, the new ALCOA plant became the only option for work.

Stock tanks dried up, the rivers stopped flowing, and the pastures became barren patches of dust where green fields of hay should have grown. By the time the rains returned, the number of Texans who sought their livelihood as farmers and ranchers had fallen by nearly two-thirds. As a result of the drought, many new reservoirs were built to stockpile precious water resources. Underground aquifers were exploited, increasing their utilization five-fold. Yet the absence of rain to maintain the soil's moisture would ensure that farming and ranching remained a gamble.

Despite the ongoing drought, large downpours came in 1951 and 1952, providing water to the San Gabriel River. This was important, because it meant we could still go fishing, if you could time it right. The best time to fish was when the water flowed at about one-third up to half bank, meaning the tiny Gabriel River became a torrent of energy as the Gabriel watershed funneled runoff en route to the Gulf of Mexico. This generally happened about three hours after a good two to three inch rain.

It was the perfect outlet for a construction company crew, because when there was a large rainfall, outdoor work had to be called off anyway.

~~~

Hank listened intently to the radio.

"Everybody. Shut up!" He yelled.

It was the noon weather report. Seems a cold front was en route, bringing with it a plethora of moisture. The meteorological elements were conspiring to bring a host of rainfall to Milam County:
~~~

The front should arrive about sunset, expect temperatures to drop into the low-to-mid 50's overnight, but the big story is the rain. We've been waiting for this one. This is one of the few times we'll ever predict a 100-percent chance, but you can guarantee it's going to be wet out there tonight. Widespread one to two inches in Williamson, Milam, and Robertson County, and up to three inches further west to Austin and the hill country. Showers will continue overnight and clear out in the late afternoon tomorrow.

As the report went on, Hank's smile slowly grew. When the meteorologist signed off, he was beaming. He couldn't care less that work would have to be cancelled tomorrow. The river would be up, and we were going fishing.

We departed the cabin in our two-man fishing boat just after 8 a.m. The rain gauge showed 1.8 inches, which was about perfect. The river wouldn't be raging, but it would definitely be navigable. We made our way upstream to the best fishing hole on the Gabriel, a deep murky straightaway covered overhead by a row of massive cottonwood trees draped as a canopy.

Old timers in the area said this hole went all the way down to the aquifer, at least 30 or 40 feet. The aquifer provided life-sustaining fresh water keeping the deep holes full even in times of drought. It was the same aquifer all wells in this area tapped, including the San Xavier mission two centuries before. The remains of that mission lie just 200 yards up a hill from us.

If old Snively really existed, he had certainly been down this way before, and no doubt the Spanish missioners caught catfish from this very same hole.

No one really knew how deep the hole was. We'd never known anyone who could swim that far down. Deep holes are good for finding catfish, as they are primarily bottom feeders. They love the dark, cool waters, but they'll come up to the surface in search of food if they sense a commotion such as the kicking of a grasshopper's legs or a worm on a hook. The long whiskers make them very perceptive even in zero visibility.

We pulled in a decent haul by noon. Hank was half drunk, drinking beer most of the day. I had a few as well. We often had to relieve ourselves right there in the river. At one point, we both had to go about the same time, so Hank stood off the front side and me off the back, to keep the boat from tipping over. We commenced our restroom break.

"Damn, this water's *cold,*" Hank said, giggling drunkenly to himself.

"Yep. It's deep too," I replied wittily, one-upping him as always.

I guarantee you he'd been planning that witticism for some time, just waiting for the right moment to use it. Now he'd spend the next two days trying to come up with an even better reply to get me. He hated the fact I was always quicker on the comebacks than he was; it pissed him off.

This is the same hole I suspect George Sessions Perry wrote about in his novel, when his characters Sam Tucker and Clappy Finley first spotted the monster catfish *Lead Pencil.* It was a yellow cat so large, its whiskers were as big around as a lead pencil, hence the name. Folks around here knew the novel was based upon real observations by Mr. Perry, as the entire book was a direct examination of life along the San Gabriel River.

It was while they were walking along the bank beside the long hole that they saw something that stopped their hearts beating. A catfish of the most gigantic proportions floated to the top for a moment, and then with a gentle, undulant motion of his great tail went back down. And now in their little world there was a new being, an incredible monster, and one to scheme against on sleepless nights. For to whoever caught Lead Pencil fame would be assured. - ***Hold Autumn in Your Hand, Chapter 12, pages 103-104***

Catching a large catfish can grant one near fame in Milam County, and that's as true today as it was during the Great Depression. In the book, Sam and Clappy vowed to keep their sighting a secret, in the hopes that one of the duo would land the big fish without attracting a horde of fishermen to compete for it. As Sam Tucker would soon come to know, you must be careful whom you trust. Despite assurances from Clappy that the fish would remain a secret, he clandestinely went about his own ambitions to catch the prized fish.

So that flappy-mouthed Clappy had been with Henry last night telling him about Lead Pencil, and Henry was trying to get rid of the boat at once, before it could be used in fishing for the big fish. If Henry was going to be fishing from the bank, he wanted you to also, despite the fact that both the boat and Lead Pencil were your own discoveries. Flappy Fin had told their secret for a mess of momentary awe. - ***Hold Autumn in Your Hand, Chapter 12, page 105***

Sam would inevitably hook the large fish, but he would not be able to lay claim to it. You see, he traded it away to Henry in exchange for a first pass at his Henry's lovely garden. Henry wanted what Sam had, the respect and notoriety as a capable fisherman. While Sam wanted what Henry had, enough food for he and his family to survive through winter.

Again, as life imitates art, many locals who couldn't read, or hadn't bothered to peruse Mr. Perry's book, often took the story to be true. The legend of gigantic catfish, 70 pounds or more, was spoken of as if it were from the Bible itself. Myths of large catfish continued unabated and likely will as long as the Gabriel flows.

Late night beer joint conversations and card games are notorious for giving life to these tall tales. Hank had his own share of sightings, though he had never hooked a large fish. He was a fan of Mr. Perry, and in homage to Sam Tucker, Hank referred to his seeming nemesis as the offspring of *Lead Pencil*. He appropriately named the uncaught fish *Dick Pencil*. Suffice to say given Hank's maturity level in that day and age, it wasn't long before *Dick* became the surname.

Our personal drought in hooking the big fish was headed for a change. As the day went on, our haul of respectable five and six-pound channel cat would include an eight-pounder. It was nothing too spectacular, but the sun was just now beginning to set. The cold front was clearing out and rays of sunshine could be seen darting through the clouds.

The freshness of the crisp air was splendid, and this is the time of day when the big fish come out to eat. We baited up our lines with larger portions to attract, with any luck, a 20 pounder. We were required by the fisherman's code to report it accurately, so 25 would sound about right.

Hank caught sight of the shadowy outline about the same time I did. It lurked just below the surface. The gigantic whiskers were all that was visible as it investigated our presence. It zigzagged back and forth underneath the boat, lazily, and then darted below quicker than a flash of lightning, spooked by something on the surface.

Moments later, it would return, and began the dance again. Not wanting to further alarm the fish, we spoke in a muted whisper. We could barely hear one another, and must have looked like a couple of idiots.

"Hey. Hey! You seen it?" Hank asked.

"Yeah. I see it."

"Sumbitch is the size of a hog. I reckon that's ol' Pencil Dick himself."

"What?"

"Dammit. Pencil Dick."

"Who?"

"No, it's. Never mind. I'm reeling back in to re-bait."

"Don't, what?"

"I said I'm reeling back in."

"I can't hear a word you say."

"Stop moving. What the hell....shut the hell up you're gonna scare him off."

Hank reeled his line in, slowly. He almost had his hook re-baited, when *Pencil Dick* dispensed with the pleasantries. I felt a tug on my fishing rod, and then the line went limp. It snapped taught a split second later. I might as well have had a bowling ball on the other end.

Pencil Dick was hooked.

He pulled so hard on the line, I lost my balance. The boat lunged back and forth as I tried to regain it. Hank braced himself against the sides of the boat, trying in vain to offset me. Without a firm grip, he dropped his pole into the water. I tried to keep my stance spread far enough to keep from toppling overboard, but *Pencil Dick* kept on pulling, first left, then right, fighting feverishly to get free.

We didn't have much of a chance. Trying to gain some leverage over the mighty fish, I leaned out a bit too far to the starboard side. He changed direction. Into the drink I went. Hank was too far against the port side, and once my weight lifted from the boat, he careened into a backwards cartwheel. As he hit the water, the little schooner flipped over on top of him. Our beer and tackle boxes were now on the way down to the bottom.

When Hank managed to get his head back above water, there were no more subtle whispers.

"Hot dammit, don't lose him! Pull that slack in." Hank shouted.

It was at first a gargling gibberish coming out of his mouth as he tried to get the water out of his lungs.

"Hold on to it! Shit! Don't let it go!"

I had the reel in one hand, and treaded water with my legs. I used my free hand to doggy paddle to the shore as *Pencil Dick* gave me a reprieve. Hank made it over to the bank first. He tried to grab the reel from me as I got near the bank. I refused to give it up. This was my fight.

Hank fished his net from the water and took position alongside me, ready to strike. He tried to pull the rod from my hand several times.

"Mac! Here, let me have it! Come on, you're gonna lose him! Don't lose him! Here, let me have it!"

I wanted this one for myself.

After 15 minutes, my palms were bloody from the constant twisting of the rod with that bowling ball of a fish on the other end. I eventually got the line reeled within striking distance of Hank and his net. He waded in and manhandled that fish into the net. He had the biggest smile I'd ever seen.

Pencil Dick gave a mighty fight right up until the end. Its bony appendages caused the both of us to bleed. As it wailed in desperation for its freedom, the fins sliced our forearms as we hustled the beast to the shore. It took both of us to hold it down, in a net, on the bank, and then Hank drove a lock blade pocketknife into its head.

The flailing stopped.

We slumped over onto the bank exhausted, and dehydrated. Fishing is hours of boredom broken by minutes of downright pleasure. By that measure, this had been the best fishing trip I'd ever been on together.

The mighty *Pencil Dick* had been slain.

~~~

That night, we fried the big fish up at the cabin. Hank invited all the men over. We always ate what we killed, or served it up for the crews. This was the best tasting fish I ever had. It was the taste of victory; hours spent saddling the river in a rickety old boat, followed by half an hour of *mano y mano* warfare.

The aroma of fish still stained my hands, and dried blood stained my clothes; all part of God's wonderful creation. It
~~~

was a great night; the smell, the taste, the blood, and the warm glow of a campfire on a brisk, cloudless night with the sound of crickets chirping in the distance.

We placed the head of old *Pencil Dick* on a fencepost for good luck, next to a water moccasin hide. When flipped upside down, this custom was said to make it rain. We weighed the fish at 67.5 pounds, and rounded to 75. By now, the legend of *Pencil Dick's* size has probably grown to well over a hundred pounds in some dusty bar in Milam County. No doubt it took half a dozen men to reel him in.

16. HANK'S HISTORY

All Scripture is breathed out by God and profitable for teaching, for reproof, for correction, and for training in righteousness, that the man of God may be competent, equipped for every good work. ***2 Timothy 3: 16-17***

The first time I met Hank, I noticed the ring on his finger, noting he was a Freemason. This tradition went all the way back to his family's emigration from northern England in the 1800's. Scotland was the birthplace of Scottish Rite Freemasonry. A large percentage of early Texas settlers were Masons. The Brazos River Valley became home to many of the brethren in the period leading up to the Texas Revolution.

The Craft would continue to grow into the 1900's, but towards the end of that century the ranks of membership waned. The American economy shifted to a more technical landscape during that time. Ultimately, the decline of blue collar craftsmen and a dearth of American manufacturing would turn a once exigent body into more of a fraternal organization.

Masonry was the original construct for the labor union, a band of men who worked with their hands. Lodges were self-organized with their own elective leaders *to pay the craft their wages and see that none go away dissatisfied, peace and harmony being the strength and support of all institutions.* Modern-day unions once stood as the bedrock of working rights for the common man.

As Masonry shifted from being the bedrock of American society, some unions devolved to smell of corruption and cronyism. Such a statement would be branded blasphemy in Milam County once ALCOA came to town. The steelworkers union provided protection for former farm hands who now found themselves in the employ of such a large corporation.

Despite its changing landscape, the Masonic Lodge never parted ways with its deep and guiding principles. It is not a secret society per se, but it does uphold many ancient and secretive traditions. It is also not a union, nor is it political or religious.

Hank took Masonry more seriously as he matured. He took the helm as Master of Lodge #978 around the time of his 30th birthday. I became his Senior Warden.

~~~

Not long after Hank and I met, my curiosity got the best of me. Something had bothered me about our first meeting, and I finally got up the nerve to ask Hank about it.

"That first day we met at Steve's Place, when Elmo called you Hiram," I began to ask.

"Yeah. What about it?" Hank replied.
~~~

"Well, it just seemed, it got my attention because I had just gone through the rites of initiation. I assume they call you that because you that as a reference to Hiram Abiff."

"Nope."

"So, is it related to the Lodge?"

"No."

"No?"

"Nope. That's my name."

"I don't get it. Your name is Hank."

"No, my name is Hiram. I was born Hiram King Benson. That's what the H.K. stands for. But no one calls me Hiram, except some of the older guys who were around when I was born."

I guess stranger things have happened. After all, his family was full of Masons. The importance of that name could not have been unknown to them. Perhaps it was just another in a line of coincidences.

Another man with the same name was beginning to grow in popularity, though I doubt more than a handful of people knew it. His music was heard far and wide, especially around this part of the world. His name was Hiram King Williams, but his friends also called him Hank.

~~~
~~~

The night following our victory over *Pencil Dick*, we still nursed our wounds and basked in the afterglow. Hank and I finished up the two-day fishing bender and entered into a debate over Masonic history. He was once again under the influence, this time it was Jim Beam, which made him even more talkative and recalcitrant than usual.

He entered an almost manic state when drinking and fired up about something. Since he became Master of the local lodge, he had taken to deep study of its history. Naturally, he would regurgitate his learnings out loud, as he did everything. He wanted me to follow in his footsteps and become Master the following year. It entails a sizable amount of education in the esoteric symbolism and unwritten word of Masonry. The secrets and traditions cannot be passed on in inscribed form, only in the spoken word.

It was an honor I would ultimately turn down. It would lead to a fraying of our relationship. It would not sever us entirely, but it would mark the beginning of the end of the closest relationship I've ever had, and I am positive the same was true for him. We would not part ways until 1958, and it would be to something completely unrelated.

Hank sold the business in 1960. He went on to start a family. I went back to teaching schoolchildren, and he went back doing whatever it was that kept him happy. Fishing, drinking beer, running cattle, and traveling across the country in his airplane. Unlike Hank, I would never marry nor have a family. It wasn't in the cards for a traveling man like me.

While Mason's must profess a belief in the divine, the specifics are left up to the individual. A man who does not profess a belief in a higher power cannot be made a Mason. Even so, I had no issues taking the oath of a Mason. I had always believed in a higher power. There was nothing about Masonry that violated my own personal beliefs. However, Hank wanted me to take a larger role in the Craft, and it was just something I wasn't prepared to do. I thought deeply over it, but my obligations lie elsewhere.

Despite being diverted many times on my road less traveled, I had not given up on the reason I first pursued Masonry in the first place. As the conversation that celebratory night veered off course, I asked Hank if he'd ever heard of the legend of a magical Jewel in any of the Masonic history he had read. My own search had turned up nothing but wildly varying stories from locals about floating lanterns and fire-breathing ghost bulls. I'm sure Hank had heard the same.

While it felt I may be chasing a phantom, the Almighty was about to correct my course and put me back on the right path.

"I've never heard of a jewel like that in any Masonic tradition." Hank answered.

"I didn't figure. It's just, when I was in Europe I came across something that has befuddled me now for many years. It is what led me to Masonry. It was an old chest with Masonic markings, and I..."

Hank interrupted me.

"But that is not to say, that I may or may not know of a jewel that exists."

My first thought at his reply was that given his inebriated state, he was just messing with me. I had come to know that when he began speaking in this matter, with "I may or may not know", you could be certain he did know something. As I mentioned earlier, when he got excited about something, his poker face left the building.

"Beg pardon?"

"The Jewel. I know of it."

"You do?"

"It's a jewel that has supernatural powers. I know all about it. I call it Hiram's Jewel."

I was intrigued. Maybe he did know something.

"You are the only person I've ever discussed this with. Tell you the truth, you're the only one in the world who has ever even mentioned such a thing. It was brought to this land in the 1850's by the great Sam Houston."

"This land, you mean Texas?"

"No. I mean the land you are standing on."

~~~

Hank had a story to tell.
~~~

First, he demanded to know what I knew about this supposed jewel. He was basically telling me "you go first." So I did. I told him of the chest I'd found back in Germany, and how I fought my way across Europe and ended up in Hitler's bunker. I told him of the Monuments Men. I regaled him of the trip across the Alps. And finally, I told him of the Jewel itself, the glowing splendor, and the raw beauty of its mangled form.

I told him of the many documents, and how I folded those pieces to hide them in the cargo pockets of my fatigues to sneak it all out of the country. I took it upon myself to translate and re-write most of those documents so the history would never be lost again. The papers yielded a trove of information. They provided first-hand experience from the holder of the Jewel in time periods dating back thousands of years.

The Jewel turned one's thoughts inward. Each holder of the Jewel, it seems, had become compelled to write down its history. It is the same urging I feel now, and is part of the reason I write this book. The Latin and French came alive, and I reminded myself of the beauty of different languages, and why I was drawn to learn them all early in my existence.

Hank listened to my story, never saying a word. His look became more serene. His gaze went from unsuspecting, to intense. When I finished, Hank remained silent for a while. Eventually, a smile came across his face, and he shook his head for a moment, as if in disbelief.

"All this time, most of my life, I thought I was crazy. That my grandfather was crazy. That I was suckered in to some grand myth. That all the bizarre shit that has happened to me was, I don't know, demons possessing me, or something like that. I've been waiting for that other shoe to drop for a decade. I've mostly just tried to forget about it."

Hank took a sip of the whiskey, winced his eyes and grimaced, turning his head to the side as the 80-proof liquor cascaded down his throat.

"I guess it just did."

Hank then told me his own story. It was of a very similar Jewel. He had found it while looking for Indian arrowheads on the banks of the San Gabriel River when he was a boy.

"I was right down there, where the Gabriel turns back east."

He pointed northward.

"There's a low water crossing that was pretty well dry. Me and Suzie were down there looking for arrowheads. I must have been about 14 or 15. I had seen a glowing the night before. Everybody around here sees that glow from time to time. Back then I thought it might be Old Snively. I was too scared to go after it at night, being a kid and all, but the next day I went down there to look around."

"I've heard of Snively. They say he was a treasure hunter and haunts the area," I replied.

"Yes, that is what they say," Hank retorted.

"I figured it was, but how can anyone know for sure? I mean, surely you believe in ghosts, and spirits, in angels and demons."

"Yes, I do. I believe in them. I haven't always, but after that day, I sure as hell did. But I don't believe in the ghost of Snively. That is just a myth."

"Why do you think that?"

"People around here, they've always wanted to believe that legend. Who doesn't want to believe in the idea that there is gold scattered around here?"

Perhaps Hank was right. It is no surprise that this land of dreamers would yield a salvo of tall tales. The area was populated in the mid-1800's by Stephen F. Austin's charter. He brought 300 families to the edge of Indian Territory in the ever-expanding United States.

Perhaps the tallest tale of them all is the legend of Snively. These stories were passed down through the generations and permeated the local culture to become urban legend. Yet now, Hank and I were realizing the truth is far deeper and has far more meaning than a hundred wagonloads of buried Mexican gold.

"I found out what was causing that glow. Down in the river bottom, as I rooted around for arrowheads, I spotted something shiny in the roots of an old pecan tree. I had to wade into three feet of water to get at it. As I drew near, I felt, I don't know how to explain it. Closest thing is to say I felt drunk. Dizzy. It just felt strange."

I was hanging on every word. I recalled the same feeling in 1943, as I approached that chest at Eagle's Nest. He continued.

"I snatched up the object. The feeling intensified for a moment. I felt I was floating on air. The Jewel was muddy, and beat to hell, but I could tell it was rich. It looked old. I held it out of the water as I waded back to the crossing, and the feeling suddenly went away. That's when things got weird."

"How so?"

"I felt a cold chill. My stomach seemed to drop out of my body. Suzie started barking ferociously. Up on the opposite bank, staring down at me, were a pack of coyotes. There must have been at least six of them. They were staring at me, with these evil eyes. I figured them for rabid. Those things don't usually come out in the daytime."

"What happened?"

"They made their move. They attacked. Suzie ran out to meet them head on. She peeled off three of them, and they fought. The other three circled me. I could have kicked myself for not bringing a shotgun. I thought I was done for. The first one leapt into the air, his mouth headed straight for my throat."

Hank stopped to take a drink. There was a growing intensity in his voice, which caused it to crack. A tear appeared in the corner of his eye.

"But then, at that moment, the feeling came back—a sensation I can't describe. An overwhelming surge of adrenaline is the best way I can describe it. It was like I was on autopilot, and watching this unfold as an observer. I grabbed the animal in mid-flight. My arms wrapped around its torso. It twisted, and I got a grip on its hind legs. I slammed it into the ground with a force that shattered its skull."

"You serious?"

"I swear to God I'm telling the truth, Mac. Then the other two attacked. It happened quickly. I caught the first under my arm. I had so much strength, I can't explain it. I ripped its head from the body. The second had a hold of my lower leg and sank its teeth in deep. I grabbed him in the same manner as the first, ripping apart my own leg as I pried its teeth free. He was wounded. I kicked him so hard it must have shattered his internal organs."

"Suzie, and those other three?" I asked.

"Suzie didn't fare as well. She managed to kill one of the coyotes. But the other two got to her. She chased them other two off after they saw what I did to their buddies. But not before she was mortally wounded. She made it halfway back to me before she fell over and died."

I could see tears forming at the corner of his eyes.

"That was the best dog I ever had."

Hank stood up.

"So now you know. Whether you believe it or not, I don't really care. But there it is."

"Hank, I believe you. I might be the only man in the world who'd believe a story like that, but I do."

"Thanks, Mac. Now, I'm sorry but I don't know that I really feel like talking about this anymore. Unfortunately...."

He paused.

"What?"

"Unfortunately, the reality set in, and you've just forced me to drag this all back up. I had this great, awesome, power. But I didn't know how to use it. I could only use it to *destroy*."

17. AIDEN BENSON

I tell you that, while I believe with you in the doctrine of state's rights, the North is determined to preserve this Union. They are not a fiery, impulsive people as you are, for they live in colder climates. But when they begin to move in a given direction, they move with the steady momentum and perseverance of a mighty avalanche; and what I fear is, they will overwhelm the South

– ***Sam Houston*** *1861*

I was amazed at Hank's story, but nonetheless, I was not at all surprised. When I had my encounter on that mountaintop in Germany, it was much less impressive, but the feeling of Divine power coursed through my veins. Yet the presence of evil did not appear. I stood ready. The evil which I feared, the Nazis, were all but defeated. That piece of the Jewel had only recently arrived at Eagle's Nest.

However, the forces of darkness were in wait on the San Gabriel River that fateful day for Hank. They abided with patience for almost 150 years. Once the Jewel betrayed its hiding place, and bequeathed its power to Hank, those forces converged. Unable to match his newfound power, evil adapted to the new battlefield. It would regroup, and quickly make plans to attack him anew.

Now, I may speak of this evil as an abstract construct, but I assure it has a name. We will get to that later. To see Hank re-live that experience in a raw display of emotion reminded me that he was but a man. I think it reminded him as well. I'd never seen this man cry.

He mentioned that he was 14 or 15 years old. I could likely give him an exact date. The Jewel, while severed in twain, acted as one body. The Jewel that I found was removed from Versailles in 1942 on the same date. Hank would have been 15 years old at the time. It was on that date it awoke, in unison, from slumber.

His parents' deaths were not accidents. They were victims of the enigma which Hank had unwittingly stumbled across. He never told another soul of this Jewel. It put the fear of God into him. I am not sentimental about his loss. I know now that the second piece of the Jewel must be near. It was finally within my reach. For the first time in almost 2,000 years, there was an opportunity for the Jewel to be reunited unto itself.

~~~

Hank summoned his strength, wiped the tears away, and continued his story.

"I was frightened. I didn't know what to do with this thing. It nearly drove me mad. I kept it hidden away for several years, but it changed me from that day forward. After that
~~~

attack, my parents were killed, then my grandfather. But it's, it's almost as if I had a guardian angel. Every time something bad happened, my fortunes changed. Grandpa dies and leaves me most of his land. I was rich at 17. And he left me an explanation, written out in his journal. For the first time in my life, I understood. Unfortunately, it was..."

"What was that, Hank?"

"I said, unfortunately, it was too late. I had already done something that I have regretted all of my life."

"What was that?"

"It takes a certain understanding, a mental discipline to use these powers. I didn't have it. It is just raw power that, left to the hands of man, can only wreak havoc."

Hank looked at the ground. He wouldn't make eye contact. He was deeply disturbed.

"Look, Mac, I don't reckon I should admit this here and now. In a moment of weakness, I did something..."

The emotions weighed heavily on him. The tears were about to flow again, but he pushed them away. I wanted to comfort him. Here was a man on the verge of confessing, yet I wasn't sure he was going too.

"I used it, for, something....it was a bad thing to do."

Hank's hands were shaking. He clenched his fists. There was complete silence. Slowly he stood up, and walked away.

He had let on as much as he was going to for the night.

He stumbled into the cabin, slammed the door, and went to sleep.

~~~

The next morning I awoke at the crack of dawn. Hank was already awake. He had a pot of coffee brewing over the wood stove. He had sobered up completely. The wood stove crackled as sparks from mesquite coals occasionally escaped the stove. Mesquite is one of the hotter burning coals, and is somewhat volatile when it gets roaring.

One thing about Hank, he was rarely hung over. He had a magical ability to wake up bright and early no matter how much he imbibed the night before. Seated at an old, wooden picnic table, he had a very thick old book he was reading intently.

Cattle grazed only a few feet away, as they began their daily migration across the pasture, passing by the cabin en route to the south end. Most of the path was shaded by pecan trees, and the herd was never more than a few hundred feet from water. The Gabriel ran north through the field. Occasionally the cattle would get hold of pecan leaves that hung just low enough to reach; causing a visual distraction that made it appear the wind was blowing.
~~~

Pecan leaves were like dessert to these thousand pound lawnmowers.

Yet there was no wind, as the plume of smoke from the woodstove went straight up into the sky. It was a perfectly calm morning. As he sat near the fence, I could see a smile on his face as he turned a page.

"Morning,"

"Morning," came Hanks' reply. "Get you a cup of coffee."

"Mesquite roasted, I see. What you reading there?"

"I got some pecan in it too. It's a special blend, son."

"I'll pass. You know I can't handle caffeine that well."

"It's decaf."

"Yeah, right. If I saw you drinking decaf, I'd have to call the hospital. Cause that'd mean you done lost your mind."

"That's a fact. Well, then. Let's talk about this thing we discussed last night."

"Certainly. You remember that? You were three sheets to the wind."

"Hell if I was."

"I've seen you worse."

"I had a wonderful dream last night. An angel appeared to me."

"*Really*."

"No shit. Actually, it was an archangel. It was the Archangel *Raphael*. Have you ever heard of him?"

"I have. Absolutely. What did he tell you?"

"He told me you were trustworthy. He told me I was safe to tell you. The secret, you know, of the Jewel."

"And?"

"You don't seem too surprised."

"No."

He looked at me suspiciously.

"Why not? Anyone else I told this too would think I'm bat shit crazy. Why not you?"

"Look, I've always believed in angels. And I know they talk to humans. So, no, I'm not all that surprised. In fact, from what you told me last night, the fact that you can communicate with angels comes as no surprise to me."

"These dreams are not new to me, you know. They come along from time to time."

He took another sip of coffee.

"Remember back when you first moved here, and we were getting all those jobs, and winning all the bids?"

"Yes I do."

"Well about that time, I started having the most amazing dreams. Raphael appeared to me and gave me all the advice, all the answers I needed. I wish I could say it was my own doing, but the truth is, it all came from him."

"The Lord works in mysterious ways."

"Mac, I'm going to trust you. I know damn well you want to know where this Jewel is. Am I right?"

I was a bit caught off guard. To be honest, I hadn't thought of it this way, from his perspective. It was true, though. It was what I had sought all this time.

"Yes. Yes, I do."

"OK. Then let me tell you my biggest fear. My biggest fear is that I can't tell the good guys from the bad guys. Let's say you were a demon masquerading as a human, siding up to me and pretending to be my friend, only so you can take the Jewel from me and use it for God knows what."

"I wouldn't."

"Of course you'd say that."

"I promise you, Hank. I am your friend."

"Okay. Good. It's just that..."

Hank stopped talking. An eerie silence took hold. He didn't say anything. He just stared at me for a few seconds then turned to gaze off into the distance. He was in a trance of some sort. Suddenly, he turned his attention back to the book.

"OK. Let's continue, shall we. This here book I'm reading is the journal passed on to me from my grandfather, Aiden Benson. It's all in his writing, and it's pretty bad at that. I take it he interpreted most of it from some ancient writings. You can read it, or I can just tell it to you. I've read this so many times, I could damn near quote it all verbatim."

"Go ahead, Hank. I'm listening."

~~~

After the Texans gained independence from Mexico, victory led to annexation with the United States in 1845. While conditions in Texas were still harsh, a steady influx of American settlers continued unabated. Civilization began to take hold as the threat of Indian raids subsided. The Spanish-American War would ultimately solidify the boundaries of the Lone Star state.

Born in 1846, Aiden Isaac Benson arrived in east Texas in his early teenage years when his family migrated from northern Alabama. His stay in east Texas would not be permanent. With Lincoln's election in 1860, the Civil War began.

A divided Texas chose to secede from the Union, leading to the ouster of Governor Sam Houston who opposed it. Perhaps the governor had seen his share of bloodshed in the War of 1812 and the Texas Revolution, both in which he was wounded. In this new war, a nation would be fighting itself, in some cases, brother against brother.
~~~

Most of the major Civil War battles were fought far from the borders of Texas. Out the outbreak, Aiden was too young to fight, being barely 15 years old. Instead, he remained at home to take care of the family stock. He followed in his father's trade, becoming an exceptionally talented carpenter and craftsman. He also took odd jobs around the area to earn money for the family.

One day Aiden was called to a job for a crotchety old gentleman. This man lived in a fine estate, and no doubt had some manner of wealth and notoriety. The job paid well and it wasn't every day he got to work with finer materials. Cost appeared to be no object.

Young Aiden worked at the old man's house for the better part of three weeks; fixing the roof, the outhouse, tending to horses, and doing whatever the old man required. Each day he was presented a detailed list of chores. The old man spent most of his time sitting in a rocking chair, doing what appeared to be writing, and with great interest.

Occasionally he would glance up from his writing and, if their eyes met, he would nod in the direction of young Aiden as he toiled away in the Texas sun. With a pipe in his mouth most of the time, the old man kept covered with a blanket, his mighty cough echoing about. Aiden had seen the symptoms of pneumonia before, and he knew that if this man had it, at his age, he likely was not long for the world.

The old man was dying.

On a hot July day, the old man called Aiden into the house. His face was pale, and he did not appear completely coherent; even more frail and weak than usual. He reached his hand out. Aiden shook the old man's hand. Despite the look of frailty, his grip was strong. Young Aiden had not the first clue as to the weight of history that sat next to him.

"Son, I've watched you toil the last few weeks here. I chose you because your father..."

The old man stopped to clear his throat, and coughed several times before regaining his composure.

"Your father, he is a good man. But he is too old...too old for this task."

Aiden assumed the man was speaking of the task of labor, which he had been waist deep in for the past few weeks. No doubt it was indeed more suited for a younger man.

"Thank you, sir. Yes, I must say, this heat makes it nigh untenable."

"Make no mistake, son."

The man pointed out into the courtyard, his arm moving back and forth three times.

"This is not the task of which I speak. What I speak of, it lies henceforth before you."

The old man cleared his throat again. His mind was sharp, but his physical ailment exacted a heavy toll to bring his thoughts into spoken word.

"I must now pass to you, to you and through you, that which you must protect. Unfailing devotion it requires, of the highest order. It is my gift, though..."

"Sir?" replied Aiden.

"Though, it may damn well be a curse. You must prepare to guard accordingly."

He motioned to a chest next to the fireplace. It was not very large. It appeared rugged, and worn. Two chains engrossed it, which met in the center tethered with a lock.

"What is this, sir?"

The old man summoned his strength once again. He asked for Aiden's hand to help him stand up. Aiden held the man firmly, and brought him to his feet. The man walked feebly over to the chest.

"This, this is the treasure you seek, my son. You will find it awaits you."

Aiden examined the chest. He doubted a great treasure would be stowed in a box that was destined for the scrap heap. Nonetheless, he did as the man said.

"You must first find the key. Then you will know. The grand Architect shall guide you in your travels."

"Has it a key?" replied Aiden.

"It does."

"Will you give it to me?"

"I was not so given it, nor can I so impart it. You must seek out Brother Ben Milam. Amos 3:7."

Aiden tapped on the lock. Despite its appearance, it was solid; a miniature fortress, sealed shut with rusted iron. Aiden did not know a Ben Milam, but if the man were a brother Mason, then he would be able to track him down. Yet, it seemed an odd request. Why would he give a man he'd just met something of value, and why wouldn't he just keep the key himself? He was intrigued.

The old man grabbed Aiden authoritatively, and stuck his finger into the boy's chest, clearly pointing at his heart.

"Son, take the chest. Then fetch my wife. And *Godspeed.*"

"Yes, sir."

As Aiden departed, the old man, whispered unto himself:

"May peace and brotherly love prevail. In the name of God, and the Holy Saints John."

He raised his right hand to his head.

"So mote it be."

~~~
~~~

Aiden did as the man said, and retrieved his wife. Upon his return, the man had fallen asleep. He was unable to bid the gentleman farewell.

He finished work for the day, and went home, carrying the chest with him upon his horse. It didn't weigh that much. Whatever it carried inside, it certainly was not heavy. En route to the homestead, he stopped for grain. When he arrived he asked the storekeeper, a Mason, if he knew a fellow brother named Ben Milam.

"I have heard the name. I believe Ben Milam was a Colonel in the Texan Army" replied the man.

"What does he do now?" asked Aiden.

"Nothing. He died at the Siege of Bexar during the Texas Revolution. I believe he was buried there, in San Antonio."

Aiden was perplexed. He reckoned the old man must have been senile with such a request; to seek a man who had been dead for more than 25 years. Nevertheless, he couldn't unlock the chest without this key. Over the next week, he thought off and on about the mysteriousness of the old man's request. He couldn't let it go, and it began to occupy his mind. The following weekend he decided to return and ask the old man what he had meant.

He made his way back to the man's home to inquire.

18. HOUSTON'S GIFT

When Aiden arrived back at the stately home, there appeared an odd sight. A crowd of well-dressed men and women were gathered. In what seemed untimely for July, they were all clad in black. Aiden was entirely out of place, wearing the clothes of his trade; a straw hat and coveralls, shod with dusty work boots. He proceeded to investigate, and soon discovered it was a funeral.

The old man passed away during the week, likely not long after Aiden departed.

Aiden was not altogether surprised. The old man, in a severely degraded state, did not appear long for the world. The attendees to the procession appeared stately and well-to-do. Despite his appearance, Aiden was ushered into the house by one of the many.

The old man was now in the Celestial Lodge above, buried with the honors of a Master Mason. He could no longer answer the question that was consuming young Aiden. And now, he might never know what the man had meant. It might be nothing; the incoherent ramblings of a man near the end of his life.

Yet, that explanation would fail to satiate his curiosity. Aiden longed for something important to be in that chest. He wanted an adventure, a mystery; anything to add an element of action to his otherwise menial life. He vowed to figure it all out.

News of the man's death soon spread throughout the land. He was a great man. Aiden was simply too young to know his story. After all, in those days, even famous people rarely had pictures of themselves for all to see.

The man's name was Sam Houston.

~~~

Aiden was captivated with a determination to find out just exactly what was in the chest. He was eager to get it open. These thoughts ran through his head as he made his way home. He planned to pry it open just as soon as he got back. Surely it would be a simple task for a craftsman.

As fate would have it, he would not open the chest that day. Along the path home, he writes of meeting a man traveling in the opposite direction. The man was a stranger, but waived Aiden aside and asked for tobacco. When Aiden replied that he had none, the man asked for whiskey.

Aiden did not carry these things.

The man asked for water. Aiden, having grown impatient, directed the man to the nearest creek bed, and readied his horse to continue. Finally, the man asked for something to eat. Aiden did not wish to share, and continued his journey. After a few steps, the horse itself stopped, and turned around un-commanded. Slightly embarrassed at his own horse's impudence, he reluctantly pitched two
~~~

pieces of jerky at the man, and prepared to again head down the trail.

"Wait," replied the man.

"Sir, I must be getting on. Good day now."

"Have you heard the good news of Amos?"

"Amos?" replied Aiden.

"Amos three. *Verse seven.*"

"Okay then, sir. How do you know of this?"

"Answer *me*, good sir. Have you read it?"

"Well, no. I haven't. But I...I intend to directly."

"When will you arise from your sleep, good sir?"

"I'm afraid I do not understand."

"A little sleep, a little slumber, a little folding of the hands to rest, and poverty will come upon you like a robber, and want like an armed man."

When he finished speaking, Aiden lifted his head to reply.

The man was gone. He was nowhere to be seen.

"Hello? Sir? Are you there?"

There was complete silence.

A quiet fear ran through Aiden's veins, leaving him cold and nervous.

~~~

Whatever secret Sam Houston meant to pass on, it now took a new priority for Aiden Benson. This past week had been too bizarre for his liking. When he arrived back at the homestead, he took the family Bible off the shelf and turned to Amos 3:7:

Surely the Lord God will do nothing, but he revealeth his secret unto his servants the prophets.

He looked at the chest. It had not moved. He wanted to open it. He hated this feeling of fear and uncertainty. He would use brutish strength to force it open and end this charade.

Deep in his fiber, Aiden felt an admonishment that he was not to open this chest. Instead, he was to seek out Ben Milam, as General Houston commanded. The gravity with which Sam Houston gripped him was the embrace of a Master Mason, a greeting not extended to those who were not of the fraternity. Alas, Aiden was not yet a Mason.

He had, however, been passed certain vestiges from his father. He was aware of the swift penalties for violating the oath; having the throat cut from ear to ear and the tongue torn out by its roots. Such penalties were entirely figurative and used only to symbolize the separation of mind from body, with the tongue no longer being able to
~~~

communicate with fellow Masons. The true punishment was not physical; it was for one to be banished from the Craft, forever.

Aiden had an epiphany; perhaps the key, as well, was symbolic in nature. It was entirely possible that a man such as General Houston would speak in the figurative sense, and not the literal. He must learn everything he could about Ben Milam. Something about that man must hold the cipher to Houston's riddle.

He discussed more with the shopkeeper, and decided to visit the grave of Benjamin Rush Milam. Such a trip required planning, and he'd have to wait until the fall before striking out. Aiden never made it to autumn; at least not in Texas. He was now old enough to serve in the Army, and in late 1863, before he could begin his journey to San Antonio; he was on his way to Louisiana to fight for the Confederate cause in the Civil War.

A boy would leave Texas, and a man would later return.

~~~

Three weeks before Sam Houston's death, General Ulysses S. Grant raised the Stars and Stripes over Vicksburg, Mississippi, having defeated the entrenched Confederate forces. For the Union, it was a hard fought victory which lasted more than six months, culminating with a six-week siege of the city. This was the second major setback for the rebels in as many days. General Robert E. Lee's invasion of the north at Gettysburg was decisively thwarted as well. Coming on Independence Day, the
~~~

victory was a major morale boost for Union forces and equally as demoralizing for the Confederacy.

After capturing Vicksburg, General Grant received a promotion to Major General, and the following letter:

When you first reached the vicinity of Vicksburg, I thought you should do, what you finally did—march the troops across the neck, run the batteries with the transports, and thus go below; and I never had any faith, except a general hope that you knew better than I, that the Yazoo Pass expedition, and the like, could succeed. When you got below, and took Port Gibson, Grand Gulf, and vicinity, I thought you should go down the river and join Gen. Banks; and when you turned Northward east of the Big Black, I feared it was a mistake. I now wish to make the personal acknowledgment that you were right, and I was wrong.

Yours very truly, A. Lincoln

Despite this defeat, the Civil War raged on and six months later, Aiden Benson mustered into service with the 18th Texas Infantry at Fort Jerusha. He was rushed into battle almost immediately when General Nathan Banks launched the Red River Campaign as a diversion from Grant's plan to surround the Confederate Army. On March 14th, the small band of soldiers including Aiden was surrounded at Fort De Russy. Union soldiers attacked the Fort, breaching the walls. They prepared to slaughter the small group of rebels.

Fortunately for the Benson legacy, the white flag of surrender was raised before this slaughter could take place. Aiden was taken a prisoner of war, and sent to the

Picayune Cotton Press prison in New Orleans. He was released in July as part of a prisoner swap one year after Vicksburg fell.

Truth is, the Union didn't want to be charged with the care and feeding of thousands of prisoners. As the tide turned, they saw fit to return these fellow Americans to their homes, in hopes that the rebuilding of America could begin.

While in prison he committed, as his first order of business should he return home, he would carry out the orders of General Houston. Indeed, barely more than a year would pass until Aiden would return. His home was now destitute, in the state of Texas that verged on anarchy. The coming Reconstruction would be a difficult time for people in the south.

He would keep his promise the very day after his return.

19. The Key

Who will go with old Ben Milam into San Antonio?

– Benjamin Rush Milam, December 4, 1835

It was three days ride to San Antonio.

Again in the summertime a year hence, he should have waited for the cooling air of autumn. His patience would not oblige. As such, the trip south and west to San Antonio was hot and dusty. He had to cross the Colorado, Blanco, and Guadalupe rivers. Despite being worn out, he would not rest until he found the item for which he searched.

In the storied city of San Antonio, heroes of the Texas Revolution stood in the face of certain death at the Alamo. Today, many of those soldiers have monuments in their honor thanks to the *Daughters of the Republic of Texas,* but back then, they were simple headstones. Buried during a war, few people were certain of the location of Ben Milam's resting place. It took two full days for Aiden to find a local man who knew the place, and he led Aiden to a cemetery.

Aiden waited patiently until dusk, when the light was dim and passersby had gone home for the evening. A thunderstorm rumbled in the distance. Drops of rain would strike his head every few seconds. His time this day was running short. Near the edge of a row of headstones, he found the final resting place of Colonel Milam.

If the secret rests with Ben Milam, then he could certainly get no closer to his answer. The head stone was a large granite rock with an engraving that simply told the date of Milam's death. There were no secrets here, nothing that would give him a clue.

There had to be more. He would not give up this easily. Aiden made sure no living souls were present to observe him, and then began to pry at the edges of the stone. It must have weighed 200 pounds. After a few minutes, he finally made the stone move, but only slightly. He needed a bar of some sort to leverage himself and flip the stone onto its side. The fast moving storm had made its way near. Flashes of lightning now lit the sky as they cascaded, and the crash of thunder came ever closer.

Darkness was setting in and he had to move quickly. The rain increased steadily. A lone mesquite tree stood near the center of the cemetery. A limb from the low hanging branches would do. He wedged the makeshift cantilever under the stone, and was able to tilt it, placing rocks underneath in succession.

Once flipped onto its back, at the upper apex of the hallowed ground, he saw the faint outline of a small box. He pried it from the earth. An explosion of lightning struck less than a mile away, and the deafening boom paralyzed him briefly.

On the box was carved another verse: *Matthew 13:44.* He opened the box. Inside was a piece of cloth. It was now being soaked by the increasing downpour. There was a hard object wrapped within, and he began to unravel the cloth.

His clothes were now soaked through with water. He felt the cold of the darkness, when the sudden shriek of a bird pierced the air. Aiden looked up to see a vulture perched on a branch of the mesquite tree. It stared at him, ominously, as though it were looking at a man soon to die. *Vultures were bad luck.*

He picked up a stone to throw at the menacing bird. At his move, the vulture flew away, into the night. He dropped the stone, and the piece of cloth, as lightning struck the mesquite tree just seconds later. It exploded in a fury of splinters, knocking him to the ground. The sound pierced his ears and all he could hear was a constant ringing sound.

He thought he was dead.

~~~

It felt like a dream. Aiden awoke the next morning on the floor of a church in San Antonio. The storm had frightened his horse and it fled into the night. A Catholic priest saw the young man caught in the storm, and quickly brought him inside the cathedral.

It was no dream. The cloth was still in his pants pocket. He again attempted to unfold it. To his surprise, the
~~~

wrapping contained an old, rusted key. He felt a charge more powerful than those bolts of lightning. General Houston had not let him down. It was the *key*. In a state of near-euphoria, he was now eager to depart for home to discover what was hidden in that chest.

Then he remembered something else from the night prior. He walked to the back pew of the cathedral and picked up a Bible to look up Matthew 13:44.

The kingdom of heaven is like unto treasure hid in a field; the which when a man hath found, he hideth, and for joy thereof goeth and selleth all that he hath, and buyeth that field.

An odd verse, he thought, all things considered.

The horse managed his way back to town after the torrent subsided. Aiden found the equine wandering through the streets, stopping for water outside a saloon. After thanking the priest, Aiden continued on his journey. It was a splendid trip home. The cold front had brought in clear skies and mild temperatures. The rains had not been widespread, so he had no problems crossing rivers with his trusty horse. He had never been in a better mood. A feeling of adventure, of meaning, and of accomplishment filled his spirits.

The key in fact opened Sam Houston's chest. Aiden was correct in that it contained no treasures of gold, as it was entirely too light. What it did contain, was a plethora of documents. At the top, was a document which made Matthew 13:44 come strikingly into focus.

It was the deed to a piece of property for which colonization rights had been unclaimed since the 1830's. It seems General Houston had carved out nearly a thousand acres from this parcel of land through his time of leadership during Texas' upheaval. The deed listed one *Aiden Isaac Benson* as the owner.

The location was in Milam County.

Beyond the title deed were numerous historical documents. Aiden paged through them, a mix of languages he couldn't even pronounce, let alone read. Many of the documents were in English, so he set about reading the story left him by Sam Houston. The daunting weight of history within his reach slowly came into view.

~~~

During the time of Sam Houston, Milam County was on the edge of the frontier. The area had been inhabited for more than 10,000 years. Tonkawa and Lipan Apaches became residents in the 14th Century, followed by Caddo and Tehuacana several hundred years later. Spaniards first arrived in the late 1600's. They established missions along the San Gabriel River in 1746, then known as the Xavier River. There would eventually be three missions along with a Presidio to be occupied by the Spanish military nearby.

Father Mariano de los Dolores y Viana wrote enthusiastically of the abundant wildlife and promise for agrarian use of the fertile soil. As fate would have it, severe drought planted itself upon the area at a most
~~~

inopportune time. Due to drought, growing threat of Indian attacks, and the infidelities of Captain Rabago, as mentioned earlier the missions were hastily abandoned several years later.

This fertile land would not lie dormant forever. Near the turn of the 19th Century, Americans began to move out and settle the territory of Texas, as the new nation began its westward expansion. In 1824, Stephen F. Austin brought the first wave of colonists to east Texas, granted by the Mexican government. As more and more non-Mexican colonists arrived, the nature of man to fight himself won the day, and the Texas Revolution followed not far behind.

During this time of upheaval, General Houston and the Texans moved assets strategically about the countryside. Not only did they preserve battlefield assets, but the Archives of the early republic as well, moving them in a shell game from town to town. Once the battles were over, the general moved one final shell to keep the Jewel of Hiram out of the reach of enemy hands.

The enemy was no longer the Mexicans, but rather it was the enemies of *good* whom he sought to outwit.

General Houston felt the same inhibition towards the Jewel as had Marcus Aurelius more than six centuries prior, though Houston lacked the extensive empire Aurelius had. Texas was, however, quite large with vast expanses of unsettled territory. He devised a master plan to shelter the object, replete with riddles and clues, to keep the Jewel at bay. The final part to his plan would prove to be the most difficult to orchestrate.

Houston had to find an unassuming young man to take up the charge. He required one who demonstrated a certain purity of heart; not overly ambitious, nor cunning, but a man of impeccable character. The general searched in vain during the latter years of his life, to no avail. Even entrusting such a Jewel to the brotherhood of Masons, while subject to the rights, lights, and benefits of the Craft; they remain susceptible to evils of the darkness in the heart of man. His inner circle consisted of men he trusted, but their ambition gave him pause. He wanted someone completely naïve; a *tabula rasa*, as it were.

Houston's health deteriorated quicker than anticipated, and he was ultimately left with few options. Unwittingly, that fateful July day in 1863, Aiden accepted work for General Houston. The boy seemed an adequate foil, and the general had to make a move. Houston left the fate of the Jewel to the Lord as he went about signing over those documents. He then snapped the lock shut; the key already far away per his well laid plans.

The primary aim of Houston in later life, as Aurelius before him, was not the passing of a legacy. It was, conversely, *obfuscation*. This Jewel in the hands of the wrong man would cry havoc. It is why, even on their deathbeds, they took final efforts to hide the Jewel's location.

You see, General Houston merely guided Aiden to the land, more than a thousand acres, but he would never disclose to him where it was buried. It was his hope that the land would remain unbothered for hundreds of years, so that the Jewel would rest in peace, not susceptible to being accidentally found. While Houston could not send the Jewel as far as Marcus Aurelius, he cast it out to an area that would remain sparsely settled and undeveloped for many years.

This was the most failsafe measure his mind could create, and with it set in motion, the great Sam Houston passed on.

20. Mary Benson

Aiden decided to take Sam Houston's offer to settle in Milam County. Not only had he been granted land, but the general left enough currency for him to start a new life. Nearing the age of 20, it was time for him to stake his own claim in the world. There was just one problem. He was of marrying age, women would be scarce where he was going.

There was only one woman he'd ever loved.

Her name was Mary, and he had not seen her since he was six or seven years old. The memories of his youth led him to believe she was the love of his life. From time to time, they would write one another, but he had not heard from her since before the Civil War. Her family fled their home during the fighting, and he believed her to now be in Tennessee. It was a risky proposition to travel halfway across the country, in search of someone he had not seen in over a decade. She might well be already wed, dead, or worse she might refuse his proposal of marriage.

In a way, going in search of Mary would be its own treasure hunt, and Aiden brimmed with confidence. At his age, he'd already survived the Civil War, met Sam Houston, and taken a leap of faith in pursuit of his destiny. With each success, his self-assurance bloomed. In his mind, stealing a woman's heart should be an easy chore.

Four months later, he had tracked her down to a dry goods store in Huntsville, Alabama. He observed from afar. She was an amazing sight; he was simply flabbergasted at the beautiful woman Mary had become. Even better, she was not yet married. She was, however, courted by a man whose father owned the cotton textile mill, an arranged sort of relationship between the two families.

Upon seeing this, Aiden set to eliminating his competition. Her beau was an imbecile born with a silver spoon. He was weak, and possibly a drunkard. He cared less for Mary than card games. He was a skinny chap, as was Aiden, yet the latter was unafraid to engage in a pugilistic affair. He was focused solely on the success of his mission to woo this lady. Truth be told, and she would later confirm, she would have joined him regardless as there was no love in her heart for her current man.

Nonetheless, Aiden waited one night outside a saloon where the man played cards. Near midnight, the man stumbled out of the saloon. Aiden challenged him to a fight. The coward refused and attempted to run. Astonished at such spinelessness, Aiden tackled the man, and swung his fist directly into the man's jaw. The beau immediately fell limp and rolled into a ball on the ground, begging to be left alone.

Aiden could no more beat on a weakling than he would cut his own skin. This man lacked any backbone whatsoever. Yet, Aiden had to be certain he would not return to Mary. So he held the man's head in a watering trough, and after a few seconds, let him up for air. He told the man to leave town, to forget about Mary, else he would be back to finish the beating. The grateful beau fled, even offering an apology as he left. He would hole up at his family plantation for three days, scared to venture back to town.

Aiden had to make his move. The next day, he surprised Mary with flowers as she left the store. Mary was yet unaware of Aiden's presence in town. She'd not recognized him about town as he slyly carried forth his plan.

He indeed made his move, and suffice to say; two months later they were married in a church in Huntsville. An able strategist in her own right, she made Aiden spend two weeks courting her, and nigh every dollar he'd brought on the trip to seal the deal.

He told her many a tall tale regarding his accomplishment; his unfinished moral compass at the time made him believe he had to lie to her to win her heart. The truth is, she cared not for money. She suffered the same sentimentality of youth as Aiden, particularly given the family hardships she'd endured since.

Mary and Aiden fell in love.

Of course, her family disapproved, at least on the outset. They thought any man who spent weeks traveling across the country in search of a woman was too lazy ever to be successful at anything. Even less, they doubted his ability to survive busting sod in the rugged frontier of Texas. Aiden didn't care, and neither did Mary. She wanted a man who'd risk his life for a better future, and a man who'd already demonstrated such tenacity surely had more to offer.

~~~

Mary was the niece of Admiral David Farragut. Her family had known the Bensons in the northern Alabama territory, near Tennessee, long before the Bensons left to charter a new life in East Texas. Her grandfather Jordi Farragut was born in Spain. He was a short, squatty, man, albeit equipped with a genius intellect and undeniably adventurous.

Jordi took to the sea at a young age. He soon found himself trading goods throughout the Caribbean at a time when piracy was rampant. As hostilities between the colonists and the British reached a boiling point, he was forced to choose sides. Near the outbreak of the American Revolution, he joined the Americans. With his littoral experience, he was commissioned a naval officer and in the process Anglicized his name to George in lieu of Jordi.

George was captured during the Siege of Charleston in 1780. After his release, he continued to fight for the embattled revolutionaries at Cowpens. The Battle of Cowpens was an epic fight. It has been compared to Hannibal's tactical genius at Cannae, as both battles led to a defining psychological turning point in their respective wars. At Cowpens, the founding generation of Americans pressed its mettle against British masters. Ultimately the American victory ignited a domino effect of defeats for
~~~

Cornwallis in the south, ushering in Washington's victory at Yorktown and the birth of America.

After the battles of the Revolution subsided, George Farragut was assigned by Thomas Jefferson to staff the port of New Orleans in 1805. He received this duty in part because he spoke fluent Spanish. This meant he was equipped to deal with the locals who distrusted English-speaking Americans.

This was during a time before the influx of colonists into Texas and a few years before the War of 1812. His posting at New Orleans was part of a larger strategy of expansion for the United States. It would ultimately result in the Louisiana Purchase; the largest acquisition of land in U.S. history. The young American state attained land from the French spanning from the Mississippi River to the Rockies, as it continued its march westward.

Manifest Destiny.

It would be a bittersweet assignment for George. Soon after assuming the post, his wife died of Yellow Fever. Dedicated to the job, George would remain at his post and send his children back to Tennessee. They were eventually placed in the care of a foster family, though most ended up returning to live with relatives. George stayed behind, spending his last days in Pascagoula, Mississippi, and living to the age of 53. He died in 1817.

As mentioned, one of George's children was David Farragut. He would become a famous sea Captain as well. Described as notoriously aggressive and difficult, he rose to the rank of admiral during the Civil War, fighting with the Union. Famous for the battle cry "Damn the torpedoes, full speed ahead" at the Battle of Mobile Bay, he was the real-world incarnation of Leeroy Jenkins. The admiral's zeal for adventure and heroism—a characteristic of his father—were traits that would later emerge in Aiden and Mary's lineage. The pedigree of their progeny would be abundantly fruitful with a proclivity for action.

Aiden and Mary both descended from a proud heritage which gave rise to the most prosperous nation in the history of the world. The nation would become a point of light and a beacon of inspiration built by such individuals as Benjamin Franklin, James Madison, George Washington; and the somewhat lesser known George Farragut. Sadly, the country was also built upon the backs of slaves. This tragic legacy would be remedied during the Civil War, as the country would tear itself apart to grant freedom to all.

21. Milam County, Texas

So I say to you, ask, and it will be given to you; seek, and you will find; knock, and it will be opened to you.

– Matthew 11:9

Aiden Benson would never have been mistaken for a ladies' man, so it is truly a miracle that he ended up married to the best of the lot. He was mostly aloof, a man given to thoughts of adventure rather than prurient interests. It would not dawn on him until near adulthood that he was even attracted to women. He was a truly innocent boy; that innocence only slightly tarnished when sent to fight a battle of not his choosing.

Even once he matured enough to entertain thoughts of the opposite sex, his sense of honor forbade him from such tacky pursuits. Such was a possibility in the 1800's, a time when Maslow's hierarchy still meant survival had to be certain before one could pursue pleasure. Had he been plucked from the era and transplanted to the modern day, he might have turned out much differently. Man wants for very little today, and every indulgence is available with the most minimal of effort.

During his imprisonment, it was only through keeping a journal that he deciphered his own inner being and resolved that should he ever escape with his dignity intact, he would accomplish two things: find the secret of Sam Houston, and marry the one woman he knew was intended for him. Yet, he knew not whether either of these even existed.

Something within told him he would find both waiting for him after the war.

Seek and you shall find.

~~~

Aiden and Mary's journey back to Texas was fraught with peril, though both were starry eyed and impervious to the hardships. She was not initially keen on moving to the edge of the Texas frontier where Indian raids were still a threat. She also knew should she turn down Aiden's proposal for marriage, he would go west regardless, and likely she would never see him again.

No longer were Indians and enemy soldiers the biggest fear in Texas, but rather the threat of crossing paths with outlaws in a region where law was in a fledgling state. Despite not being fully aware of what he sought, the mystery left him intrigued. He could not force away the selfish thought that maybe, this journey would leave him enriched. Such was not his primary objective, though human nature afforded him no reprieve from such self-centered assumptions.

His search for the treasure would slow from an intense hunt to a lifelong passion. What began for this young man as a youthful adventure of excitement and mystery, would
~~~

become much more difficult and evasive. Had he been gifted at that point with an ability to see the future, he might have turned his horse around and raced for the Louisiana border.

Mary's well-to-do family sent her along with a small dowry. One thing she learned quickly is that Aiden would seldom relent once he got an idea in his head. For whatever reason, he seemed fixed on settling the frontier in pursuit of his prosperity. In turn, he learned soon that she was not one to base her charter in life on others' ideas of what was proper; and she wasn't afraid to get her hands dirty.

Once they arrived back in Milam County, Aiden's first stop was the county seat of Cameron. He there formally registered his title deed with the courthouse. Milam County was no longer the rugged frontier of a quarter century before. By the time of the Civil War, Milam had more than 3,600 residents. Between 1850 and 1860, the amount of settled or improved land increased six-fold, yet still represented less than three percent of the total area.

Aiden scouted his new homestead for three days before he decided where to build a new house. He planted the foundation for his structure on a small hill raised against the river's flood plain, but nested only 50 feet from the water's edge. In times of high water, the ripples of the Gabriel's flow might nip the edge of the house, but its rise would be halted by drain-off in numerous gullies.

He was no geologist; he put faith in his own discretion and a little nod from the gods. As luck would have it, that same house would stand for almost 100 years. Its base was overcome with water only once, and its demise came not at the hands of the mighty Gabriel, but the crushing blow of the pecan he'd planted that same year. In that respect, one might argue the Gabriel indeed crushed the home. The tree's root tapped the supple water of the river and caused the tree to grow to a stellar height. Correspondingly, the drought of the 1950's shrank the Gabriel, and in turn caused the mighty tree to topple as its root system dried up.

Mixed in with the predominant pecan trees were mighty oaks, which would be cut, hewn and mauled into the structure for his future family. The Benson farm was supplied with water by the spring-fed Gabriel. The land would soon bring forth a bounty of crops from its fruitful soil, washed over with sediment from ages of flooding in the Gabriel bottom. Over the years, Aiden would fell many a tree as he cleared the land to plant crops. Mary took to the new life undeterred by the difficult road ahead.

Aiden likely would never admit his wife brought more accomplished military experience and history to the family. He viewed her in a much more passive style, and was drawn to her elegance and beauty. A nobler lady he could not imagine, though in her blood ran the genetic line of kings and generals. Their offspring would boast vestiges of these traits, leading to moments of excitability and recklessness.

On that topic, when you have as many years under your belt as me, you learn the apple doesn't fall far from the tree. I must confess to you that the ancestry of Mrs. Mary Benson is downright fascinating. Some of these thoughts are speculative intrigue, based more on a sophisticated hunch than direct records. Precise lineage is specious in the early 1800's, but there is one interesting thing which jumps out at me, and I must tell you because it seems too perfect not to be true.

While her grandparents are known, not much is known of Mary Benson's parents. Her mother would have been a sister to Admiral David Farragut, a child likely missing from the record books during the tumultuous years of the Revolution and Jordi's station in New Orleans. She would have been born sometime in the early 1800's, and likely died a decade or so before the Civil War.

It is my belief that Mary's father was of the Grissim clan from Kentucky, and died fighting in the Civil War. The Grissim family is much storied. Descended from line of Owen Tudor in the 1600's, it makes the children of Mary Benson a line of English royalty. The same line would also spawn Jeannette de Lafayette Grissim, whose daughter would be the mother of one Howard Robard Hughes.

Part of this speculation lies in the overwhelming similarities between Howard Hughes, and Aiden Benson's great-grandson, Troy. Since I've had the pleasure to meet both of these men, it's about all the proof needed for me. Now, you don't know much about Aiden's great-grandson just yet, but we'll discuss him later in the story. His adventures with Crash Carter are soon to be legend. You can decide for yourself.

Both of these men were geniuses, obsessive-compulsive by nature, with an almost unhealthy fascination with airplanes. They were stubborn to a fault, failing to give up even after numerous crashes and other setbacks. At heart, two headstrong and determined individuals who lost their parents at a young age; who developed a sense of direction of their own accord.

Howard Hughes captured the imagination of generations over the span of decades. It is my guess that in a completely different way, Troy Benson and Crash Carter are about to do the same. The difference is the latter duo will do so in the twinkling of an eye. Such is fitting for a society that moves both upon the back of, and at the speed of, an escaped electron.

The speed of light.

22. HOME ON THE RANGE

Many years passed as Aiden and Mary proudly built their homestead. The honeymoon period had long since vanished, and frontier life's hardships made them realists. Nonetheless, the love that took hold was true, and they pressed on despite numerous setbacks – droughts, floods, and lack of civil society and neighbors. He knew how to cheer her up, and in those days, new clothes were a rarity. He returned home from town one day, and retrieved a new dress from his saddlebag.

A baby in her arms, Mary let slip a smile as he walked to the door.

They were now the parents of two small children, with another on the way. Eventually they would have three more. Mary loved children, and not just her own. She had already become a schoolteacher. First to teach her own children, but as other families settled in the area, Aiden built a schoolhouse on the property and Mary started taking in any child she could.

The railroads came in the 1870's, and Milam continued to grow. Many of the settlers were uneducated folks, and Mary's instruction made the Benson family grow in stature quickly in the remote territory. Outside of raising her own family, teaching would become her lot in life. Her passion became education, to instruct the young children through basic reading and writing, and even a bit of math, all skills which were rare in this part of the world.

While she lacked her husband's mechanical genius, he lacked her patience, empathy, and ability to communicate effectively. He also had a difficult time focusing on any one discipline, nor on the fundamentals. While his thoughts and theories might have been genius, his writing ability was still at an elementary level. Over time, she would not only help him perfect his writing, but he'd learn Spanish and Latin as well.

Milam County developed an above average public school system, and this was in no small part due to Mrs. Benson's determination. Nearly every Milam County settlement boasted a school by the end of the 1870's. Mrs. Benson traveled from town to town throughout the year to help establish curriculum.

Aiden was an entrepreneurial man. He parlayed his endowment from Sam Houston into numerous successful and profitable ventures. He dabbled in farming and, eventually, in livestock. He built the first cotton gin in the settled area which was used for over 60 years. Aiden would use his wealth to buy up land, and gambled some of his profits trying out new and cutting edge technologies of the era.

Farming was his first love, and it was by chance that he expanded into cattle ranching operations in 1876. He was in Austin handling land deeds, when he made a too-good-to-be-true deal while drinking whiskey with some cattlemen. He had a few dozen head of cattle back at the ranch, primarily for his own family's milk and beef supplies. He now found himself buying another hundred head from a herd that was passing through the area en route to Montana. They were planning to establish a ranch in that *cattleman's paradise* as they called it.

He spent the evening chatting with one of the captains. It was a sign posted to the outfit's wagon which sparked the initial conversation. Not only did it have a humorous vignette which mentioned something about renting pigs, but also had a Latin phrase; *uva uvam vivendo varia fit*. As this garbled corruption made no sense, and Aiden now understood Latin, he made quick friends with the Captain.

Aiden always appreciated a man who didn't take life too seriously. The outfit started the drive with 2,600 head of stolen Mexican cattle and needed to sell a few to finance the upcoming trip. He made a deal with the Captain for the hundred head and had their cowboys peel them off to drive over to Milam County. Two years later, he heard the men had successfully established their ranch in Montana, although one of the captains died after crossing paths with a band of Indians while scouting the territory ahead of the herd.

Aiden and Mary would meet their first tragedy in 1884. Their eldest son, Miller, ran away and joined a trail drive passing through Austin on the Chisholm Trail en route to Kansas. Miller was already on the verge of being disowned by his father, having been reported stealing whiskey from a gin palace in Rockdale. It was the last in a long line of infractions committed by the renegade and directionless child, starting with a propensity for dishonesty from the time he could speak.

Regardless of how Aiden and Mary reared him, Miller Benson was a derelict from the day he was born. He inherited bad genes from Mrs. Benson's side of the family, according to Aiden. While he admired his wife for her redeeming qualities, both intellectual and physical, he knew that several of her kinfolks were prone to being idiots. This attribute of his wife he was willing to overlook, or perhaps, he didn't have much choice at this point.

Even the best of farmers sow a bad crop every now and then.

Aiden loved genetics. From a young age he had noticed traits passed on through animals the family had raised as livestock, or even the wild animals which he tried to domesticate. He often opined about what he saw, and kept records in his own journals. He'd observe the behavior of everything from feral cats, to owls, to squirrels. In each, he found a certain subset brave enough to interact with humans, and he would gain their confidence by leaving food. Eventually these animals would spawn, and through successive generations, he found himself surrounded by more and more animals that flocked to him like Noah.

The same idea worked with cattle. Over the years, he could literally feed his herd from the palm of his hand. Cattle are smarter than people think, and they would only eat from Aiden's hand, which irritated the heck out of Mary. They simply did not recognize her as their master.

Those tricks never worked with his eldest son. When Miller ran away, he took up with a cattle drive leaving out of Austin. He made it as far as the Red River, before he was run out of the outfit by the captains for stealing another man's wallet. He was on the verge of being hanged, when the Captain realized Miller was Aiden Benson's son. Aiden was now a well-respected name in the cattle business, and was trading with the famous Charles Goodnight.

This knowledge bought Miller a reprieve from the noose, because the captain would not administer frontier punishment without Aiden's blessing, lest he have hell to pay at the hands of Mr. Goodnight. Instead, the captain sent the derelict on his way, knowing that in these parts, his fate would follow close behind. Miller headed north to Indian Territory, a land as lawless as his own ambitions, in search of his destiny. Aiden's reputation was now out of his reach.

Back in Milam County, the same realization dawned on Aiden. A directionless boy such as Miller would soon become an outlaw, and his time would be limited. He still wished the best for his eldest son. He prayed he would change and become a good man. Yet, he had serious doubts given his observations of the kid since he was a child that he would get, or much less deserved, any further leniency. His pattern of pernicious thoughts and actions were bound to fetch a reckoning.

Miller was the product of the worst elements in the genetic line – stupidity, and malice. Aiden had six other children to look after by now. He'd given Miller everything he could. Miller had many chances to reform, and he never took them. He was simply incorrigible, and unable to adapt to a more civil society.

Unfortunately for the Benson family, and as predicted by Aiden, Miller met that fate at the end of a rope in 1886. Arrested by a U.S. marshal for murder, cattle rustling and other serious crimes, Miller was sentenced to be executed by Judge Isaac C. Parker, the famed "hanging judge" who presided over the U.S. District Court of the Western District in Fort Smith.

~~~

While Aiden might have quietly blamed his wife's lineage for Miller, Mrs. Benson wasn't the only side of the family with genetic imperfections. They were the only side thus far exposed. Aiden's side of the family also had a few itinerant genes that predicated mental ailment, though they would not become visible until a few generations later.

One example was a distant nephew born in the early 20th Century named Forrest Benson, who went on to write popular novels, and even became a candidate for Alabama governor in 1970. However, the fool ran for governor as a white supremacist and had a long history of sometimes violent association with the Ku Klux Klan. He was soundly defeated and lampooned in the media for his madness.

Aiden himself would have never supported such association. Even during the events leading up to the Civil
~~~

War, he agreed with Sam Houston in that Texas should not join the secession efforts, and not just because it was madness to fight the Union, but because it was morally wrong to endorse slavery. To hold such useless beliefs some hundred years later, as did his great nephew, well that was just lunacy.

Aiden's mental faculties would be tested over the years. He found himself in a constant state of flux; torn amongst the growing responsibilities of a large family, his expanding stature within the territory, and his innate desire for adventure. His duty to family and community caused him to neglect his adventurous side, but the Jewel of Hiram continued to pull at his curiosity. It lie buried within the ground upon which sprouted the fruits of his labor. It kept in on a righteous and prosperous path.

In the daily grind of raising a family and expanding his land and holdings, Aiden would lose sight of that key ingredient to his success. He had dutifully followed Sam Houston's wishes, taken charge of the designated land, and now almost forgotten why he came here in the first place. Thus, the genius in the General's final masterpiece explained.

Aiden Benson would never find the Jewel.

Found or not, the sacred ground provided his family a blanket of protection and a great fortune. In his earlier days, he charted numerous possible locations. Over time he lost his bearing as he began to clear large swaths of pecan trees in order to create more farm and ranchland. He would forget about the Jewel completely until later in his life, but it was there, nonetheless, hidden safely away from view. The Jewel would only reveal itself at the time of its choosing.

At the turn of the century, Aiden Benson had expanded his land to include more than 1,500 acres. The 2nd tragedy of his life occurred in 1915, when Mary died of cancer. She did not die suddenly, and the ever-deepening state of her frail body exacted a mighty toll on his conscience. He was heartbroken. His true love was gone; the woman he'd traveled halfway across the country to find had left him alone.

They had lived a long life together, yet he would have many years remaining. He didn't want to go on without her, but he had no choice. He almost wished he had never taken that trip back to find her, so he could forego the pain he felt today. Such thoughts he pushed aside as nonsense.

Two more of his children would die before they reached the age of 40. None of them turned out as well as expected, having been born into the trappings of a decent life. His dedication to family began to wane. His subconscious compensated by devoting thoughts to the Jewel. As he aged, with his legacy firmly in place, his attention focused clearly on finding the Jewel. He became obsessed with it; for what reason, he couldn't say.

His longing for the Jewel caused him to lapse into fits of mania. He regaled those near him with great visions of wealth buried beneath the ground on which they stood. With Mary gone, he longed for another of his first loves; a long lost childhood memory. He wished to find it despite neglecting it for nearly a lifetime. He was overcome with a deep-seeded desire, just as he had when he first courted Mary. It was though the Jewel was within his grasp, but evaded him, and he would have to move Heaven and Earth to find it.

As he passed the age of 80, his search was still fruitless.

Discovery of oil and lignite in Milam County in the early 1900's gave Aiden a glimpse of heavy equipment which could pry deep into the Earth. There was only one way for Aiden to find the Jewel, and that was to simply dig for it, far and wide. In the 1930's he sought to do just that. As his years on Earth were dwindling to a close, he invested a substantial fortune in equipment that allowed him to dig deeper, and deeper, tilling up the blackland soil, and overturning land that had never been disturbed by mankind.

He unearthed many things; lignite coal and entire skeletons of mastodons. Lignite would eventually make his grandson, Hank, a wealthy man and dinosaur fossils would have been of great interest to modern day archaeologists. Yet he found no Jewel. These items were cast aside as mere inconveniences to him as he searched for something of much greater value.

Alas, the treasure he found was not the treasure he sought.

He was dismissed as a crazy old man by his children, who nevertheless continued to live off of his generosity. They turned their back on him public, and waited for him to die. Most had long since moved away. Rather than take his side, they sought to distance themselves from the Benson name, lest they be ridiculed for their relationship to an estranged old coot that lived out in the country.

As he sat alone in his quiet hours, rejected and abandoned by his own family, he poured through the brittle parchment left him by Sam Houston; falling prey to the General's last feint. His wife had remained by his side for 50 years, and before she left the world, interpreted the Spanish in which most of it was written. In his last days, he re-wrote as much as he could, detailing the history and chronology, hoping that a clue would present itself to the location of the Jewel.

But it would be for naught.

Approaching 98 years old, he saw the light. He was finally blessed with a clear vision. He was now ready to die with the only respect that matters. *Respect of self.* He wasn't crazy. He was merely a foot soldier in a game played by powers far greater than mere mortals.

The vision showed him that he would never find the Jewel, *but his grandson would.*

His grandson was the only heir who could carry the charge where Aiden left off; a man who was aptly named for the Jewel he sought. At the time, he was but a child, an orphan left behind in Aiden's care. He would now be granted the same burden which Aiden had been handed at the same age. The boy was one Hiram King Benson.

But his friends called him Hank.

In Aiden Benson's last days, he made it so. The burden passed to him eight decades earlier was lifted from his shoulders. He died with the knowledge he had fulfilled his duty, and left secured the Jewel beneath the ground, keeping it safe from even himself.

Despite his years, he would not die of old age.

PART 3

23. Boots on

And if anyone takes away from the words of the book of this prophecy, God will take away his part from the tree of life and from the holy city, which are written in this book.

– Revelation 22:19

Aiden Benson went out with his boots on. He died in September, 1944. He was found slumped over the steering wheel of a wrecked 1939 Ford pickup. It crashed into a tree on his property, which grew at the base of a slowly tapering hill. While the cause of death for a 98-year-old man should not be difficult to ascertain, the local magistrate scratched his head over this one.

Aiden had blunt force trauma to his torso, as well as cuts across his forehead. The truck was badly damaged; the entire front end smashed into the front wheel wells. An initial ruling stated he suffered a heart attack while driving and crashed into the tree.

In a twist, the coroner overruled the justice of the peace. He could find no evidence of a heart attack. He pointed to numerous things, such as scuff marks on Aiden's boots, indicating his foot had been on the gas pedal, and the truck remained in third gear at the time of the crash. If the driver had a heart attack, it is unlikely a vehicle with manual transmission would continue moving forward. He noted that both hands were still on the steering wheel. By these indications, Aiden was still conscious and alert when the crash occurred. The vehicle was traveling at 40 miles-per-hour upon impact.

As such, the coroner ruled this death a suicide.

Now, it might have been left at that, except for an odd sequence of events that followed. Just as dogs awaiting scraps from the dinner table, Hank's children salivated at thoughts of their upcoming payday. He'd barely entered *rigor mortis* yet they'd already planned on which assets to sell first. They didn't have the work ethic to keep a ranch in business. For them, Aiden's death was great news.

They were truly mortified to learn that Aiden bequeathed the lion's share of his wealth to Hank; their nephew and Aiden's 17-year-old orphan grandson. In Aiden's will, he stipulated very specifically who got what, and only Hank would retain the original San Gabriel River property granted him by Sam Houston. He rightly should have given his entire estate to Hank, but Aiden fell prey to the same empathies as many parents. He gave the others an equitable share of the surrounding property; primarily out of pity.

For his generosity, he would be despised by those children after his death for the unforgivable crime of not giving them more. When you feed a stray dog, it keeps coming back. Teach a man to fish, and so forth. The fools could never grasp the value of this land lie not in dollars, but in a mystery from the ancients that they could never fathom.

That mystery was not listed in the will; it is impossible to bestow such a thing. However, hidden among paperwork attesting to his material possessions of land, money, and artifacts was Aiden's journal. It was from this journal Hank now relayed to me his intriguing story, and which held the secret; it provided a bridge to the Jewel from Aiden to Hank.

Old, brittle parchment by this time, the journal was the real treasure of Aiden's lot, and the only thing he cherished at the time of his death. The journal would yield not only a marvelous tale, but provided a moral guidebook for Hank's life. In principle, at least, he followed it more closely than some righteous men might follow the Bible. Every word of the hallowed manual became sacrosanct to Hank.

When Aiden died, he was alone in the world. While Hank and Aiden would scarcely speak to each other in life, the words of Aiden came alive beyond the grave to escort Hank through his coming tribulation. Tragedies which beset the young Hank at an early age would soon be vanquished, but not before they reached a crescendo which would galvanize his morality in stone at the tender age of 17.

Barely old enough to walk, Hank had witnessed the burial of his mother beneath an old oak tree on Alligator Creek. A few years later his father would be buried at the Masonic cemetery near Little River at Port Sullivan.

Finally, his sole progenitor and only father figure, Aiden, would leave him. He would turn to this journal as the only source of paternal guidance remaining.

And now, the final tragic turn would round the corner as the aunts and uncles hired lawyers to challenge Aiden's will. Once the period of mourning was over, perhaps even sooner, they filed lawsuits and enacted vengeful attacks against Hank. They even spread spiteful rumors that Hank was responsible for Aiden's strange demise. As a result, a full inquiry into cause of death was undertaken.

The result of the new forensic analysis would be more thorough, and overruled both the findings of suicide, and the heart attack. Experts demonstrated that Aiden was merely feeding cattle when his truck became stuck in a patch of mud. Even two months later, the ruts were clearly visible in photos taken by investigators; dried into the blackland soil they were as good as a fossil record. As Aiden felt the truck tires lose their grip, he "gunned" the engine to get enough traction to clear the sludge, spinning the tires ever more quickly. It was at this point that the gas pedal of his truck became stuck.

The truck eventually broke free from the slippery muck, and found ample sod in the rolling bluestem prairie grass. It quickly gathered steam going downhill. With the engine revved, Aiden could not shift out of gear. He tried in vain to free the pedal with his feet, his other now on the brake pedal. The ride was too bumpy for him to reach down with his hands. The brakes of the truck, which harnessed only the rear wheels, were heavily eroded after this quarter mile run. The right drum completely failed, being no match for a revved V-8 engine. The truck entered a slowly arcing turn to the left as it continued to gain speed.

The truck decelerated from 40 to zero instantaneously upon encountering the massive tree. Without a seatbelt, Aiden Isaac Benson, age 98, died instantly.

He had both hands on the wheel, and rode it right up to the end.

~~~

Hank had been talking for nearly two hours and it was almost sunup.

The mesquite wood crackled, sending a shower of sparks from the belly of the old wood stove. Hank grabbed the tea kettle and poured another cup. It wasn't normally his style to burn mesquite, as he preferred his beloved pecan.

Regardless, every year he stacked cord after cord of either. Having cut his own pecan wood, he received the mesquite from Mexican Joe. Mexican Joe was a neighbor who always owed money and was far more likely to pay in goods and services than cash. He was a hard worker. Hank was always willing to entertain a trade, particularly as splitting wood was difficult work.

Hank believed pecan wood burned just as hot as mesquite, which is actually true. Common thought has prevailed that mesquite is the hottest burning of all wood types. To argue this would never yield an accord, just as arguing which genus of pepper will set a man's tongue ablaze more
~~~

adeptly. Whether one imbibes a habanero or cayenne, many circumstances dictate the level of heat an individual experiences. Only fools argue such things.

To its distinct advantage, pecan is not given to shooting out embers that would cross the room and singe arm hairs. This much is rather easy to observe, even for a fool. To its disadvantage, pecan wood is nigh as durable as mesquite, as cut pecan soon deteriorates to brittleness. Within three years of being felled, it is little more than dried honeycomb.

Mesquite, on the other hand, only gets harder as time marches on. It is an undeserved encore for the mesquite tree, which lives its entire life as a nuisance to the land. It only finds a suitable use in death. Conversely, pecan trees are universally beloved for the nourishing fruits they provide over hundreds of years of life.

Little things such as these were the lens through which Hank Benson looked at life.

He offered me a cup of the black stuff. I obliged. It was strong, with a smoke-tinged aroma that caused my eyes to open wide. It held far more caffeine than I was accustomed, which was now a necessary ingredient to my given state.

Day was about to break. The owls now hooted a fevered pitch, eager to catch one final meal as they prepared to slumber. They investigated the two coffee-drinking interlopers in their midst. As the first rays of the sun signaled its grand appearance, they perched near us, knowing their nocturnal duties would soon be at an end.

Sunrise in the country was always an awesome sight to behold. Today would begin cloudless. Through a section of the horizon, not a tree dotted the vista between us and the rising sun. Our eyes fixed upon the coming moment. The extra-terrestrial sphere bolted through the horizon, showering us with a luminance straight from Heaven.

We could see for many a mile, across the rolling hills of Milam County. We were at the crossroads where blackland made bedfellows with the Post Oak Savannah's sandy loam prairie. It marked a stunning end to night; just as the coming end to Hank's story, he'd saved the best for last.

While waiting for the inevitable sun, I felt certain Hank would soon reveal something incredible. Pieces of this puzzle had worked their way into position, though several key pieces were still held in Hank's mind only. If I were a betting man, I'd wager that Hank held pocket Aces and was trying to represent he only had a low pair. I saw through this, because he was never good at bluffing.

The picture was thus not yet clear to me; and for good reason. Unlike a hand of poker, Hank kept his past close to his heart. He took every measure to ensure that only a trusted friend would learn these things. This trust was granted to me long ago, and I now suspected it was because he knew the truth of my existence.

A quiet eeriness dawned.

Indeed, I had a secret just as he. You all know this full well; though at this moment Hank was unaware of just how much I knew of the Jewel of Hiram. I now reckon he knew more than I suspected. What confounded me is at which point he had figured me out. I've always prided myself to being a bit smarter than the average man.

The Lord puts people on this Earth to fulfill His own ends. Mankind is quite capable of cunning from time to time, and Hank could be a gifted tactician in many respects. In his long-winded reflection, he had turned the tables. I mistakenly let my guard down, and my mission was now in jeopardy. Hank did not let his guard down. One should take caution to doubt the abilities of anyone put here by the Supreme Architect, as was Hank. Such responsibility takes an uncommon level of discipline and levity.

I'd come to learn later many of Hank's foibles were simply well-crafted disguises.

It was my sole purpose in this life to reconstitute the Jewel of Hiram, and I'd at one time suspected it was Hank's as well; but it was not. My mission was to commandeer the Jewel and his was to keep it hidden. I now must confront the fact despite my God-given gifts, Hank had the upper hand. He was playing from the defensive, and I was on offense. He was a protector, and I the pursuer. All he had to do is keep the Jewel far out of reach.

He had the patience his grandfather did not possess. There were no riddles for Hank to decipher. His test was one of true faith, and temptation. Tragedies from an early age solidified that faith and held off the temptation of the

Jewel. When visions from the Divine now told him something, Hank *believed*. He believed that in due time the complete Jewel would be made whole; but not in his lifetime. The Master of the House would bring to fruition the unveiling of the grand artifact on His own terms and at the time of His choosing. Hank might not be a man of God, but was wholeheartedly a man who furthered God's end.

As this came into focus, I realized he would never turn its whereabouts over to me. The reason suddenly became clear, and my misunderstanding was merely a matter of perspective. Hank would soon depart this Earth, yet I would remain far longer. Hank intended to take to the grave his secret, a charge he would not let down. The marathon came to an end, and he hit me with the news I already knew. I wanted more, but he would not give it. He would not proceed.

Hank delivered the rest of the story, as Paul Harvey would say.

"I will never tell you where it lies."

"The Jewel?" I replied.

"The Jewel, Mac. You know damn well what."

He took a sip of coffee, and peered at me.

"Okay."

"Good. You understand then. It's nothing personal."

"No. It's not."

"So where do we go from here?"

"Well, then. I'm not going to show you mine, either. "

"That's a fact."

"Hank. We're on the same side here. You know this."

"That well might be. But the road to hell is, well, you've done road construction. You know as well as I do what it's paved with."

"I'm used to disappointment. Somehow I figured this would turn out differently."

"I know. Brother *Ralph*, I know. This is difficult, but we can't..."

Hank paused, uncomfortably. Then he continued.

"I think it's time we go our separate ways. The temptation of this thing, it's sometimes unbearable."

"I understand."

I nodded slightly, in agreement. I don't cry, but this was of those rare times where I felt that type of emotion. I reached for his hand. We shook hands, but there was no goodbye. He turned and walked back into the cabin. I got in my truck, and drove down the road. I departed the farm, and kept on driving. I would not return.

Just like that, it was over.

It was the last time I'd ever see the man.

I would not return until his death, many years later.

24. PENANCE

Be afraid, for he does not bear the sword in vain. For he is the servant of God, an avenger who carries out God's wrath on the wrongdoer.

-Romans 13:4

He called me by my real name, *Ralph.*

How he figured that one out is beyond me. It was a secret I'd kept from the world and he might be the only other man alive who knew. He was right about something else. That is, we were the two of us, better left apart. It was time for me to leave.

The Jewel was bigger than Hank or I. By our meeting in this lifetime, the two pieces of the Jewel of Hiram were perilously close to being reunited. Such power, in a vessel capable of being wielded by man, had not existed on the planet since the time of Marcus Aurelius and the Roman Empire. It would be certain to attract trouble. Not only the always-present temptation which lurks within the soul, but the certainty that true evil would be made known of a reconstituted Jewel.

It would send shockwaves across the universe to those with the power to perceive such things.

I had overlooked this facet in my zeal. It had, after all, been a long journey for me to this point. We were not treasure hunters, after all. It was time for me to refocus my efforts to that end. His piece was hidden away safely, as was mine; our secrets protected from even their protectors. Even as friends, there was still great risk should our secrets be let free. Hank was wise, for a man, and never trusted anyone; even me. That was an endearing lesson I learned from him.

I departed the farm with a heavy heart. He was the first person I'd ever truly enjoyed being around and it was a bitter moment to leave my friend. I turned my truck onto Farm Road 908 and headed back to west Texas.

~~~

Hank sold his interest in his construction company to the Guthries in 1960. He married, and had several kids. Throughout, he continued to buy land with his money. Over time, Hank acquired thousands of acres across Milam County and eventually bought back most of Aiden's land the thankless aunts and uncles sold off. He lost a small fortune in his ensuing divorce.

He became at times alcoholic and anti-social, a fact that no doubt helped end his marriage. He drowned his sorrow in the skies, buying several airplanes. He pursued ever more dangerous stunts, unsure if it was the adventure he sought, an escape from the real world, or both. All the while he never ventured too far from the little cabin where he toiled away as a youngster, and where he and I would fish and drink beer and whiskey.
~~~

After years in the construction business, he became a cattleman and dabbled in farming. He never needed the money but everything he touched turned to gold. He couldn't lose, and that confused him more than anything. It worried him because it was further proof God existed, and that though he be a sinner, a layer of Divine protection entombed him. He would spend his time alone out on the land. He thought deeply. He wrote.

One of Hank's true difficulties in life; he was among the few men in history to know, to have seen proof, of God's existence. No longer did he need faith, nor hope. The spiritual man and atheist alike can argue about who is right and who is wrong, but neither side can prove their case with any fact. That is the essence of faith and the beauty of it. Hank knew without question the power of the Divine exists.

In many ways, this was more difficult than not knowing. Even Satan knows God exists, but he sure as hell isn't going to Heaven. A man who thinks deeply enough must answer two questions at some point – is there a Heaven, and am I going there? It was the latter which kept Hank up nights. Afflicted by the curse of human reason, he knew he would be judged one day as surely as the devil.

Figuring this out early in life, he at times wondered what else he had to live for. The only question remaining would not be made known to him until the Master of the House appeared. Over time his understanding would evolve and he would find something to live for: first a business, and then a family.

He would sell the business, and soon find himself estranged from this family. Still, he was able to vicariously enjoy the small things, like clipping newspaper articles of their accomplishments. His only son would die tragically at an early age, but not before leaving behind two grandchildren. Hank would again find something to live for as he became a guardian. Hank had been the vessel for Aiden and he now had his own bridge to continue the mission of the Jewel; a reason to live.

No matter how much he wished to give up the ghost, the Lord always pressed Hank to keep going.

~~~

Earlier I mentioned when we first met, Hank had told me of doing things he had to do. He never spoke of those things to me. He wrote me a letter near the end of his life. He now wanted to clear his conscience and did not want to meet his Maker with this stain. To him, confession to me was as close as he'd ever get to God himself. It was classic Hank – hedging his bets.

His confession was simple; he had used the Jewel for an evil purpose. I'd come to expect as much. He began his letter with the following verse:

But when the righteous turneth away from his righteousness, and committeth iniquity, and doeth according to all the abominations that the wicked man doeth, shall he live? All his righteousness that he hath done shall not be mentioned: in his trespass that he hath
~~~

trespassed, and in his sin that he hath sinned, in them shall he die. - ***Ezekiel 18:24***

When he first learned of the Jewel's power, he was consumed by anger. He also was overcome with a feeling of omnipotence. Uncertain of the powers, he proceeded to test their limits. As he would find, they were nigh unlimited – for good, or for evil. Just as man has free will and discretion in his life, the Jewel could only magnify a man's ability to pursue his ends. There was no governance of this fact except that which already existed in a man's heart. His anger was his own, and not the Jewel's.

This was soon after the death of Aiden. It was during the legal fight with his own kinfolks soon after Aiden left him the majority of the inheritance. He told me he won the day because he learned the legal system. That was far from true. In a moment of weakness, he summoned the power of the Jewel to exact revenge.

An attorney representing his aunts and uncles paid Hank a visit. The egotistical lawyer vowed to destroy him, seize his land, and assured Hank he would never take possession of his legacy. If there is one thing Hank disliked more than being threatened, it was wanton arrogance.

As I stated earlier, when he inherited the land, Hank was only a 17-year-old kid. He was now the target of angst among aunts and uncles, who had all been angling for rights to the property. They were prepared to stab each other in the back over it, but didn't expect a climb over their nephew first.

Such malfeasance is as old as the Jewel itself. Adonijah, the elder son of King David, conspired to steal the throne from his younger brother Solomon. In the same manner, the aunts and uncles tried to use legal tactics to undermine their father's last testament. Even an ironclad will didn't stop them from trying to usurp his intentions.

The attorney made his play. He was soon dead. Hank did not disclose how. The body was never discovered. It did not end there. Drunken with power, he next used the power to go after the relatives who had caused the problems in the first place. Two of his relatives' houses, at the same time, were consumed with fire.

He watched from afar, the reflection of flames dancing in his eyes as he felt the pull of wickedness. He appeared at the doorstep of a third, the one who stirred up the conflict, and issued a dire warning: "Leave this place, and never return. Or you will die." The fear delivered by Hank is the reason those relatives left the area. They dropped their suit against him. He took possession of his legacy and charted his own course. He never spoke to the rest of the family again.

He was then consumed by an overwhelming guilt.

There is a fine line between taking life as a righteous warrior to vanquish an enemy of the Lord, and murder. The latter is a sin. When his rage subsided, Hank realized this. He would come into contact with the ancient writings passed from Aiden and would learn the truth; his actions were unnecessary. He had sinned in a most unrighteous manner.

After I strayed, I repented; after I came to understand, I beat my breast. I was ashamed and humiliated because I bore the disgrace of my youth. ***– Jeremiah 31:19***

His reliance on the Jewel would come to a halt. He came to realize that the temptation was far too dangerous; so he buried it in the ground. He began a slow conversion from anger to virtue, buoyed by the power beneath his feet. It was during this steady transformation I first met Hank, still foul mouthed and hot-headed, but progressively finding his way.

In the philosophy of Stoicism, there exists a universal structure which orders all things. Righteousness can be achieved solely through virtue, by fortifying character and attaining a deep wisdom. What matters most is the virtuousness of the soul, not the material possessions one might accrue. A sage has reached the height of this virtue, and lived life indifferent to the events in the world around him. He lives a life free from his own passions.

Hank Benson became a sage; an existence that is by no means glamorous.

Righteousness for a man of God follows closely with that of the Stoic, with one key difference. In addition to a life of virtue, outward fulfillment for the man of God must be met with certain needs, such as love. It is perhaps why Hank struggled to become a man of God. He never felt loved.

He lost his parents, his family attacked him, his marriage failed, and most of his children rejected him. The love of God, while ever present, was nigh impossible for Hank to see given the monumental burden placed upon him. I guess I was the only one whom he truly trusted, and loved, though he'd likely never admit it. It's why he chose to write me this letter.

Yet the pursuit of righteousness is far different from salvation. This would become another sticking point with which Hank wrestled. The Lord makes it simple, repent and believe, but until one gives up the struggle to go it alone, they are lost.

Not by works of righteousness which we have done, but according to his mercy he saved us, by the washing of regeneration, and renewing of the Holy Ghost. – ***Titus 3:5***

He didn't regret the end result of his life. What he regretted; he had used the power of the Jewel as a shortcut, failing to have faith that God alone would deliver his vengeance upon the wicked. It is difficult for a man who'd developed this stoic calm to admit. In the true sense of his philosophy, he realizes that even a sage is not immune.

It is no coincidence this doctrine was subscribed by Marcus Aurelius, perhaps as a result of the same emotions and desires now found in Hank. The two men held the Jewel nearly 2,000 years apart. Both were deeply affected by it. This Stoic school of thought flourished in the Roman Empire about the same time the Jewel made its way to the peninsula.

The letter closed with this:

If we confess our sins, he is faithful and just and will forgive us our sins and purify us from all unrighteousness.

– 1 John 1:9

This letter now verified to me that near the end, Hank found redemption. What haunted him most of his life he was able to make amends in the simplest of ways. Free of a burgeoned conscience, he was clear to depart in peace. This was the last time I ever heard from him. He died three days after I read this letter.

I only found out about his death because it was all over the news.

~~~

Old Hank must have written his own obituary before he died. I got a laugh out of it. Short and sweet, with the same dry humor he always had:

Hiram King "Hank" Benson hit the ground near San Gabriel, Texas, in 1927, without a dollar to his name. He is the grandson of Aiden and Mary Benson, early settlers in Milam County following Aiden's service in the Civil War. He is survived by his grandchildren, Lieutenant Troy Benson, US Air Force, and Doris Sanderson and her husband of Wyoming.

He owned and operated Benson Construction Company from 1945 until 1960, helping build the ALCOA plant in
~~~

Rockdale in 1950. He is a past Master of the local Lodge #978.

Hank was an avid pilot and fisherman. He farmed and ranched many acres along the San Gabriel River bottom. For many years he claimed to have caught the biggest fish ever on the San Gabriel River, but now confesses that it was actually his good friend, R. Cyrus McCormack, who actually caught it.

His last wish is to have his ashes scattered on the land he loved. The funeral is soon, and I will be in attendance. I've been asked to be an honorary pallbearer, an easy task seeing as there will be no casket. I can't help but think this is an inside joke, as Hank would relish the thought that we were all letting him down one last time.

~~~

When Jesus saw the crowd around him, he gave orders to cross to the other side of the lake. Then a teacher of the law came to him and said, "Teacher, I will follow you wherever you go." Jesus replied, "Foxes have holes and birds of the air have nests, but the Son of Man has no place to lay his head." Another disciple said to him, "Lord, first let me go and bury my father." But Jesus told him, "Follow me, and let the dead bury their own dead."

– Matthew 8:18-22

Hank died much the same way as he lived most of his life – on a piece of machinery. In this case, it was a tractor, and about half a 12-pack into plowing one of his beloved Milo
~~~

fields. The man had lived quite the life, and his final deed would be worthy of the evening newscast no doubt. It would have suited him just fine.

Even at 80 years old, the man still plowed, shredded, planted Milo, and cut hay. It had become his passion in life to work and live on the land, though he always found his way to Steve's Place (now called Domel's) at the end of a long day to drink a few beers with the other old timers. It was essentially a chat room for farmers. Elmo was long since gone.

He died of a heart attack early in the afternoon. It was a pleasant late April day. There would be no need for further inquiry of the coroner with this one. He was tilling a field to remove encroaching weeds in preparation for a stand of Milo.

As per his annual routine, he planted the Milo before he planted his garden, because a late frost might come before Easter. It wouldn't harm the Milo, but it could wreak havoc on his tomatoes and jalapeno peppers. He never missed planting either of them, but he always wished for late frost just to kill the grasshoppers before they could hatch out. A mild winter meant more insects in the summer.

Despite Hank calling it quits and slipping the chains of human form, the tractor he occupied had yet plenty of life in it. Unlike an automobile, a tractor has a throttle. Once set forward, the engine will not stop for anything, except the clutch or brake, neither of which this particular driver could manage in his then condition.

The tractor kept going another six miles with Hank slumped over the steering wheel, his body bouncing with life over every obstacle the John Deere encountered. Miles of barbed wire he barged through came unattached from their posts, and tangled up in the plow. He accumulated an impressive array of items behind him – a lawn chair, a gate, garbage can, and of course, Perry Coffield's mailbox.

Old Perry actually thought Hank died and ran over his mailbox on purpose, out of spite, as the two of them had a few cross words from time to time. Perry was the mayor, and as die-hard, blue-dog Democrats, they always buddied up around election time. Around here, local politics ran second to only high school football as primary entertainment.

The mighty John Deere took down 12 fence rows in total, then crossed a county road, taking with it one of the marker signs. It clipped McQuary's turkey house, letting loose a swarm of poultry to wonder the countryside. Later that night, the local coyotes had a Thanksgiving feast. The Deere then became wedged in McQuary's feed silo for nearly 30 minutes, allowing several folks to draw near with video cameras. None were adequately brave to get near enough to cut the engine as the tires still spun with fury.

The Deere would wriggle free and proceed across a hay patch, at which point the plow became unhitched and the tractor pressed on alone. With a flattened front left tire, it began a slow turn to the port side. The final hurdle was a small stream, easily negotiated, before dueling to a draw with a 100-year old pecan tree.

The tree was some 14 feet in diameter, and neither side would yield right of way. The diesel engine, with a belly full of fuel, would have kept spinning the tires perpetually, or until they ruptured. By now a gaggle of farmers had gathered in hot pursuit on this final victory lap, and were able to cut the engine. Hank had made it halfway to Thorndale by the time all was said and done.

He must have been smiling proudly as he loosened grip with the terrestrial scene and floated on up to Heaven.

~~~

He was gone, and I was now the sole remaining steward of the Jewel of Hiram. The only other man on the planet who knew its location was now a ghost. He passed on his legacy to his grandson, Troy, and his sister Dottie; but it was Troy who would receive the burden of the Jewel.

I only had a passing knowledge of this kid, who was born after I left Milam County. Suffice to say, apples don't fall far from trees. This kid was Hank Benson reborn, complete with all the foibles and defects, raw human emotion and unbridled ability. As his grandfather came up the hard way, this kid would be born into a much less austere life.

At least, at first.
~~~

25. THE FLEDGLING

April, 1987, Milam County, Texas

Long before he ever met Crash Carter, Troy Benson wanted to be a pilot. He built his first airplane when he was seven years old. The young man had his head perpetually in the clouds, and as with many of his ill-fated endeavors, the approach to this airplane might best be described as *Ready-Fire-Aim*. Generally speaking, just as most things in his life, this one would not work out quite as he had anticipated. Yet, he remained undeterred.

A school bus rambled down the gravel road, leaving behind it a contrail of billowing dust. The driver, eager to finish her route, came to a halt in front of the Benson homestead. They were some 10 miles northeast of the nearest town and just on the edge of the school district's boundary. It was the last stop on the route.

With nothing for miles but row upon row of cornstalks and rolling pastures parched by the arid climate, a herd of cattle grazed lazily and moved across the plain. Newborn calves suckled the teat for fresh milk, while tails whipped back and forth as industrial strength flyswatters. The bus came to a stop in front of a rusty mailbox, halfway smashed in during some drunken teenage hooligan's mischievous odyssey the week prior.

Out here there isn't much law, but there were plenty of guns. While teenagers didn't have a shopping mall or arcade to misspend their youth, smashing mailboxes was as aberrant as most behavior escalated. Anything more and you'd likely find the business end of a .12-gauge shotgun, or worse, stampeded by an angry bull. The gun was mostly for show, but a bull was deadly serious. The old Aggie war hymn *Farmer's Fight* is not just a song played at football games.

The door of the bus opened with a gaudy screech, as two small children emerged with backpacks and lunchboxes, and raced toward the gate. While Troy could easily outrun his younger sister, he let her keep up right to the end. Having completed her duty for the day, the driver put the yellow dog brute into reverse, and sped away, the wheels grasping for traction, throwing rocks and dirt behind it.

"First!" Troy yelled, touching the gate just a split second before Dottie.

"No fair, Troy! You cheated on purpose!" she screamed.

"Give me five," he said, holding out his hand. Dottie quickly recovered from her loss, and smacked his hand. She never backed down from a challenge from her older brother. She tried to emulate him. Dottie was so nicknamed because Troy could not pronounce the "s" in Doris when she was born.

"Up high."

“Down low; tooooo slow!” he proclaimed, yanking his hand away at the last moment.

“I’m telling mom!” she yelled, climbing through the gate. She was off running again, down the quarter mile or so of gravel road that led to their house. Troy kept up, skipping along behind her, letting her enjoy the lead again. As they neared the end of the drive, he slowed to a walk.

“*Wait a minute*, Dot,” said the boy to his younger sister.

“What for?” she replied.

“Come here for a minute. Help me move this box into the road.”

Troy walked to the side of the road, where knee-high coastal Bermuda grass kept hidden an object. It lay discreetly next to a pile of old junk iron their father kept near the bend in the road.

“What are you doing that for?”

“It’s a secret. Just help me move it.”

“OK.”

Dottie helped her brother drag a box ramp into the gravel road. The road was bordered on either side by barbed-wire fences to keep cattle inside. This ramp was integral to Troy’s plan for the day. He spent most of the time this week in school sketching the details on his notepad rather than paying attention to the teacher.

Despite the temperature outside reaching more than 100 degrees, they had yet to lose a bead of sweat. They were well-accustomed to the Texas climate. There would be two hours before mom arrived home from work. Dad was gone until the following morning, as he was working swing shift at the ALCOA plant. He left the house half an hour before they got off the bus.

His father, an ironworker by trade, and cattle ranching hobbyist, taught Troy the basics of welding. He was an artisan of the steel, and in time Troy might follow in his footsteps. At seven years old he lacked any finesse or craftsmanship but could bead two pieces of metal together fairly well. He'd been practicing over the past few weeks, and today he would put his newfound vocation to the test.

Dottie watched curiously from the porch as Troy strung grounding leads from a welding machine out to their Go-kart. Her gaze became more intense as the diesel-powered welding machine sputtered to life, releasing a puff of black smoke. The Go-kart was her prized possession, and she made sure to let Troy know that it was *theirs* and not *his*. Her primary concern at the moment was if Troy was going to break the Go-kart. However, she also wanted him to make it go faster, as he had proven so when he removed the rev-limiter two weeks ago which their father still had not discovered.

This was a day and age when kids could be left at home alone after school let out. Cars and houses were unlocked as well. There hadn't been more than a handful of murders in Milam County in the past 10 years. Not too long before, some out-of-towners tried to rob a convenience store. The clerk had wounded one of them with a .22 pistol, and, in a panic, they killed her. One died of lethal injection several years later, the other plead to life in prison. "Don't mess with Texas" applies very much to those wishing to commit capital offenses. Nonetheless, the recent murder is why a gate now cordoned off the Benson property.

Dottie looked away as the welding rod made contact with steel, unleashing a vibrant flash of light. The diesel engine bore down in a guttural change of tune to provide more electrons, releasing yet more plumes of black smoke. Their father always made them look away when he was welding, as the bright flashes could blind a young child just as surely as sitting too closely to the television. Finally, her curiosity could abide no more, and she walked out to get a closer look.

"What are you doin' *Troy*?" A rhetorical question, delivered in an attempt to mimic her mother's same tone of voice.

"I'm makin' the Go-kart into an airplane."

"Nuh-uh. Like Grandpa Hank? Can I fly in it?"

"Yep. Just like Grandpa. But mine's gonna be better and go faster. "

"Don't break the Go-kart Troy. Daddy said it's mine too."

"Go back in the house, Dot, and shut up."

"Momma said you better not mess with Daddy's stuff. I'm gonna tell on you!"

"You do, and I won't take you riding when I get this thing fixed."

"But, momma said....OK, I won't tell."

"Go inside and watch cartoons."

This operation was simple in theory. He had identified two suitable pieces of junk iron that would serve as wings. It took him the better part of an hour to weld the "wings" to the frame of the Go-kart. In his mind, that was all he needed to attain flight. He had seen airplanes on television enough times to know that wings were the key ingredient; it was the only thing that separated them from cars. With that task accomplished, he shut off the welding machine and inspected the aircraft. He had about 20 minutes until mom got home.

It took four pulls on the starter handle before the *Briggs and Stratton* engine cleared its lungs and crackled to life. Dottie heard the commotion and came running out of the house in Pavlovian style. She slammed the screen door against the house, eager, as always, to go for a ride in the Go-kart.

"Wait a minute. Go get your helmet. This is an airplane, now. You'll need it in case we have to do a crash landing."

"OK. Don't leave without meeeee!" pleaded Dottie as she turned and ran back to the house.

He previously used the ramp to jump his bicycle, but had never tried it with the Go-kart. He figured with enough speed, the machine would be propelled into the air and the wings would do the rest. Seven-year-old ingenuity is not known for its comprehensiveness, and Troy, well, he was more of a trial-and-error type of kid.

Dottie jumped into the passenger seat, and Troy turned to "taxi" down the 200-yard straightaway. As he drove down the road, he pretended to do a pre-flight systems check, just as he remembered Grandpa Hank doing when they went flying. He turned the steering wheel, looked off to the sides, tapped on the seat, et cetera. These tasks were essential, as he recalled. He wasn't sure why, but it sure looked cool when Grandpa did it.

At the end of the road, he turned the Go-Kart around and pressed the gas pedal. The Go-kart reached top speed almost immediately, which was about 23-miles-per-hour. Dottie had a huge smile on her face, and kept yelling "faster, *faster*!" They rumbled down the road.

As they approached the ramp, Troy held tight onto the steering wheel and clenched his teeth. This was the moment of truth. He pressed harder on the gas pedal, but it was already as far as it would go. Hitting the ramp, the front wheels launched into the air.

He felt a jolt, as the ramp collapsed immediately under the weight of the machine. Dottie was thrown from her seat, as the front wheels left the ground but soon yawed hard to the right, putting the machine into a cartwheel. She tumbled into the ditch. Troy was still at the wheel when it barreled through a barbed-wire fence with its rear end first.

A few minutes later, their mom arrived at the scene. She screamed when she saw Troy, covered in blood, limping back up to the house. Dottie was hysterical, but uninjured, and screamed about how they had "flown the airplane". This made absolutely no sense to mom, and only added to her own confusion as she tried to assess the situation.

Troy had lacerations on his arm, his leg, and across his chest. She quickly bandaged him up, and took him to the hospital. His dad had to take off work to come to the triage unit at Richards Memorial Hospital. When the doctors were finished with him, his mother and father came into the room. He could see the disappointment in their eyes, but at the same time, they were thankful he wasn't killed or more seriously hurt.

His father, hearkening back to his own days as a boy, knew there was precious little he could have done to prevent Troy's unbridled spirit. Nor was there likely anything he could do in the future. The kid was always going to push the limits, and that was something he'd have to accept. It required an overnight stay, 32 stitches, and he had to wear a leg cast for three weeks.

His mom was not of the same opinion, and found it difficult to contain her emotions. She cycled between tears joy and relief, and bordered on anger. Fortunately, she held her tongue, and gave him a hug and a kiss instead of a smack. She wasn't given to swearing all too often, and knew it wouldn't have come out right. Being raised a strict

Protestant; she was never very good at swearing. Once, she had been enraged that Troy shattered the windshield of her car trying to hit a bird with a slingshot. She managed to call him a *little son of a bitch*. That faux pas had Troy's dad in tears of laughter, and eventually, herself as well, once she realized what she unwittingly called herself.

Dottie had a few bumps and bruises, but was entirely non-dissuaded from trying it again. She proclaimed as much to Troy and promised she wasn't the one who told on him. Her cover up wasn't exactly Watergate material. He liked his little sister, and they were best friends at that stage in life. Their relationship would have its ups and downs, but this moment in time would come to define a certain respect each had for the other. This infantile state would come to salvage their relationship many years later.

Troy's first hospital visit left an indelible stamp on his memory. His father, who could at times be overbearing, held his temper well, and sought to make this into a learning experience for his son. He bought Troy a book, *What Makes Airplanes Fly*, a book which Troy devoured in a day. He immediately saw the error of his design, and vowed that he would yet slip the bonds of earth.

26. BECOMING A MAN

The hospital stay was not as vivid, nor jarring, as the trauma which would visit him three years later. It would leave a more permanent scar, one that would never truly heal. He would leave the hospital and become a near celebrity back at school. The other kids would sign his cast as he regaled them with stories of the ill-fated flight.

He and Dottie would go on to many more adventures over that time, as their father, much to mom's chagrin, could not seem to pass up bringing them new toys.

After the duo "lost" a three-wheeler ATV, dad was forced to draw the line. Dottie finally confessed that it was at the bottom of a pond, despite her promise not to tell. After that, mom stepped in and crafted a new playbook. They were given bicycles, and helmets, and told to stay away from the county roads.

By that time, Troy was old enough to start handling some of the smaller farm equipment. It was hoped the additional responsibility would temper his inclinations for mischief. His dad taught him to drive the old Massey-Ferguson tractor used for shredding pastures to remove excess grass and weeds. Troy took to operating equipment as a duck to water. He could soon operate just about any piece of machinery in the stable, but his farming career got off to a rocky start.

As his dad turned him loose to begin shredding, he stood off to the side, and gave the thumbs up. Troy lined the tractor up to hug the edge of the pasture, engaged the power-take-off, and pushed the throttle forward. He shifted his focus on the far end of the field, wanting to ensure he cut a straight line. So focused was he on the straight line, he neglected to notice the shredder lodge itself into the barbed-wire fence and was now unraveling it post by post.

His father began an all-out sprint to catch up with him, waving his arms and yelling, but the tractor was far too noisy. Troy tore out 75 yards of the fence before he caught a glimpse of his dad in the corner of his eye, and quickly pressed the clutch in to bring the tractor to a halt. He spent the next week stretching barbed-wire to repair the fence, a lesson which made him learn to pay closer attention to details in the future. Manual labor has that effect on people; it should be employed by more parents.

The misadventures of Troy and Dottie all came to a grinding halt just when they were really hitting their stride. As part of their new list of chores one afternoon in late fall, they raked up a large pile of leaves. Dottie exhausted herself jumping into the pile time and again. Troy was too old by this time to enjoy jumping into leaves. They raked the leaves away from the yard and over to the barn, where their dad had recently stocked 300 square bales of Coastal hay. They proceeded to light the leaves and burn them, just as they had seen dad many times before.

Troy poured a small can full of diesel, which caused the pile to erupt in flames and thick black smoke. Dottie stood in amazement, and wanted to see more. Troy continued to pour small cups of diesel on the fire, sending a flash of flame and plume of smoke. To Dottie, it looked like a magic trick. Troy soon lost interest in amusing his little sister and told her to keep an eye on the fire. As the fire burned down to embers, Troy returned the rakes to the shed and unraveled a water hose to spray the flames out. Dottie wasn't finished with the fire just yet, and grabbed the cup that Troy had used to throw diesel.

The only problem was she didn't know the difference between diesel and gasoline. Their dad had tanks of each sitting in the shed. She picked the can that was labeled *GAS,* unaware of the dangerous difference in flashpoints of the two liquids. She was unable to repeat Troy's magic, as the gasoline merely fizzled when it was poured onto the smoldering embers. There was no flame present to ignite it. She continued to pour more, and more, until she too gave up and lost interest.

As she walked away, the latent heat warmed the dangerous petrol, and the fumes were ignited. A fireball erupted, and the fire spread embers into the freshly-packed hay shed.

Troy returned to spray out the pile of leaves, and did not notice smoke wafting from the barn. The tightly packed square bales, once ignited, would take much more than a watering hose to snuff out. A few minutes later, dad, who was now on day shift at ALCOA, saw the smoke from three miles away. As he came driving up the road, he quickly sped up as the horror dawned on him and prepared for the worst. Acting quickly, he sprayed himself with water and entered the barn to release the cattle from the corral. As the animals stampeded their way out of the gate, he went back in to get as much equipment out as possible.

When the first truss collapsed, he was still inside the barn. As he was climbing over the flaming wood, a second truss collapsed, trapping him inside. The Thorndale Volunteer Fire Department arrived mere seconds later and heroically dragged him from the inferno. The fire had already consumed most of his clothing, and he was unconscious from smoke inhalation by the time he was on the stretcher. He was rushed to the hospital.

~~~

The barn was a total loss, but the animals were spared thanks to his quick action. Mrs. Benson met with the doctors. The prognosis was not good. He sustained third degree burns to more than 70 percent of his body. Should he survive, he would be permanently disfigured.

Troy and Dottie were brought to the hospital, and their father asked to see them. Through the patches of white gauze, Troy could still see the outline of his father's face, and could make out a smile. Holding his son's hands may have been perhaps the last full measure of this man's life. The last words his father spoke to him, he couldn't remember. Years later, he wished he had paid closer attention, but he remembered the basic message:
~~~

You are special. Don't ever give up on yourself, or let people tell you that you can't do anything you want, because I haven't. And I never will.

The doctor's ushered the family out and moved him to the operating room. They tried in vain to save his life, but he died the next day.

His death unbound Troy from the chains of a father figure. It would become a double-edged sword which would forever shape his world. He was free, unfettered from any moral compass, to chart his own path to virtue.

They say a man does not truly grow up until his own father passes away. Perhaps unhealthily, Troy kept these feelings bottled up for many years. He didn't cry at the funeral. He was old enough to understand that death was permanent, yet somehow he convinced himself that this had not really happened. His sister did not understand any of it. She held out hope that her dad would be back some day.

His mother sank into a deep depression. She became numb to the world. She was placed into counseling by relatives, given medication, and for a while things seemed to turn around. It wasn't from abuse, nor lack of supervision that Child Protective Services showed up one day and took Troy and his sister away from her. Dottie, it seems, had been bruised up while trying to catch a baby calf, as she had seen Troy do many times before. She merely wanted to imitate him.

Their mother failed to notice, or perhaps care, as her kids at that point were nigh untenable. They acted out in ways that many kids do when faced with such a tragedy. The bruises caught the eye of a meddling teacher at school.

Losing the children brought the widow Mrs. Benson near the edge of sanity, pushing her into another bout with the depths of her demons. A downward spiral ensued and the strain became more than she could bear. After failing to show up to work for three days, her body was found where her husband's ashes had been scattered. It was a little pecan grove near the San Gabriel River where they would often picnic as love-struck teenagers. She took her own life with a .410 shotgun.

Grandpa Hank stepped in and adopted Troy as his own. Dottie became a steward of her grandmother. The two grandparents had long been divorced, so the once inseparable siblings would rarely see each other. Their lives would take devoutly separate paths.

There would be few happy days for Troy for many years. He devoted life to the one thing that could actually make him smile – airplanes. He studied them with a passion almost unhealthy for a kid his age. While other kids were playing the latest *Nintendo* games, Troy was neck deep in the study of thermodynamics and high-bypass turbofan engine designs. It was the only thing that gave him levity.

He made friends with a kid that lived across the river from his grandpa's farm. His name was Cy Carter, and they were about the same age. The kids at school called him Crash. Cy didn't have a mom, and his dad spent most of his time in the Gulf of Mexico working as an underwater oil rig welder. Young Cy pretty much had his run of the farm, and managed to get to school about half the time.

Cy was the polar opposite of Troy. The two didn't actively associate at school, but out on the farm, they were inseparable. They would tinker with Grandpa's tractors and ATVs, when they weren't off hunting dove or fishing. Troy often wished he was more like Cy. He had no rules, and no ambitions.

As Troy came of age, his grandfather treated him in a strictly authoritarian manner. They were both emotionally closed off, never talking about problems or tragedies of the past. Grandpa Hank knew the only way forward is one step at a time, so he cut the boy little slack. He encouraged Troy's academic pursuits, himself knowing the value of the written word.

The emotional side of life was repressed ably by Hank's stringent demeanor. He siphoned off Troy's energy through hard farm labor, long hours in the hot Texas sun fixing barbed-wire fence, chopping wood, and at times, plowing the fields and planting Milo with a John Deere tractor. Such guidance, peppered with lessons of life, steered Troy to excel in school, not desiring to spend his life in the fields.

As they entered high school, Troy and Crash saw less and less of each other. Troy played football, and began to take his studies seriously. Crash couldn't have cared less, aside from Ag Shop, where he could out-weld the instructor and fix just about any engine in the place. The two grew apart, and by the time graduation came around, they were but distant memories, each heading out into their own life's direction.

Time would unravel quickly; it wouldn't be long until they'd be reacquainted.

27. LEARNING TO FLY

For all who take the sword will perish by the sword.

- ***Matthew 26:53***

Central Texas, 1989

The farm continued to grow and was by now a sprawling ranch in the middle of Milam County. Troy and Hank had one thing in common; the airplane. Hank realized soon enough that it was the apple of the boy's eye, and as such, his own renewed love affair with the old beauty took hold. Old Green, as he called her, was his baby since she came off the assembly line of the Cessna facility in Wichita, Kansas. Old Green's home was out on the farm, just as a stabled show pony. She couldn't run with the thoroughbreds, but she sure was pretty; and sexy in a way that only an aviator could understand.

A legitimate landing strip was not necessary. The 180 Skywagon's abundant horsepower made getting off the ground in a hayfield an easy chore, but Hank normally just taxied right up to the county road for takeoff. Not many people out here would notice, nor care enough to complain. Besides, at the time, he drank beer with the county judge and was a member of the volunteer fire department. Those were basically *Get Out of Jail Free* cards for any infraction below felony.

Long before Troy took interest, I had the pleasure of many flights in Old Green. Hank acquired her midway through our 10-year companionship, in 1954. I might have been the first person foolish enough to climb aboard. The Skywagon had a high power-to-weight ratio for that day and age, with more than 230 horses in its Lycoming IO-540 horizontally opposed six-cylinder engine. Hank used every last one of them. So long as he wasn't drinking, his flying skills weren't too bad. No matter how many beers he'd had, he usually sobered up enough to land gracefully.

Hank had the flying bug and Troy inherited the same gene, without question. Troy had the benefit of an intricate understanding of the laws of flight, to which Hank had zero when he first took to the skies. "Book smart" as Hank would say, was all horseshit. Just saddle up and ride, you'll figure it out or die trying. Hank had nothing but basic instinct and a desire to fly; and a ton of money to buy a plane, of course.

The two had their first flight together when Troy was five, before he became an orphan. Hank liked to showboat a bit, and made sure it would be an unforgettable experience. Hank's theory held that the boy needed to realize flying, while safe as driving if done correctly, was inherently unsafe to those who lacked respect. One must be vigilant and prepared to act at a moment's notice, without hesitation or fear, should things go awry.

As Troy entered high school, he set his sights on earning a private pilot's license. By this time, his brain harbored enough knowledge of aerodynamics to pass for an undergraduate Aero major. He never stopped thinking about it; reading and learning until he was crammed full of density altitude and spin recovery techniques. His encyclopedic knowledge of the physical properties involved in man's flight through life gave him a thirst which could only be quenched by putting knowledge into practice.

Nonetheless, youthful intrigue and theoretical knowledge are no match for wisdom and experience. By the time Troy was ready to take flight with Grandpa, the old man had it down to a science. Even cranking the engine was a work of art. Mixture rich, magnetos off, and spin the prop three times over to put just a touch of gasoline into the cylinders. With that, the engine would fire to life with just a touch of the starter.

Landings in Old Green were optimal with 30 degrees of flaps, touching the wheels just as the stall warning horn sounds. The tires settled so smoothly that a passenger wouldn't know they had touched down, save for a barely audible squeak of the rubber. Hank was quite the artisan when it came to flying Old Green.

Troy's practical experience was zero, and trying to learn from Hank was a futile effort, as he did it all by gut feeling; just as a master chef who can't recite a single recipe. Troy completed the FAA Ground School before he learned to drive a car, but would have to be 16 to legally get a student permit to actually fly. He long ago set his sights on Old Green for lessons.

Hank then enrolled the boy in an Instrument Flight Rules class, and hoped the mathematics and associated intricacies would put the brakes on the boy's zealousness and constant bugging. Perhaps it would stifle the young man's fixation on the airplane, and keep his mind occupied on the ground, school, and learning. Yet, Hank was no Aristotle; Troy bit off the entirety of the advanced course and swallowed it whole. He stood ready for more.

Hank's roadblock was an abject failure and he was left with no other choice. He'd have to let the boy start taking flying lessons. He told the instructor to "really let him have it", a desperate last ditch Hail Mary attempt to stop the inevitable. Troy grinned from ear-to-ear when the instructor demonstrated the power-on stall. They progressed to near-aerobatic maneuvers at the limits of the Skywagon, and the boy refused to be knocked from his perch. His psyche was now hooked on the feeling of weightlessness and increased G-forces.

Troy was struck with an insatiable appetite to find his way back to the air.

~~~

With his aeronautical needs fulfilled, Troy was able to focus in school. Intellectual challenges were bracketed by the other major pull in small town Americana; football. Thorndale was the quintessential small town, with one stoplight and half a dozen beer joints. The whole town showed up on Friday night for the high school's football games, and just about every kid played the game. During this era Thorndale went undefeated to win state
~~~

championships in 1989, 1994, and 1995, under the legendary coach Don Cowan.

On the first summer "two-a-day" practice of his freshman year, Troy ran the 40-yard dash in 5.2 seconds, to which Coach Cowan proclaimed "get that boy some linemen gloves." His glorious football career was over before it ever started. Most of the team held out hope a bit longer. On that first day, a healthy percentage of the team fully expected to receive a Division-1 football scholarship. Statistically, maybe one student every 10 years made it to a D-1 field. The reality settled in sooner for some than others.

Yet even a master tactician and motivator such as Coach Cowan could never hold Troy's attention the way Albert Einstein could. Troy first became intrigued of physics while in junior high when he began to think about the paradox of time travel watching Arnold Schwarzenegger in *Terminator 2*. Aside from time travel, the movie's rendition of a nuclear detonation fascinated him, furthering a desire to understand the mysteries of subatomic particles and the massive energy they contained.

Once he discovered Einstein's Theory of Relativity, the natural world became much larger. He moved beyond the rudimentary physics of aerodynamics which sprouted from his innate desire to fly airplanes. He created his first scientific hypothesis during sophomore year, a juvenile attempt which might best be described as ecumenical, and worst, as heresy.

He blended the teachings of the skeptic Einstein with that of Martin Luther. The speed of light became his apotheosis. If *God is Light*, as his preacher postulated, then God must be everywhere; timeless, and ageless, as is light. All life requires light. The speed of light is the only way to gauge the vast distances of the Universe, and nothing can travel faster than the little *C* in MC-squared.

He couldn't pull this haphazard theory together and eventually grew tired of abstract thinking for which he lacked the means to test firsthand. While inclined and gifted, a savant he was not. He had far too much practical leaning to become engrossed in things he could never prove. So he turned his attention back to Bernoulli. Without a doubt, Bernoulli provided a more provable exegesis, and could be verified every time Old Green managed to leap into the air.

Daniel Bernoulli was an interesting character. Despite being born in 1700, his many contributions to science led to the advent of two 20th Century technologies which would revolutionize the world. These include the carburetor for internal combustion engines, and the airplane wing. Both of the now 300-year-old engineering marvels were alive and well in Old Green.

Bernoulli's study of fluid dynamics and decreased pressure in a moving stream were far more useful to Troy. Junior year he was expelled from school for trying to build a mini-jet engine in the science lab of Thorndale High School. It was more of a ramjet as it had no moving parts. He simply attached a Bunsen burner to a Venturi-shaped cylinder and lit it.

The experiment ignited a trail of exhaust and the unconstrained jet writhed about the science lab as a firehouse with no fireman. It quickly spread to a shelf of books but was mostly contained by the brick walls. The fire itself did little damage; the real damage came from all the water the volunteer firefighters used. They also tore through the back wall to get at the fire. The water destroyed the entire cupboard of elemental chemicals in storage, protected from fire suppression from above, but not when it's blasted from the side at 200 Psi.

Mrs. Culp was the senior science teacher, and she found herself caught between a rock and a hard place. Here sat one of the brightest students she'd ever tutored, who showed real intellectual curiosity and aptitude. Yet, he had just incurred $13,000 in red ink to her department's budget, and at the same time shown no regard for the rules of the scientific method. A real scientist not only asks if he *can*, he asks if he *should*.

She understood what was at stake. This type of genius is rare, and requires special care and feeding at the right moment. Unaddressed, such raw ability struggles to find its course, like a ship with no rudder. It is crucial that a course correction be made at this infantile state so the boy becomes as an asset of the good guys, and does not fall into league with shadows.

With the right touch he might stay the course and continue his journey.

~~~

"Stay away from the Marines. They don't give a crap about their people."

The words of the late Claude Guthrie echoed *ad nauseam* by Hank once his grandson got the idea in his head to join the military. While Claude was proud to be a former Marine, he warned others to stay away. It was a calling meant only for those who could survive a meat grinder; a breed apart.

The same sentiment strikes many parents, who, while they look highly on military service, the thought of putting their own children in harm's way hits too close to home. It's a natural parental instinct which even Hank Benson was not immune.

Regardless of Hank's apprehension, Troy would soon graduate high school. He desired to enter the service as an officer. His goal was to command the skies in an F-15E Strike Eagle, the most fearsome aerial platform in the world's arsenal. It not only owned the air, but could interdict ground forces with death from above at Mach 2.5.

He accepted a scholarship to the ROTC detachment at Texas A&M University, which boasted a Corps of Cadets larger than the enrollment of West Point, Annapolis, or the Air Force Academy. It would be a rude awakening. Those who have been through basic training in any military service will tell you that the objective is to break one down mentally and physically. The goal of the establishment is
~~~

to put new candidates into a pressure cooker, though on Day One, it felt more like a frying pan.

The basic mental and physical tests allow cadre to see who will react effectively when pressure is applied. Equally as important, they must ensure the individual can function cohesively in an environment that requires teamwork. The military is a well-oiled machine that relies on each part to function. For good reason, there have been no superstars in the service since Audie Murphy in World War II.

"Cadet Benson!" shouted the drill sergeant.

"Yes, Sir!" replied Troy (now Cadet Benson).

"Why are you such a weak, ignorant, sissy!?!? "

"Sir, I do not know!"

"Wrong! That's not the answer to a 'Why' question! Let me re-phrase, *why* are you such a weak, ignorant, sissy!?!?"

"Correction please, Sir! Sir, the answer is, 'No excuse, sir!'"

"Good answer.! Now get down in the front leaning rest, and stay there!"

"Yes, Sir!"

He was not one to quit. Four years after he left Thorndale, Troy graduated from Texas A&M University. He earned a degree in aeronautical engineering with a minor in Spanish. He spoke Spanish almost fluently from his childhood days working with Mexican Joe and the other farm hands back in Milam County. He was commissioned a 2nd Lieutenant.

He was awarded a coveted pilot slot by the U.S. Air Force, and would begin undergraduate pilot training only three months after graduation. His grandpa Hank was the only family member to attend his graduation on May 31st. It was the only family he had, really, save for his sister who couldn't make the trip from Wyoming. While being pulled in numerous directions to celebrate with his friends, Troy found his grandpa in the crowd.

He knew the importance of acknowledging the man who looked after him all those years. The man who also taught him to fly now stood before him. Troy would soon enter an elite group comprising the tip of the spear in the most feared flying force in the history of the world.

As the two men shook hands, Troy felt something he had not experienced for a long time. He felt a sense of completeness, that through all of his life struggles, he had finally arrived on the world's stage, and his ship had arrived.

"Well, congratulations. You done good," Hank managed to say.

"Thank you, Hank. *Grandpa.* Thanks for coming." Troy replied.

"No problem. Any time."

"You want to come by later we're having a reception downtown?"

"Nah, no, y'all go on, I just wanted to stop by."

"Okay, well, you sure?"

"Yeah, hell, y'all go on. I'll see you at Thanksgiving."

~~~

Thanksgiving never came to pass.

Four months after his graduation, in a single day, terrorists would hijack four commercial airliners and crash two of them into the World Trade Center on 9/11.

The United States Air Force would answer the call, and Lieutenant Troy Benson would be preparing for war.
~~~

28. AMAZING GRACE

*And they made his grave with the wicked and with a rich man in his death, although he had done no violence, and there was no deceit in his mouth. –**Isaiah 53:9***

After 9/11, the global landscape would change for the next two decades. A period of complacence would be replaced by a time for alarm. America ushered in a new generation of war heroes and Troy Benson would be at the tip of the spear. His entire life had been spent in pursuit of aviation and he found his new home in the cockpit.

His skill as a pilot would be surpassed by only his bravery in combat. He became a war hero at 24, earning the coveted Air Force Cross in December 2003. Alongside the award came the respect of an entire operational community; both in the skies and from the snake eaters on the ground who fell under the blanket of his top cover. His actions are the stuff of legend, but that is another story in and of itself; it is not obligatory to the story at hand.

Yet his downfall came quickly.

He was dishonorably discharged in July 2004 for conduct unbecoming an officer and a gentleman, and failure to obey an order. When his career was taken away, the pilot inside him was crushed. He soon followed a wayward path that led him overseas; a man without a country searching desperately for a new meaning. He was too embarrassed at the time to move back home, unsure if he would be embraced or shunned.

Now a civilian, he found work with a government contractor in Turkey, a place as good as any to hide from his embarrassment. By June of 2005 he was back on solid ground, as the Cargo Hub at Incirlik Air Base kicked off to support operations downrange in Iraq. Troy would be an equipment operator working long hours to transload cargo onto C-17's.

Unfortunately, he soon found himself in even more trouble. While partnered with a Turkish man he befriended, he ended up an unwitting foil smuggling contraband over the border between Turkey and Iran. It was the zenith of the Global War on Terror and Iran was a key antagonist. As such, Troy ended up in custody of the CIA in May 2006. The agency locked him away for almost a year in an undisclosed location despite pleadings from his former commanding officers that he was innocent. His record as a combat hero mattered not.

Needless to say, 2004 through 2006 is a period of his life he'd like to forget.

And he would be wrong.

Those years of tribulation laid the cornerstone of his future. By the middle of 2007, he emerged from prison with a new lease on life. It was not all that different than the experience of his great-great grandfather Aiden Benson. The elder Benson returned from his Civil War imprisonment in Louisiana to settle in Texas and become a steward of Sam Houston's mystery; the Jewel of Hiram.

Trials and tribulation often precede great men and their accomplishments.

His incarceration would soon be at an end. The CIA released Troy to return home for his grandfather's funeral. Ultimately, it would be a permanent release. By now, Troy was a political liability for the powers-that-be as the 2008 presidential campaign was underway. Candidates sought to distance themselves from any war-related headlines. He was absolutely no threat to the country. The CIA finally realized they were not dealing with an international terrorist, just a misguided young man who ended up in the wrong place at the wrong time.

~~~

Milam County, Texas, August 2007

The young man was now sitting in the front row with me, just a few feet away. I'd never met the kid, but he had the same eyes as his grandfather; brownish green, with an archetypal look of feigned interest. The feigned look was indeed a feint, as his falcon-like vision observed every trait and every action within his purview. His brain quickly processed each observance as friend or foe even more quickly than an infrared countermeasure.
~~~

I'd seen this quality before; in his grandpa Hank. He was a true warrior in all aspects, whether here, at a funeral, or at 10,000 feet in the cockpit of a war machine. I have not a doubt he processed me as "low threat"; a quality I've come to embrace in my time on this planet.

We were situated with the rest of the pallbearers at St. Paul Lutheran Church, basically a crew of old farmers from Steve's Place; among them were Muff Daniels, Lawrence Stanley, and Shorty Biar. Naturally hyperactive, Troy found it uncomfortable to sit still and even more so whilst surrounded by a huge crowd of mourners. He could feel their eyes boring holes into the back of his head, whispering *is that him?*

His nerves were primarily agitated because he would soon have to stand up in front of this crowd and speak. There were many faces he recognized, but he was never good with names. Ten years make even the most photographic memory lose a clear picture. Regardless, they all seemed to know who *he* was.

The mighty organ pierced the silence with the melody of Amazing Grace. Tensions waned. Hearts opened. Everyone became suddenly thankful for everything they had. This hymn had the ability to bring every man and woman together. As the music came to an end, a few old ladies cried. Their husbands yawned and checked the time.

My reflections turned inward as well. For a moment, I stopped thinking about the things I needed to learn about Troy, and reflected on the life of Hank. This was Hank's funeral, after all. It is important that we remember the deceased, and pay them homage when it ought to be due them.

Hank lived a good life.

Many of his close friends had long since passed away, save for me and a few other old timers. He never went to church, but today the church was overflowing. If sellout crowds redeem souls, then this sinner was already in Heaven. I doubt that is how it works, but it will do just as much for the soul as a lifetime of good works.

Photos of Hank as a young and spry 30-year old adorned the lectern area. Former employees, rugged construction workers with calloused hands, had the twinkle of tears in the corner of their eyes. The man that gave them a job, put food on the table, and gave them sustenance had passed on to the great unknown. By any measure of life, Hank made a positive impact on the whole town.

If only these folks knew the half of it.

Pastor Mahan finished his brief sermon in typical German-Lutheran liturgical style. Hank had not been a regular churchgoer, if at all; in fact, he hadn't been to a service in several years. Pastor Mahan didn't have much to work with despite Hank being a bona fide member of his flock. He had tried to reach out and witness to Hank on many occasions, but was always rebuffed.

Pastor Mahan knew that Hank was a Mason. Some Lutheran priests give fault to Masons, and do not allow them to be members of the church. For what reason, I am not sure.

Where there is the Fear of God to guard the dwelling, there no enemy can enter. – ***St. Francis of Assisi***

Hank lived a life of the sword. As do I. As does his grandson. Guarding the door is the most basic task in the Lodge of Freemasons. It is a task which goes unappreciated. It is that duty for which Troy Benson stood trial, and lost his career; and to which Hank went unrecognized, praised for his benevolence alone; and not for the death and destruction he prevented.

The Bible admonishes us to seek fellowship, but Hank rarely obliged. While certainly not a Nazarite, as was Samson, he was never violent. There was no untruth in his word. He lived in isolation; a life in his own prison. He lived it in plain view of the world.

Not all work of the Lord is glorious. Those tasked with less than pure responsibilities often fight difficult struggles in reconciling their given obligations. How other to ascribe to the executioner, who takes life as part of his duty? Does he not ensure the masses are kept safe from evil?

Or the soldier, who takes the life of an enemy which would otherwise seek to kill the innocent?

Such men are instruments of the Lord's wrath. They righteously carry out his vengeance. In a world of evil, war is necessary. It is necessary far more often than not.

Hank was one of those instruments.

His heart was pure. Yet even for him, his Judgment cometh, and that right soon. His bones returned to dust.

~~~

Given the events of his leaving the Air Force, Troy hoped to make this trip quietly. It was a difficult chore, because half the town of Thorndale would be at his grandfather's funeral. His plan to duck-and-cover showed little sign of promise.

He was not keen on the idea of being on display for the entire town to see, but he certainly could not skip out on his grandfather's funeral. He needed to do the old man justice, and deliver a eulogy that would reflect the life he lived.

His sister was here as well. Her presence gave him strength. It was good to see her. Heck, he was happy to see just about anyone who knew him other than the failure he saw in the mirror. It would be the first time in many years they had met. When times were tough, he reached out to his little sister for a word of reassurance on an overseas call, and vice versa. Dottie was no longer the little girl riding in the Go-kart; she was the life raft he reached out to in his time of need.

Dottie and her husband arrived the day before the funeral, and picked Troy up at the airport. They caught up and reminisced about happier times. Troy got to meet her new husband, Lane, who seemed like a decent enough fellow. They were married and living up in Wyoming,
~~~

having bought a ranch with a herd of Red Angus and Hereford cattle.

Troy and Dottie met with their grandfather's attorney the morning of the funeral. To their surprise, Hank left his entire estate to the two of them. It was a very basic will, which the attorney handed over in Hank's original handwriting: "The boy gets the land and all the stuff, the girl gets the money."

They both looked up after reading it, and laughed.

"That's Grandpa," exclaimed Dottie.

"Yes, that's him. Short and sweet," replied Troy.

"He had a way with words, I can assure you. You two ought to be damn proud of your grandpa," said the attorney. "That guy, well, we are sure going to miss him."

The attorney assured the two he had taken those instructions and written up an airtight will. Few would know better than he, as he'd served as the Milam County District Attorney many years previous. He was now a private practice attorney in Cameron. His given name was Llywelyn S. Hollis, an affable and energetic man in his late 60's. He was a long-time friend of Hank's. Lewis, as they called him, gained Grandpa's trust in the most interesting of ways.

Mr. Hollis was a man who followed the law. As district attorney, he prosecuted Hank for fleeing a police officer back in 1987. Hank was celebrating his 60th birthday at the time and was driving his Harley on County Road 486 after a weekend of fishing and whiskey.

Hank never looked in his rearview mirrors. As such, he didn't bother to stop once a local cop gave pursuit for the offense of going 70 in a 55. Deputy Dog didn't catch up to Hank until he was in the driveway of his home, but nonetheless, the loyal Dog promptly arrested Hank for evading arrest and fleeing a police officer.

Hank spent the night of his 60th birthday in jail.

~~~

Pastor Mahan experienced a rare moment of anxiety.

He invited Troy and Dottie up to pay tribute to their grandfather. He'd known the boy would be here, and he understood the tragic past of this family. However, allowing a layman to speak in church was always risky, as they might lack the tact to which a congregation is accustomed.

As Troy stood up, he unfolded the eulogy he typed the day before. He'd gotten maybe three hours of sleep over the last two days, mostly because he stayed up late writing, and reliving all the memories he had of his grandpa.

He paused.

It was an uncomfortably long pause. A few heads in the church pew looked left and right, wondering if something was amiss. This town hadn't seen Troy for 10 years. Back then he was but a young, recalcitrant buck aimed on
~~~

conquering the world. The last time he spoke publicly in this town was when he gave his valedictory address to the high school graduating class.

That was a doozy of a speech. He kept a copy of it and re-read it two days ago. It gave him goose bumps; not because it was Churchillian, but because it was so clichéd and naïve. Looking back, he now wondered how many knowledgeable folks in the audience thought to themselves "this kid has no clue about the real world." Such is the understanding of the world for a 17-year-old.

For the man who knows nothing, anything is possible.

Ten years of reality sat between him and that valedictory address. This speech would be far more real than the former. As the pause finally came to an end, Troy prepared to release his first words. Some in today's audience thought they were about to witness a public emotional breakdown; some probably even hoped.

Since news of the death a few days ago, Troy wanted this eulogy to be perfect. He spent every free minute since, writing, and then re-writing every word. The guest of honor, as imperfect as he was, deserved nothing less. His grandfather was the man he respected above anyone else on earth. Troy burned the midnight oil to make sure his ramblings were a tribute, and not a mourning.

And of course; it had to be topped with a dash of humor.

29. THE EULOGY

*Life is a comedy to those who think; a tragedy to those who feel. - **Jean Racine***

Troy spoke from the heart.

"They say a good ball team plays to sellout crowds. Well as I look around here today, I'd say that Grandpa packed them in pretty good."

He had no great life lessons to pass along. He wasn't running for office. Nor did his message have much of a Biblical reference, save one. This was all about remembrance. The congregation gave him a sympathetic laughter, a patronizing reply just to break the tension. He limbered up a bit. It was a huge relief to get those first words out; it should all be downhill from here.

He moved on to the next.

"You know, I've never done a eulogy before, so I'm a bit nervous. But grandpa used to say that even a blind hog can find an acorn."

More laughs sprouted forth from the congregation, this time, a few even appeared genuine. Self-deprecating humor seemed to be a winning ticket, which is good, because that was the foundation of his entire speech. The past few years had taught him that if you can't laugh at yourself, you'll find life more difficult than necessary.

"You know, Grandpa was a lifelong Democrat. A *Blue Dog* Democrat, as he would say. But he never ran for office. He said the only way to tell a politician is lying, is if you see his lips moving."

A few people laughed, but not enough to pause. So he kept going.

"He wouldn't stand to hear people talk about paying too many taxes. He told me the only year of his life he never paid any taxes, he also nearly starved to death. He was fond of the old saying the only thing you are guaranteed of in life is death and taxes. The day after he died, he called to say those are both true."

He stopped cold, and looked up, in serious manner. Only a handful of folks realized immediately it was a punch line. Odd stares sprinkled about the congregation, but the laughter grew as more people got the joke. The mood shifted, and he was on a roll.

He dropped in a non-scripted line.

"You know what else he said; 'He who laughs last, doesn't get the joke.'"

Even more laughter. The crowd was breaking.

"My grandpa was a pilot. He liked to tell jokes about aviation. He regaled me once the story of an old World War I pilot, who liked to tell war stories about fighting against the Germans, and in particular a dogfight with some German Fokkers. Grandpa asked the man if the Germans had the best pilots, and if the Fokker was such a great airplane, 'How did you manage to shoot them all down?' The old man replied, 'Well, I only shot down two of those Fokkers. But by the way, they wasn't Fokkers, they was Messerschmitts.'"

Pastor Mahan perked up a bit. He briefly considered standing up to politely put a stop to it, but decided it might be awkward. He let Troy keep speaking. He hadn't crossed any lines. Yet.

The crowd kept laughing.

"Grandpa was a lifelong rancher, but he made his money in construction. He used to say he had to keep a full time job to pay for his ranching habits. He believed people spent too much money on fancy tractors and fertilizers. He always invested in land, regardless of how it looked, because, as he said, 'They ain't makin' any more of it.' In his opinion, the way to make money with land, and cows, was simple. Keep grass in front of 'em, and a bull behind 'em."

The audience continued to laugh. Those old time farmers all could relate. Knowing Hank, whether he said those words or not, every person in the room who knew him could envision it. Pastor Mahan blushed, but the crowd had spoken.

"One year, Grandpa regaled us of the drought in the 1950's. It was so dry you could walk across the San Gabriel

River. 'Drier than a popcorn fart,' he would say. I believe he actually prayed to the Lord to send us a 'turd-floater' to fill the tanks back up with water."

Pastor's smile dissipated and he gazed towards the floor. He was getting more uncomfortable by the words. He silently said a little prayer, "Lord, let this end well."

"Some of you older gentlemen probably worked construction for my grandpa. I was once told a story, I can't remember who it was; maybe someone can verify if it's true. When his company won its first contract for ALCOA, he was young, in his 20's. The contract was to provide mine services and other work at the plant. First day on the job, a fire broke out where they were digging for lignite, and here comes Hank and a couple of his workers, hauling ass down the road. He didn't stop at the guard gate; he just drove right through it and smashed it to pieces. Within minutes they had the fire put out, and one of the ALCOA operations execs came by to congratulate the men for a job well done."

"Mr. Benson, you and these boys did one helluva job. You really showed some guts out here today."

"Thank you, sir," Hank replied.

"I'm glad you won that contract. Tell me, what are you going to do with all that money you'll be making?"

To which Hank replied. "Well, sir, first thing I'm going to do is fix the brakes on this goddamned truck."

Pastor stood up, but the congregation was roiling with laughter. Troy acknowledged Pastor Mahan by putting his hands up in Nixonian fashion, gesturing for a little forgiveness.

"Sorry, pastor. We'll tone it down a bit."

Pastor sat back down, a nervous smile on his face. It looked like part of the show, but it was entirely unscripted.

The speech was going better than he expected. His confidence was up. He had nothing to fear from his hometown. It was obvious they were behind him. So he started in on the next section of his eulogy.

As a seasoned combat pilot, he knew he'd passed the V1 engine failure speed. If there were any inhibitions left in his mind, this was the time to abort the takeoff, throttle down, and walk away. If not, then it was time to pull back on the stick and let this jet slip the bonds of earth. In the back of his mind, he heard his own voice through a static-laden intercom, calling the control tower; *'Shack 54, airborne.'*

"Let me take you back to a story about Grandpa Hank, and I'll throw in a history lesson as well. Some of you know I've had some time off lately so I've had plenty of time to do a little research. His farm was settled by the Indians many years ago. You've all heard of Apache Pass, just outside of Thorndale here, and the El Camino Real trading route that led from Mexico up through Louisiana. That is where my great-great grandfather Aiden Benson originally planted roots back in the 1800's. The El Camino Real was basically the Silk Road of Texas connecting Mexico City all the way up to Nacogdoches. The original Silk Road was started by the Han Dynasty. For those of you who failed history, that's in China. This was 200 years before Christ. While the Silk Road led to development of civilization across Asia, the El Camino helped expand the frontier into Texas, both up from Mexico, and from the east as the United States laid claim to the frontier through Manifest Destiny."

"Now this farm where Aiden settled was cut by the Gabriel, and the point which the El Camino crossed is what we now call Apache Pass. The Apache were here because of the fertile blackland soil and native pecan trees in the lowland river bottoms; but the area has always been flood prone. That was until the Army Corps of Engineers built an upstream dam in 1980. I believe it was this dam Grandpa was referring to when he spoke of the salvation it brought to area farmers protecting their crops and homes from massive torrents of water during Texas thunderstorms. And it's to which he was referring every time he mentioned the words *God dam*. You all know he referred to it quite often."

Pastor had given up worrying, and had clenched his ears shut at this point. The crowd listened intently, thoroughly enjoying the history of their own community. So much of it existed here, yet many never gave a thought to what existed. And, they continued to laugh.

"Hank's farm is now the last stop on the river until the Gulf of Mexico. It's the longest *un-God-dammed* stretch of river in the state. It pours into Little River, and then the Brazos, before its final terminus in the Gulf. Now, those of you who worked for Grandpa know he was prone to fits of mania. That is a clinical term, mind you, but basically means that he could be a real jackass at times. This was never more apparent than during the Great Christmas Flood of 1991. Grandpa read the meteorological signs, and when the rains began to fall, he knew there was one thing he'd always wanted to do. The dam had put an end to all the flooding, which wasn't a bad thing of course, but it meant the Gabriel was no longer navigable. Like a steer after castration, it no longer had any balls. This never set right with Old Hank. He like to set trot lines and fish in the river, and now it was just a creek that ran at a constant flow."

"1991 was an El Nino year. During such, abnormally warm ocean water tends to cause more extreme weather. It was on this stage a series of cold air masses made their way south across the Great Plains and into Texas. A cold front centered itself over Georgia. Around December 18th the wave from up north stalled in a line from Arizona to the deserts of Sonora, Mexico. Clockwise flow around the Georgian front brought warm, moist air in from the Gulf of Mexico, right up in to Texas, and the low level jet stream dipped in to act as a trigger. While spot records for rainfall did not break records, the sheer area of rainfall led to one of the largest volumes of precipitation in Texas history. Many areas got 12 to 18 inches. You all remember this storm right?"

The audience acknowledged. Many were on the edge of their seats. Anyone over 30 remembered this event. It was legendary, and it hadn't happened all that long ago.

"Even by mid-March, every emergency spillway on the Brazos would still be brimming. That much water takes months to trickle down the long voyage to the Gulf. Every dam along the numerous rivers which drain the Texas watershed was at maximum capacity. I was about 11 years old at the time the rains first started falling, but I still remember Grandpa Hank summoning me to get the boats ready. Some of you remember this was just after my parents passed away, and I was living with Hank. The Gabriel was soon running half bank, which was wide enough to accommodate Grandpa's sea-going fishing boat. He called out his neighbor, Clappy Carter and his son Crash to come along with us. Y'all remember Clappy Carter don't you?"

He got a "Yes" from the audience. But oddly, there were a handful of strange glances, left and right. Apparently not many people recognized the name *Crash*. A few mouths silently asked their pew mates; "Who is Crash Carter?" This led Troy to think possibly the boy left town or no longer lived here. At any rate, they did remember old Clappy. Clappy earned that name because Hank was a George Sessions Perry fan. He nicknamed the man after Clappy Finley of *Hold Autumn in Your Hands*. The real-life version was somewhat of a rough old cob, and a heavy drinker.

The other thing Troy noticed; his Texan drawl had started to return. Years of living outside the state had somewhat diminished his southern voice, but it returned now with pride.

"Clappy knew more about boats than Grandpa, by far. I know I speak of my grandpa as a halfway crazy man, but he was downright Platonic compared to Clappy. That man was certifiable. He was the perfect foil for this little boondoggle. As an underwater welder, he spent most of his free time deep sea fishing when not working on oil rigs. His other hobby was scalping tickets to sporting events around Houston, which was the equivalent of day-trading in the stock market back then. Clappy was always looking to make a buck the quickest way possible, honest or not; emphasis on *not*. But mostly he just liked the water and the great outdoors. "

"Hank was going down that river. All the way to the Gulf of Mexico, come hell or high walls. There were no high walls coming, but high waters sure as hell were. The rain was falling upstream near all the way to Oklahoma north and New Mexico west. In half a day or so it would all be flowing right down past us, right on down the San Gabriel. It would overwhelm the banks and cause a flood that'd make Noah himself jealous."

Pastor Mahan accepted the fact that borderline sacrilege would be permitted today. Better than outright blasphemy, he supposed.

"We weren't the first to make the trip, but ours would probably be the quickest. Normally the Gabriel isn't much more than a trickle, but in December 1991, it was a raging cauldron of water 60 feet wide. Downstream, the Brazos would swell to some five miles wide in places, overcoming its banks and sprawling out into the Brazos River Valley. Grandpa Hank wasn't going to miss the opportunity."

"He had Clappy back the boat into the stream at Apache Pass. Two days earlier it was a low water crossing that today was anything but. It lies just upstream from the Old Worley Bridge. Grandpa, Crash, and I got in the boat, and fired up the twin inboards. We didn't have much maneuvering room, and the water must have been running a brisk 15 miles an hour. Logs and all kinds of debris came by at a quick pace; we could hear them plink against the side of the boat. The rain still fell in sheets as the boat listed heavily to the side. I held tight to the railing, ready to dive overboard should the whole thing capsize. It was treacherous to say the least."

"Grandpa kept the boat at a hover, trying in vain to stay near the ever expanding shoreline. Clappy put the truck in four-wheel-drive and got it out of harm's way. He parked it next to the bridge and ran back down to the boat. We couldn't get close enough to the bank to pick him up. The bow was too high above his head to jump aboard."

"He and Grandpa communicated with some hand signals and yelling, and the next thing I know, the crazy son-of-a-gun Clappy took off running towards the bridge. He climbed up to the bridge and ran to the center. Crash and I had no idea what he was doing, until Grandpa threw the boat in reverse and headed for the bridge. He put full back throttle as we approached, creeping along slowly enough underneath the bridge so Clappy could jump down. As he jumped, his boot caught the edge of the railing, turning his body to a front flip, and he landed on the boat's cabin with his left shoulder to a loud thud. Grandpa peered over the windshield to make sure he was still alive, then turned back toward Crash and I with the biggest smile I'd ever seen on his face, shaking his head, almost in tears he was laughing so hard. He pushed the throttle forward and off we went."

"As nightfall came, we'd made it as far as Little River, which is far wider than the Gabriel. Hank pressed on. We had spotlights and flashlights scouring the water in front of us. Sometime during the night, we made it to the Brazos, and by 7 a.m., despite the rain continuing, we had enough light to see. Hank put the hammer down, and we flew down the river at 40 or 50 miles an hour, winding slowly back and forth to dodge debris. The Brazos could have passed for the Mississippi. As we neared Hempstead, we were low on fuel, and Hank made a pit stop, then ordered Crash and I to walk up a highway overpass to find fuel. It took us two hours to hitchhike to the nearest gas station and back, each lugging a five gallon jug of fuel."

"We made it to the Gulf of Mexico in 38 hours, just as the sun was rising again. The rain subsided. We basked in the glow of the bright yellow ball as it made its way over the flat and unperturbed ocean horizon. Every single item of clothing was soaked through. All we'd had to eat were a few bags of beef jerky and potato chips, and Hank was out of beer. He drove the entire trip, never once looking fatigued. I had never seen the man so happy. It wasn't his style to smile much, but the past two days were an exception to the rule."

~~~

Then there was silence.

Troy neared the end of his eulogy. It came quickly. He had gotten so wrapped up in it, he was now at the end, and he started to get nervous.

The congregation was on the edge of their seats.

He grabbed two shot glasses from his pocket. He poured them full of Jim Beam whiskey from a flask. It was his grandpa's favorite. His plan went awry as his hand was shaky, knowing that despite his humor, the stark reality now dawned that his last surviving forefather was gone, and he was essentially alone in the world.

All the joking in the world could not undo that fact.

One of the fondest memories of his childhood now crumbled under the weight of that realization. He struggled to hold it back, but unlike in the past, he could no longer keep his emotions in check. They were boiling over. It finally hit him, at the worst possible time, because this is the part he didn't want to screw up, and he didn't want to cry in front of the entire town.

Tears filled his eyes. He was losing focus. He lost his cool. His sadness bordered on anger. He felt he was going to embarrass himself in front of everyone.
~~~

Sometimes, it's impressive to see a man feed on true emotion. Many in the audience began to wipe tears from their own eyes. The silence was deafening.

His hands shook almost uncontrollably as he spilled whiskey all over his fingers. This worked out so much better when he rehearsed it in his mind, absent the nerves and hundreds of pairs of tuned in eyes, hanging on his every move. He set one glass on the lectern, and with the other, raised his hand for a toast. He paused until he could speak without a quivering voice. It was no easy task.

He drank it down.

He held up the other glass.

"To Hank Benson. My grandpa. You may be gone, but we'll never forget you."

Here's to you, here's to me.
A better man I'll never be.
Hank is gone, and it's plain to see,
He was solid as a Post Oak tree.
He leaves a mighty legacy.
Close at heart he'll always be.
From these shackles he is now set free.
Here's to Hank, I drink to thee.

He slammed the glass into the floor, shattering it into a million pieces.

There was dead silence. Jaws dropped. It was the most surreal moment the church had ever witnessed.

Only the first few rows of people actually heard what he said, but it didn't matter. They all *heard* the glass shatter, and it shocked them back from their condolence-laden state of mind. The physiological impact grabbed their hearts, and ripped away the hilarity that was present just seconds before. This emotional roller coaster had just hit a crescendo.

Troy wiped the tears from his eye, gathered his sheets of paper and then, slowly turned to the center, and saluted the photo of his grandfather; it was a sharp, crisp salute. He did an about-face, and headed for the exit down the center aisle, towards the far end of the church.

A few steps down the aisle, a clap pierced the silence.

Then, another. More claps, followed by two, then three.

Then a smattering of applause erupted into clapping and cheers. Before he could make it to the door for his exit, he was being grabbed, hugged, and patted.

It had been a while since he felt the town of Thorndale's warm embrace, but just as riding a bike, it was always there. He just had to get back on and start riding. He could no longer remember what it was he had been so afraid of.

Hank was gone, but Troy Benson is back.

30. THE AWAKENING

As you go through life, two rules will never bend, never whittle toward yourself, or pee against the wind.

– Hank Benson

Three hours later, a crowd gathered on the lonely hillside where centuries earlier the San Francisco Xavier de Horcasitas mission stood. A slight breeze kicked up, throwing a blanket of dust over those assembled. They were here to scatter Hank Benson's ashes on this hill that overlooked the land he loved so much. An airplane hangar off to the south stood proudly atop a smaller hill, connected by a long gravel road which ran atop a terrace connecting it to the main highway.

Hank would have good company in his final resting place. Under this dirt lied the bones of dozens of men; Spanish missioners and Indian chiefs, and possibly those of old Snively himself. It was a storied piece of land, and Hank would be proud that many of his friends would again today have the opportunity to see it.

An old man stood at the back of the crowd, with a walking cane, held slightly askew. Between his two hands he balanced his weight forward on the cane. He wore a Veteran's of Foreign Wars flight cap. He was a tall and slender man, with thick glasses, and a steel gaze. His lean physical build no doubt contributed to his long life, having avoided serious illness and other plaques which curse mankind.

He was, until recently, healthy as a horse, but that health was now failing rapidly. Even today, he struggled to remain upright. He stood warily; eyes caged forward intently. Since news of Hank's passing hit him, he felt that he had little left to live for. That feeble old warrior was me, R. Cyrus McCormack.

I had listened, only hours earlier, to Troy Benson pour out his heart to honor his grandfather. I kept up with his days in the military, but I never met the kid before today. I doubt he knew much about me. As the ceremony ended, with Hank's ashes scattered, I would have the honor of one handshake with young Troy. Not a single word was spoken. To him, I was just another old man come to honor his grandfather.

When the ceremony ended, I went on about my way.

Sometimes the secrets of the world are within our grasp. We shake its hand and look it in the eye, yet we fail to recognize it. The boy reminded me of myself a bit, a few years after I returned home from World War II. There was no arrogance in his eyes, nor was there any fear. He was wounded, but not defeated. He had just a few ambitions, but no further anger or ulterior motives; just an understandable amount of sadness.

Tragedy changes a man's demeanor, as does war. You talk a little differently. You carry yourself otherwise as well.

Conceit is replaced by a more subtle projection of strength; a calm humility which gives credence to your own mortality. These changes manifested in Troy Benson. He was a *tabula rasa;* the same blank slate Sam Houston observed when he handed the keys to Aiden Benson. It was upon this empty canvass the Lord would soon draw a masterpiece.

Underneath the façade, cradled in a newfound sense of direction, grew virtue.

~~~

Over the years since he left Thorndale as a teenager, Troy Benson put less and less stock into what others thought or how the world viewed him. While certainly in no danger of becoming a nihilist, it became apparent to him today, that he cared far more than he realized. There was renewed sense of meaning that began to creep up from deep down. In today's mourning, there came a ray of hope that despite his missteps, he could become good again.

A journey of a thousand miles begins with one step.

– Lao Tzu

Back to the basics; one foot in front of the other.

Hank Benson had not only passed on his land, he passed on an overwhelmingly responsibility. That duty was already making its presence felt. The internal strength and fortitude Troy displayed today were the direct result of a growing new aura.
~~~

He was no longer worried.

Despite his own overly harsh, perfectionist attributes, people in this community felt a deep and enduring respect for his decisions; his decision to serve country, his decision to come to the aid of the helpless, and to face his reckoning head-on when the tables turned. He displayed the same qualities shared by generations of pioneers, settlers, and tenant farmers from this land whence he came. These rugged individualists rarely gave up hope.

They were as proud of Troy's achievements as his own grandfather, yet, just as Hank, they rarely acknowledged it. By age 24 he'd achieved far beyond what many in this small town ever endeavored throughout their entire lives. It was his lot in life, and they lived through him, as a doppelganger, through his victories and defeats. It didn't matter whether he was downtrodden or on the come. The ray of light that shone to him and through him was not an arriving train; it was a light at the end of a tunnel.

Just as spring follows winter, there began a thaw in the icy cold war of Troy Benson's mind. His newfound levity gave him pause, and a weight lifted from his shoulders. In the throes of redemption, a new weight saddled him. Now becoming self-aware of the simple things he'd neglected, his subconscious mind had but one reply;

Damn the torpedoes, full speed ahead.

~~~

I sensed the end was near.
~~~

My feeble body summoned strength for one last mission. In the distance, I could see the grey roof tiles of the old farm house sticking out through the grove of pecan trees. I'd never brought my piece of the Jewel of Hiram to this land. It was an understanding of Hank and I that the two should never meet. Hank was gone; his ashes still blew in the wind. My longing to see The Jewel reunited could no longer be contained.

I knew he had it buried around here somewhere.

It took me nearly an hour to make the short trek. I was welcomed by his dog, Suzie. She was probably the fifth or sixth animal he named the same, a mix of Collie and some type of Shepherd. A herd of cattle grazed across the bottomland. The grass was a luscious green. I felt that cool breeze coming off the Gabriel. It brought me back half a century to my days with the Benson Construction Company. I could almost hear grasshoppers hitting the water, and smell the aroma of mesquite smoke from the old wood stove.

I recalled a Bible passage from Ezekiel that describes this land to perfect tune: *I will feed them with good pasture, and on the mountain heights of Israel shall be grazing their land.* A heavy scent of pollen filled the air. The cabin was little changed. It was a beautiful oasis in the middle of nowhere; far from the prying eyes of passersby. Hank had upgraded a few things. He had satellite TV now, a new iron fence, and the lawn was sodded with pristine carpet grass.

I sat down at an old wooden picnic table. Carvings from men of ages past ingrained the weathered lumber. My journey to the past brought back old friends. Then I found it:

Pencil Dick, 75 lb yellow – 9/14/54 Hank and Mac

I can still see Hank leaning over that table, half drunk, as Pencil Dick hung on the scales inside the cabin. He carved the memorial into the table as his men frolicked and drank, ready to feast on the prize he and I hauled in that day. It was one of my fondest memories.

I stood up, and steadied myself against a pecan tree. I remember this tree. Hank had planted it a few years before we'd met. It was by now halfway grown.

Then I felt a quiver in my leg. It was the Jewel. It had begun to resonate.

I removed the Jewel from my pocket, and found it glowing. I've been left wanting for what happened next. I had a good idea what would now come to pass. In all I've seen, I still could not truly be prepared and might well cower in fear in the presence of the Almighty.

I took a few steps back and got down on my knees. The ground shook. The branches of the tree in front of me began to sway. Clouds appeared from nowhere to settle over the farm. Darkness crept in and snuffed out the light of the sun.

I held up the Jewel, as an offering, and its glowing intensified.

The rumbling grew to a roar as an oncoming freight train. Pots and pans in the old cabin rattled from their perch, and crashed to the ground in a commotion. A piercing sound entered my ears as the tree before me fractured in twain. The deafening roar of the earthquake caused all other sounds to evaporate. The tree fell to the Earth.

A bolt of lightning cascaded down the atmosphere, lighting up the sky in a flash of brilliance. The impending crackle of thunder found its way directly to me, as the bolt impacted the ground where the pecan tree had stood. I was knocked backwards from my knees, and the Jewel fell from my hand.

With the tree felled, the ground continued to shake, and I saw another glow rise up from the ground. It was the second piece of the Jewel of Hiram. In an instant, an explosion of light ensued as the two pieces came together. The intense flash turned night into day. I covered my face at the blinding brightness, certain that this was the end.

And he who sits on the throne will shelter them with his presence. ***– Revelation 7:15***

And then, there was dead silence. The clouds receded. The storm was gone.

I slowly regained my focus.

In front of me, The Jewel hovered over the ground. A ring of majestic light encompassed it. I could see the faint outline of wings, the markings of my Heavenly associates, as they held it gently. They descended beneath the ground. As they disappeared, the ground itself began to glow.

I prepared to take shelter as the ground began to growl once more. I stood in awe as the fallen tree began to quiver. Its hewn pieces began to reassemble themselves. Limb by limb, leaf by leaf, the old pecan tree became whole again, and before my very eyes, returned to the soil from whence it came.

Everything was back as it had been, except for one thing. The Jewel was no longer mine. I heard the voice, as clear as I'd ever heard it.

"My servant. Depart in peace."

My newfound energy was gone. My head became light; my eyes began to see stars. The lethargy returned. I was unable to stand. I lost consciousness.

~~~

I would awake sometime later in a hospital bed, clinging to life.

The Jewel's reunification sent shockwaves throughout the universe. For the moment it lies safely buried, and I am the only one who knows the secret. Just as a nuclear detonation, a raw display of power such as I witnessed does not go undetected. It awakened forces of evil asleep for thousands of years. They would become hell-bent on gaining this prize to use its powers for death and destruction.
~~~

Some of these forces might be right in front of you; gaining your confidence with a handshake and a smile. Troy Benson will soon learn this the hard way. He now owns the very ground in which the Jewel rests. As such, just as with Hank, there will be precious few people in this world he can trust. It is just a matter of time before he is under a full scale assault. It is now his burden to carry, yet he knows it not.

Thou preparest a table before me in the presence of mine enemies. ***– Psalm 23***

One, in particular, will soon knock at the door.

31. DRAKE RAINES

In the late 1960s, KGB head Yuri Andropov tasked the Soviet bloc's disinformation machinery with turning the rest of the world against the U.S. by reviving anti-Semitism. Andropov knew that the U.S. would stand with Israel and that he could convince the European leftists and the Islamic world that America was dominated by Jews.

- Lt. Gen. Ion Mihai Pacepa

Regardless of how the world got to this point, suffice to say the Middle East will continue to be an arena of conflict for generations; be it the Israeli-Palestinian conflict, the U.S.-Iran showdown over nuclear weapons, Iraq, Afghanistan, the Russian incursion into the Caucasus, or the unrest in Egypt and Libya in 2012.

Much anti-Western sentiment in the Middle East can be traced back to the aftermath of World War II and the ensuing Cold War. It is at least partly attributable to a deliberate propaganda campaign undertaken by the Soviet Union. Holy Wars, just as any conflict, are shaped by policies and tactics. America has historically supported Israel since the founding of the modern Jewish state in 1948.

With contrasting social ideologies, the Soviet Union became a nemesis of the United States. The enemy of my enemy is my friend. As such, the Soviet Union sought to foment anger against the United States from the Muslim world, which naturally disavows Israel and western Christians due to religious differences.

This is not to say U.S. foreign policy did not play into the hands of the Soviet game. The Soviets already formed a natural alliance with the Iranians, primarily due to Sunni-led tribal factions of the Northern Caucasus being adversaries of both the Soviets and the Shia-led governments of Iran and Syria.

The people of the Northern Caucasus for years have been treated in Russia as a dangerous and even criminal community. The anti-Sunni character of the clerical Shia government of Iran that had deposed the pro-U.S. Shah Pahlevi became a natural ally of Russia after 1979.

- ***George H. Wittman***

In such games of shadows, there are many foils. People, in general, are quite easy to manipulate, and even easier en masse. A teacher once told me the definition of Holy War is basically any situation that has no good outcome, a tongue-in-cheek observation based on the seeming recalcitrance of religious fervor throughout history. Three thousand years have passed, and here we are. The major religions which sprouted from the Dome of the Rock, supposed portal to Heaven, continue to be the source of major conflict which now surrounds it.

~~~

Bordering the Middle East lies the Anatolian plateau in Turkey. It is home to a complex geography of beauties and wonders. It ranges from Cappadocia in the center to the mountains of Ararat, then south to the Mediterranean, and west to the sensual straits of the Dardanelles which define the far border of Europe. Anatolia has a long history in the annals of civilization.

Anatolia is Greek for "east". Incidentally, the eastern side of this plateau is home to dissidents from numerous sects displaced through centuries of infighting. The cradle of civilization is more aptly today a crossroads of conflict. It is a juncture of borders with Iraq, Syria, and Iran.

The People's Mujahedeen of Iran, better known as the MEK (Mojahedin-e-Khalq) had been active in Iran since the Iranian Revolution of 1979. It was devoted to Marxism at one time, and free markets another. As typical of disparate groups, it struggled to find its bearing. Its elements splintered into numerous factions, all operating under the same general umbrella of opposition to the Iranian government. Over the years, the MEK launched a guerilla resistance against the theocratic regime of the Ayatollah, and created an underground society of freedom fighters.

Mujahedeen is an Islamic term similar to jihad, meaning *struggle*. There are dozens of unconnected mujahedeen groups throughout the Middle East. The United States assisted Mujahedeen fighters in Afghanistan for a decade beginning in 1979 in an attempt to thwart the Soviet Union. The Mujahedeen, assisted by Osama bin Laden
~~~

himself, eventually repelled the Soviet incursion, in no small part because of Stinger missiles used to shoot down helicopters.

These missiles were supplied by the United States. The Mujahadeen in Afghanistan eventually gave way to the Taliban, which ushered in a society aptly demonstrated in *The Kite Runner* by Khaled Hosseini. After 9/11, the United States would return to fight against the same people it had assisted against the Soviets. The United States should have learned a lesson, but as political cycles twist and turn, memories fade.

In Iran, after the 1979 Revolution, the MEK was largely dispersed, fleeing for its very life. Members were pursued and executed on the spot, without trial or opportunity for protest. Its fighters fled Iran for neighboring Iraq, where they set up a base of operations.

A young Iraqi General had recently seized power in Iraq. He would soon invade Iran. With the support of the United States, France, China, and many other nations, he not only invaded Iran, but utilized chemical weapons to suppress a Kurdish insurgency to the north. Again, the enemy's enemy is your friend, so it is really no irony that these same actions were used as justification *against* the General in 1991 and 2003. In those years, the same nations above supported wars to bring forth his ouster.

The General's name was Saddam Hussein.

The real reason for Coalition action is often swept aside. It was the same primary grievance of the Japanese Empire in

1941 against America, who cut off the former's oil supply. It led to the bombing of Pearl Harbor. This time, Japan and the United States were on the same side. *C'est la vie.*

Nonetheless, in 1979, the interests of Saddam Hussein and the MEK were temporarily aligned. Because of these entangled alliances, the MEK was granted asylum by Saddam in 1980. They were given free reign over a small slice of Iraq, in return for paying to him a handsome royalty. They operated freely until the Coalition invasion of Iraq in 2003. During the invasion, members of the MEK were detained, almost indefinitely, by U.S. Special Forces. They had been branded a terrorist organization, and while not combatants in this war, they were held for many years without any formal charges. The Coalition simply did not know what to do with them.

One of the more interesting members detained was an American expatriate named Drake Raines. He was a person of interest to the CIA. Years earlier he rejected a fortuitous life in the United States, and in the late 90's, moved to the Middle East in search of a cure for his ideological woes. While technically still an American citizen, he symbolically renounced his citizenship sometime in 1997 and joined the MEK, casting himself a revolutionary.

Raines was the apex of high intelligence, registering an IQ of 165. He grew up in the effete Marin County suburb of San Francisco, the son of 1960's hippies who were second-tier college professors and connoisseurs of the counterculture. They drowned young Drake in dogma, but the overtness of his parents desire to spout Kinsey, Marx, and Marcuse turned him off to such liberal leanings.

He instead branched into the hard sciences once his true genius began to blossom at Berkeley. He earned a Rhodes Scholar, having a gift for both chemistry and physics. He culminated his education with a Ph.D. in Materials Engineering from M.I.T. in 1986. He accomplished all of this by the tender age of 24. In a continued departure from his parent's lifestyle, he forsook academia and committed the near-excommunicable offense of becoming a defense contractor.

He found his true genius in the most sought-after new military technology; designing low-observable stealth materials for the newest Department of Defense approach to airpower. The magnificent abilities of his mind rivaled Fermi and Einstein. He capitalized on the fervor of the F-117 Nighthawk within the Pentagon, the mis-designated "fighter" whose only real mission was bombing. Its first generation stealth technology was combat-verified by its pursuant success in Desert Storm, flying night strikes over Baghdad without a loss.

Riding the coattails of the F-117, Raines developed cutting edge composite materials for the second generation of stealth, solving riddles that plagued the B-2 Spirit like the mysteries of Atlantis. Even more, he successfully incorporated active stealth employment into the genetic fabric which would eventually become the third generation of this maturing technology. The skin of the B-2 had to not only reflect radar, but absorb it, and do so while not peeling away during high speed flight. It had to be stronger than steel, yet lighter than Aluminum.

Such a challenge was the type of thing Drake Raines was born to solve. His designs would go on to be used in the F-22 Raptor and the F-35 Lightning II, which would replace the twin-engine F-15 Eagle and single-engine F-16 Falcon, respectively. He also became a shrewd businessman.

Rather than work as a highly-paid contractor, he formed his own Limited Liability Company. This allowed him to apply for and receive exclusive patents for his numerous designs, which were ahead of their time and highly regarded by the deep pockets of the defense industry. As airframe lifecycles can last decades, he continued to perfect his designs to meet the changing requirements of the Stealth program. Drake Raines's personal net worth soon climbed north of 50 million dollars, and defense contractors salivated over the man with the billion dollar brain.

The life of a young, wealthy, playboy, soon began to eat away at his conscience. Just as a heroin addict needs more and more, the lavish lifestyle made it increasingly difficult to attain the intrinsic high which furthered his ambitions. His societal ineptitude led to a reversion to his parent's anti-capitalistic ideology, culminating in near reclusiveness. He spent time reading manifestos of Guevara, Marx, and even Kaczynski. He began to revile those who sought to buy his intelligence for a profit, and felt guilty for the luxuries gathered unto himself in the name of national defense.

He hated all good works and virtuous deeds,
And him no less, that any like did use.
And who with gracious bread the hungry feeds
His alms for want of faith he doth accuse.
-**Edmund Spenser**

This metamorphosis accelerated in 1993 when he visited war-torn Kuwait after Desert Storm. Handlers within his own firm thought it would inspire his imagination to see a battlefield first hand. Perhaps he would realize he could make a difference in the speed and efficiency with which the Air Force might deliver a fatal blow to a strongman like Saddam, and in turn, save the lives of citizens. The trip was a sales pitch funded by the military to bring Mr. Raines back into action.

The trip backfired.

The prism through which he now viewed the world showed only the many lives his own livelihood had destroyed. With this narrowed vision, he blamed himself for providing material support to the ends of an empire. He came to loathe his existence. Increasingly ashamed of his wealth acquired at the tip of a sword, he vowed to change his life.

He launched his own humanitarian assistance non-profit group. Throughout the mid-90's, he spearheaded efforts to bring attention to the plight of the Middle East. His contacts in the defense industry gave him small, obligatory, donations, but behind their boardroom doors scoffed and laughed at his efforts. He soon realized his attempts to right the wrongs of human nature were futile. He could bend no one's ear, nor make any difference, as a humanitarian. His only stock in trade, the only thing for which he had value, was as a *Lord of War*.

His animosity deepened. The millions he made profiting from machines of war, in an America that sought to invade and destroy, left behind a wake of broken lives. He came to see America as the enemy, and his heart was tugged by the plight of the underdog. Subliminal fundamentals in thought hammered into his head from childhood began to take hold of his thinking. He grew even more disgusted that his parents were mere amateurs, who latched onto the revolution only for the gluttonous promiscuity which they enjoyed.

His parents never put themselves in harm's way. They enjoyed all too much their elitist lifestyle, spouting a worldview from the safe confines of Marin County. Drake Raines wanted to be a true revolutionary; a world changer. He had the mind, and the resources, to make it happen. He altered his plan of attack in a methodical, highly calculated manner.

He was going to war.

~~~

Just before the F-22's first flight in 1997, the Joint Strike Fighter program looked to replace the F-16 with an upgraded stealth-enhanced version. It would eventually become the F-35. More than two thousand Joint Strike Fighters were projected with a total program cost
~~~

approaching one trillion dollars over 50 years. The Joint Strike Fighter development contract was signed in November 1996. Every company bidding on the project wanted Drake Raines' patents. In late 1997, he proceeded to auction those patents to the highest bidder.

He traded the future cash flows for a significantly less lump sum payment, but it mattered not to him. The auction took his net worth up to almost 200 million dollars. Soon after completing the sale, he transferred the bulk of his wealth into overseas accounts. He then disappeared from the face of the planet.

At least for a while.

Raines had visions of picking up a weapon and joining the fight in a way he never previously had. He romanticized the idea of becoming a martyr to sacrifice himself at the altar of his newfound creed; a reckoning for the misguided life he lived. In searching for a venue to carry out this lunacy, he made contacts with locals in Eastern Anatolia, and his presence was sent through back channels to MEK operatives. The existence of an American could only mean one of two things; either he was a spy, or he was a fool.

He was intercepted by the MEK while living as a nomad near Lake Van in eastern Turkey. It did not take long for his name to echo up the chain to mid-level commanders, who would likely judge him a spy and sentence him for execution. This did not come to pass, and once his name reached the top; there was fervor within the MEK leadership. It was a golden opportunity.

An MEK commander dissuaded Raines from becoming a foot soldier; in fact, he was given no option. They convinced him that he could bring his intelligence to the fight and be far more effective to their ends. Secretly, they wanted to tap his vast sums of money, as well as his intricate knowledge of defense systems for espionage. They made him an honorary commander, and bestowed upon him the titles of a great man.

He became indoctrinated in the MEK's ideology, which was disparate to say the least. He brought a renewed focus to many decades of infighting and spent his twilight hours writing out beliefs with a pen and paper. He tailored an agenda to fit the overall ambitions of the MEK, which called for an overthrow of the Iranian government, a return of power to the people, and a hardline stance against Westernization.

He spent years living in near squalor, in northern Iraq, occasionally being allowed to go along on low-risk incursions into Iran. He felt liberated in a way his millions of dollars never bought him back in the United States. He met a setback in 2003 with the invasion of Iraq by Coalition forces. His group of bandits lived in harmony with Saddam Hussein, but the now deposed dictator could no longer provide refuge. Once captured, Raines was charged criminally as an American citizen. More than five thousand MEK members were detained indefinitely at Camp Ashraf.

Facing deportation and a lengthy prison sentence, Raines folded. He possessed a great deal of information U.S.

Intelligence wanted, and he represented a treasure trove to his captors. During the five years he was with the MEK, he became the aggregation point for information. In a plea deal, he vowed to assist the Americans in helping to topple the Iranian regime, or at least sabotage their ambitions. He revealed details of the Iranian enrichment program and assisted the Americans in gaining leverage.

He was required to continue providing information to keep his freedom. His intel would lead to the assassination of several Iranian nuclear scientists and the planting of the Stuxnet virus several years later. The Iranian government, who was aware of a rogue American operating in the region, responded in kind to word of his capture. In 2003, they attempted to pre-empt Raines with a secret letter to the U.S. government. They offered access to hidden nuclear facilities if the U.S. would utilize its conquest of Iraq to disband the MEK. The enemy of my enemy is my friend.

The Iranians were fearful of the MEK's ability to infiltrate Iran and wreak havoc. They also knew U.S. Intel was scouring the group for information, using every interrogation technique they could keep out of the newspapers. In particular, the Iranians wanted Drake Raines dead. However, the U.S. cast their lot with Mr. Raines and the MEK. The information he provided was all checking out, and it was invaluable.

In late 2006, Drake Raines slipped away from his surveillance handlers and again disappeared.

He discontinued all contact with the Americans. It was a major non-public embarrassment for the intelligence community, who rebuffed inroads with the Iranians in order to harvest intel from Raines. Displeased at this insubordination, the CIA put him near the top of their Most Wanted list. Soon thereafter, they engaged the Iranians in an effort to work together to bring Raines in.

This time, the Iranians rebuffed the Americans. A step ahead, Raines already switched allegiances. He offered a truce with the Iranians if they would remove the Iranian bounty on his head. This removal was subject to regular contact and future information that he might uncover. Undercover Iranian operatives assisted his escape.

The double cross and embarrassment enraged the CIA and the Pentagon, who put a kill order on Raines' head. He now had tacit approval to seek refuge within the borders of Iran, putting him beyond even the CIA's reach. Other intelligence assets, including a covert organization known as Red Top, began following his trail. It was difficult, if not impossible, as a several thousand strong underground militia of MEK fighters protected him.

The greatest fear of the politicos was they created another bin Laden; a highly intelligent man who was well-financed and sympathetic to causes hostile to the United States. His journey to that station in life began with good intentions, but he descended into a virile hatred of society, and America. He now sought to set matters straight, as America put a target on his head.

He vowed to respond in kind, and he was just getting warmed up.

32. COMMENCEMENT

I am starting to reconsider my desire about staying. The work is drab; the money I get has nowhere to be spent. No nightclubs or bowling alleys, no places of recreation except the trade union dances. I have had enough.

– Lee Harvey Oswald

My time was near.

Stage 4 cancer was the diagnosis. The nurses tried to comfort me. Doctors were amazed I was still alive. At this point I couldn't have cared less. I told them to keep the morphine and that toxic brew of chemicals they wanted to inject me with. I was ready to go. My hypocrisy has its limits, but I suppose I'll keep up this charade right to the end. I don't really have much of a choice.

So I sit here and write. I've left specific instructions for these ramblings. Maybe one day they'll be read by the masses. It's been ages since I put my thoughts down into words. On some level, I feel it important to leave this story behind. I'd love for it to live on after this old man's body is but dust.

The splendid servant Pastor Mahan heard of my travails and stopped by for a visit. I always enjoy a good discussion with a man of God. He starts in with the story of Job, then moves on to the inspiring pentameter of Psalms. We backtrack to the wonders of Ancient Egypt during the Exodus, and the rule of the Caesar in ancient Rome. All captured in the Bible, of course, but expanded upon by the likes of Pliny the Younger who witnessed the destruction of Pompeii by its nemesis Mount Vesuvius.

I'm fond of Roman history. There is much to learn from their rise and fall. Our journey turns northward from Pompeii, to the seat of the Empire itself. En route we visit such oddities as Caligula's pleasure ships found at the bottom of Lake Nemi, re-discovered in the 1800's, and henceforth destroyed by those damn Nazi's in World War II before they could be fully restored.

The Nazis; I'm proud to say I had a hand in their defeat. It strikes me as odd that society today has been so quick to distance itself from the carnage of that regime. A few generations of prosperity and relative peace, and it's as mankind feels he has taken some great leap forward; never again to allow suffering and murder on such a grand scale. I have sad news for you, friend. Nothing in your genetic makeup has changed. It will all happen again.

The forces of evil prey on the unsuspecting. Add a pinch of suffering, pain, and hopelessness, and mankind will again tear itself to shreds. Even as I write, the thought that this once great country could so willingly untether itself from its anchor, the Constitution, demonstrates your inability to learn from the past. Unchecked power will always lead to tyranny.

There is no great mystery why history repeats itself, over, and over, and over again.

The line dividing good and evil cuts through the heart of every human being. And who is willing to destroy a piece of his own heart? – ***Aleksandr Solzhenitsyn***

Friedrich Nietzsche suggested that men are endowed with the same basic impulses at birth, which they may pursue of their own free will in any manner they choose. Though Nietzsche himself expressed contempt for Stoicism, in this regard he finds himself in harmony with its school of thought, by one of the more well-known Stoics of whom I am fond:

But I have seen the beauty of good, and the ugliness of evil, and have recognized that the wrongdoer has a nature related to my own—not of the same blood or birth, but the same mind, and possessing a share of the divine.

–Marcus Aurelius

Some of that evil is easy to spot. Back in 1943, the Nazi uniform all but institutionalized it. It is ironic that such an overt display of evil now lends itself to mankind's slothful approach to morality. Truly treacherous evil is far more difficult to find than a swastika; and far more common. It sneaks in as a thief in the night.

Good and evil are dueling moral dualities within the soul of man. They are intangible constructs which are subject to one's perspective. Mankind has been on a quest to define what is morally right since the time of Adam and Eve.

Thousands upon thousands of years have passed, yet precious little has changed at the most basic level. Very few have done anything to stop it; save for the cadre of unseen warriors who struggle just below the surface. It has been so since the fall.

Blessed are the peacemakers, for they shall be called sons of God. ***–Matthew 5:9***

I don't mean to imply that I advocate war. Most wars throughout history lacked a referendum for taking up arms. The common understanding among man is war should be pursued as a last resort; for survival, or to oppose the extinction of one's very life and well-being. In such cases, there is no need for justification, as it is merely self-defense. War for another purpose—ideology, economics, or humanitarian—is destined to fail. There is only one casus belli worthy of an end outside of self-defense; and that is to fight evil.

Only a march on evil should be done from the offensive, but alas, it has never been done. Nation states do not engage in such ends. A crusade or intifada is not a fight against evil, but against an opposing ideology. Evil on some level has infiltrated every religion at some point, and nations have destroyed men by the hundreds of thousands in the name of religious beliefs.

The forces of darkness can only be fought by individuals, for that is where the battle begins, and ends. Evil itself is an astute disciple of warfare. Its formidable ally is complacency. The disinterested man is a footsoldier of darkness, and a fool.

Every hero must fight a villain. Who is to say which is which? The heart does not lie, but warriors, be they heroes or villains, can be found on either side of the ethical scrimmage line. One must give caution to relativism.

I offer this reflection not to tell you that all is lost, but that hope might spring eternal. Just as evil is on the march, so too are the forces of righteousness. This is self-evident in the world in which Hank Benson and I lived. Warriors such as us fought battles armed with ordained virtues in the gray areas of combat. While virtue by definition is good, some men fight for tainted desires.

Far removed from the time of the Romans, modern-day warriors inhabit battlefields of the air, in space, and even cyberspace, armed with weaponry many iterations more destructive than swords and arrows. Yet certain principles remain legitimate today, thousands of years later. Just as a trusty sidearm, those principles will always find their target when properly aimed.

And just as good and evil may be merely different expressions of the same basic impulse, a principle in itself can become either strength or weakness. Understanding the nature of one's opponent, his ideals, his beliefs, and his principles, is crucial to achieving victory.

So it is said that if you know your enemies and know yourself, you can win a hundred battles without a single loss. If you know only yourself, but not your opponent, you may win or you may lose. If you know neither yourself nor your enemy, you will always endanger yourself. ***–Sun Tzu***

~~~

Not all stories have a happy ending.

In 1944 I jumped from an airplane to fulfill a prophecy. I confess to you now that I told you a lie when I inferred that others made it out of that plane. I don't live by your Ten Commandments. Even if I did, would I be the first to tell a lie?

But the midwives disobey and let the boys live. When the king of Egypt asks them why they're doing this, they answer, "The Hebrew women ... are vigorous and give birth before the midwife comes to them." God was kind to the midwives and the people increased and became even more numerous. ***– Exodus 1:19-20***

Take caution, for the Lord very much disavows a lying tongue. Understand when you speak, your words should endeavor a righteous goal. Truth is a bizarre concept. Many a religious man believes that thou shalt not kill. Peel back that onion, and you realize that in truth, one should only not murder. The difference is found in asking *why* you take life; is it for vengeance, or is it for righteousness? Vengeance is the sole domain of the Lord.

Of all the men in that plane, I was the only one to survive. The others were all burned alive, or fell to the earth in a twisted heap of metal. I was the first out. I was the only to get out. The plane was engulfed in flames and fire from the Nazi artillery.

C'est la guerre.
~~~

The Skytrain was merely a vehicle for my delivery hence it was kept safe to that point. So too is the body of Mr. Mac; but just for a few moments more. Just as the Skytrain, his body has carried me as far as it can. My Earthly vessel is of ghost and man. I confess to you again, I never had any fear of death. My fear is only of failure to accomplish my mission. I would not die that day nor any day since; for I cannot die.

And I will never die.

And there was war in heaven: Michael and his angels fought against the dragon; and the dragon fought and his angels, and prevailed not; neither was their place found any more in heaven. And the great dragon was cast out, that old serpent, called the Devil, and Satan, which deceiveth the whole world: he was cast out into the earth, and his angels were cast out with him. - ***Revelation 12:7-9***

During the building of King Solomon's Temple, the master craftsman Hiram, being from Tyre, did not speak the same language as the people of Israel. He relied instead on a system of codes and symbols to communicate with the brethren. As there were many thousands of workers living in the city of Jerusalem, it further became necessary to establish passwords and secret greetings to enable the wardens to pay only those whom were due them. It was a matter of necessity, but that simple act spawned a legacy of rites and rituals today known as Freemasonry.

It is why I have taken it upon myself to learn as many languages as possible, so that I don't repeat that mistake.

I told you before I had many names. R. Cyrus McCormack is merely the most recent.

Begotten not made, being of one substance with the Father, by Whom all things were made. - ***The Nicene Creed***

I am not begotten, nor do I seek a standing with the Son. Unlike Him, I was made; by the Father.

I have fought many battles. I have ministered and delivered messages to men who wished not to hear it. Others accepted my dispatch with open arms. I have given pursuit to demons, bound them and cast them into the darkness to await their day of reckoning. I have destroyed, and I wrought the vengeance of the Lord with great fury.

I traveled with Hannibal through the Pyrenees. I fought with the Seleucids, and then against the same, whence they sought to destroy the people of God. I've walked the halls of the Roman Forum, trekked across Cappadocia and the Anatolian plain, sought refuge in the great castles of the Kommagene, and hibernated in the grotto of St. Peter. I've led men into battle under false pretenses and deceived mine enemy. I've slaughtered man and beast without hesitation.

I fought on both sides of the Crusades, defending that sacred land from not an opposing religious dogma, but from the hands of corrupt men who brought evil to its doorsteps. I've smitten the enemies of good and left them to await the fires of hell.

I was once known as Acerbas, High Priest of Melqart. My earthly flesh was murdered; ripped away from its earthen bond. I guided Elissa away from her murderous husband in Tyre and in my exile escaped the captivity of the Jewel. I came to the aid of the son of a righteous Israelite from the tribe of Napthali. I would again return to exile, to be exhumed by the warrior Hannibal.

I warned Adam the dangers of lurking evil in the Garden of Eden.

In the time of Solomon, I was Hiram, a servant of good.

After the War in Heaven, Satan and the Watchers fell to the earth, and polluted the perfect creation which God hath made.

The Father called me Raphael, and ordered me thus:

Proceed against the bastards...bind them fast for seventy generations in the valleys of the earth, till the day of their judgement and of their consummation, till the judgement that is forever and ever is consummated. - ***Enoch 10***

This is not the first time I have put my thoughts onto parchment. Over 2,000 years ago, as I led the Maccabean Revolt, I wrote a detailed description of warfare and tactics. It was called the War Scroll.

This time, I write my story for your generation, but the story is the same. Will you ever learn?

After 400 hundred years of hibernation, I was awakened to find the pieces of the Jewel of Hiram. It was my sole mission in Germany in 1943. I have now accomplished that mission.

In doing so, I awakened the forces of darkness which will soon proceed in their lust for power. For even men like Drake Raines, just as Mr. Mac, are merely vessels for forces beyond this world.

My powers are limited.

Every hero has a villain. My counterpart, as we speak, is sharpening his sword to track down the Jewel of Hiram, to siphon its power and turn it for ill. Remember, neither goodness nor evil are so easy to spot, even for me. The rivalry with my nemesis, an agent of darkness, will soon spill into the physical. He will come as a thief in the night.

All warfare is based on deception.

And no wonder, for even Satan disguises himself as an angel of light.

I await the time with patience.

There are two others who need my immediate assistance. Hank's grandson, and another they call Crash Carter.

Earlier, I told you that Troy Benson, in 1986, gave me a nickname. You might have been asking yourself this entire time, just exactly what that nickname was; have you not?

This is the end of the line for Mr. Mac, but it's only the beginning for Crash Carter.

The eyes close.

The light fades away.

Mr. Mac is no more.

About the Author

Mr. Felton is a graduate of the U.S. Air Force Academy. He served much of his 7 years on active duty overseas, including tours with the National Security Agency and U.S. Air Forces - Europe. He earned a Master's Degree from The Johns Hopkins University. In his youth, he was a USPA licensed master skydiver (D-22583), SCUBA diver, snowboarder, and pilot. These days, he moves more slowly. In addition to writing, he spends time operating a small business, masquerading as a chef (of questionable ability), driving a forklift, and studying world history, politics, and warfare. This fascination with history began long ago, but was reaffirmed during time spent living in southern Turkey, and Germany, witnessing the handiwork of civilizations far gone. He is a Master Mason, Christian, 7th generation Texan, and proud American veteran.

ACKNOWLEDGEMENTS

I'm afraid I owe far too much to repay, but I'll start with these amends:

I would like to thank the late George Sessions Perry for his writings about rural Texas, both in novels and articles. His words are as true today as they were 7 decades ago.

As well, I owe a debt to Dr. Garna Christian of the University of Houston who lent his vast knowledge of Mr. Perry's writing to this effort.

I would like to pay tribute to J. Frank Dobie, who wrote many volumes of Texas which were an inspiration to me.

Finally, to Jeanne Williams, my editor. Thank you alone cannot suffice, but I hope we can write many more books together. Your encouragement and refined eye have fashioned a raw story into something people might actually read. Here's to hoping they laugh with us, and not at us!

Made in the USA
Middletown, DE
18 July 2023